Color Master moved the prism from one hand to the other to allow each of them to see the spectrum. Without thinking, Ishmael reached out, feeling the tug of the colors, the familiar weight, as the splintered light—no, the *spectrum*—edged closer. He lifted his pointer finger and a green swathe leaped toward him.

Ishmael didn't notice the other novices staring at him. He didn't hear Color Master call his name. He was oblivious to everything but the color as it tugged at him.

"Ishmael?" Color Master said again. "Ishmael!"

This time Ishmael heard her and jerked away from the splintered light, suddenly aware that no one else had reached for the color. No one else had connected with the color. No one else had become lost in the colors. He ducked his head. "Sorry," he muttered, embarrassed.

"On the contrary!" Color Master said. "Well done! You're the first novice I've seen who has had an immediate connection with the spectrum. Bodes well for this group."

—from *The Splintered Light*

GINGER JOHNSON earned her MFA in Writing for Children and Young Adults from Vermont College of Fine Arts, and lives in the Seacoast area of New Hampshire with her husband, two sons, a coop of sassy chickens, and a tank of doctor fish. *The Splintered Light* is her debut novel.

BLOOMSBURY PUBLISHING

BOOK TITLE: The Splintered Light

AUTHOR: Ginger Johnson

ISBN: 978-1-68119-623-7

FORMAT: hardcover middle-grade novel

TRIM: 5 1/2" x 8 1/4"

PRICE: $16.99 U.S./$22.99 CAN.

PUB DATE: September 4, 2018

TENTATIVE PAGE COUNT: 416

AGES: 8-12

GRADES: 3-6

CONTACT: Lizzy Mason

(212) 419-5340

elizabeth.mason@bloomsbury.com

BLOOMSBURY

THE
SPLINTERED
LIGHT

THE
SPLINTERED
LIGHT

GINGER JOHNSON

BLOOMSBURY
CHILDREN'S BOOKS
NEW YORK   LONDON   OXFORD   NEW DELHI   SYDNEY

BLOOMSBURY CHILDREN'S BOOKS
Bloomsbury Publishing Inc., part of Bloomsbury Publishing Plc
1385 Broadway, New York, NY 10018

BLOOMSBURY, BLOOMSBURY CHILDREN'S BOOKS, and the Diana logo
are trademarks of Bloomsbury Publishing Plc

First published in the United States of America in September 2018
by Bloomsbury Children's Books

Bloomsbury books may be purchased for business or promotional use. For information on
bulk purchases please contact Macmillan Corporate and Premium Sales Department at
specialmarkets@macmillan.com

Library of Congress Cataloging-in-Publication Data
available upon request
ISBN 978-1-68119-623-7 (hardcover) • ISBN 978-1-68119-624-4 (e-book)

Book design by Jeanette Levy
Typeset by Westchester Publishing Services
Printed and bound in the U.S.A. by Berryville Graphics Inc., Berryville, Virginia
2 4 6 8 10 9 7 5 3 1

All papers used by Bloomsbury Publishing Plc are natural, recyclable products made from
wood grown in well-managed forests. The manufacturing processes conform to the
environmental regulations of the country of origin.

To find out more about our authors and books visit www.bloomsbury.com and sign up for our newsletters.

To you who wonder and wish

THE
SPLINTERED
LIGHT

PART I

COTTAGE

He fathers-forth whose beauty is past change:
Praise him.

Gerard Manley Hopkins, "Pied Beauty"

Ishmael's first memory was rolling down Commons Hill, its massive stone wall behind him and the open market square before him. Luc told him to do it, so, of course, Ishmael threw himself down, rolling over the bumpy ground. He saw sky, then ground, then sky and ground, brightness and darkness, faster and faster, until everything merged into one great wheel. Pure joy bubbled out of him, and he squealed tumbling down the hill.

He closed his eyes to the strange brightness and the curious darkness and lost track of which way was up and which way was down until he felt himself being yanked sideways by a reproachful hand and a switch that whipped the joy right out of him.

Ever after, Commons Hill was linked in his memory with rebuke rather than wonder, and he never rolled down the hill again. He had no reason to go there anyway—no reason, that is, until many years later, after Luc had been gone for some time.

CHAPTER

1

Commons Hill was not particularly common, nor was it much of a hill. Its gentle slope rose up at the edge of a market square that wasn't quite square, in a town that hunkered down in a barren landscape. The stone wall with its large wooden gate circled the crown of the hill, but few people knew what lay concealed behind it.

On the outskirts of this town was a small farm—a bland and barren patch of dirt with some stubborn and stringy weeds, a few decrepit and misshapen trees, and a shriveled and fading trickle of water aspiring to be a stream. Each gray dawn greeted a gray sagging cottage, a gray ramshackle barn, and a gray kitchen garden cut into the gray turf with row upon row of untended gray vegetables.

This was Ishmael's home. He had been born here and had

seen eleven years pass by here—the past seven of which were spent mostly in the ramshackle barn, tending the rickety sheep.

On any given dawn, Ishmael could be found milking and mucking and feeding and watering, but on this particular dawn, his chores lay ignored, forgotten because of a sight he couldn't understand.

A beam of light passed through the window of the barn, slipped into a flaw in the glass and emerged, splintering into rays of light that flashed upon the wide planks of the barn floor. Ishmael walked up to the glass and rubbed his sleeve over it to wipe off the dust. The light shone down with even greater intensity.

This was a brilliance he couldn't fathom, the likes of which he had never seen before. The mud and grime on the floor, the chaff floating in the air, the straw in the pens, the pitchfork and broom hanging on the wall, and even the unsteady animals flocking together—everything bore a simple shade of monotonous gray. His waking moments were gray, and his dreams were gray. But this light burst forth out of the glass, and divided into gradations of shades brighter and fresher than anything he had ever seen.

Ishmael held his left hand out to the light, and his arm became splashed in its magnificence. As far as he knew, no one had ever seen anything like this. There was dark, and there was light, and there were several shades in between—shades of dark blended with light or light blended with dark. But this thing that he saw seemed to have thrown off the cloak of dimness worn by everything else and presented itself in finery so foreign to him that he could hardly comprehend it.

He wanted to put a name to it but could not think of anything fitting. Luc would have been able to think of something if he were here. Light span? Ribbon of brightness? Shiny flash? Nothing did it justice. He stood still, the strange light splashing against his sleeve in a gentle arc, tickling him, humming, waiting for him to *do* something.

He slowly stretched forth his finger. Immediately, the light split apart, separating into seven distinct bands. Each one seemed to have a personality of its own.

As he watched, the middle band leaped upward and twirled in the air by his hand. The motion startled him, and Ishmael jumped back. The bands of light remained where they were. After a moment, he held out his finger again, and let the strange light settle on his fingertip as the wonder of it settled deep into him.

The band was heavy, and try as he might, he couldn't hold it for long. His arm fell, and the light landed on the tip of his boot, seeping into the felted wool.

The boy knelt down and held his finger near his boot, waiting for the light to rise up to meet him, but it didn't. He rubbed at it, scraping the wool with his thumbnail, but nothing happened. There it stayed.

He turned back toward the window. The bands still hovered in the light. He studied them, noticing how one flowed into the next. They were both substantial and insubstantial at the same time. They were dense, but lighter than air. He could see the light, but at the same time he could see through it to what was on the other side. Looking at it gave him a strange feeling in the pit of his stomach. It had been so long since he had had this feeling that he hardly recognized what it was.

Joy.

CHAPTER 2

Ishmael reached out to the strange light, hungry for this joy, but a tired shadow crossed the window, blocking the bands and startling the unhappy animals into even greater clamor. As Ishmael turned, the door banged open, shaking the walls of the barn.

"Ishmael!" Mam's eyes flashed in a way all too common these days. "Have you forgotten the sheep? Listen to them!" She gestured toward the animals crowding against the gates.

What had simply been background noise resolved itself into loud and pleading bleats. Their warm gaminess filled the barn, and Ishmael remembered where he was and what he was supposed to do.

His mouth opened to speak, but he had no words to fill it, and he stood there gaping.

Mam took his skinny shoulders in her grip.

"The cheese waits to be turned, the sheep beg to be milked, the laundry needs to be hung, the barn needs to be mucked out. Simon is running wild, and I am only one person." Her eyebrows knotted. "Your father is no longer here."

Guilt oozed over him, squeezing out any joy he had felt from the strange light only moments before. *Papa.* His fault.

"The longer you wait to milk the sheep, the less milk they'll produce, and once they're done milking for the year, there will be no more. It's going to be hard enough to make ends meet as it is. Why do you do nothing when our survival depends on this work?" she asked.

At that moment, the shaft of light coming through the window shifted and landed upon her cheekbone. Ishmael's attention was drawn to the bands of light fanned out upon her face, running from her hairline to her jaw.

"Answer me!" She gave him a little shake.

"It's the light," he said.

"The what?"

He pointed to the window. "Coming through the glass. It's different."

She let go of him and stepped back, away from the window. The strange light slid down her face, down her neck, and onto the planks of the floor.

"It's just light, Ishmael," she said, waving her hand through the dust motes.

"No, Mam," he said. "I think . . ." He paused. He wasn't sure what he thought, but it made him think of that time rolling down Commons Hill—the mixture of light and dark mixed with a tingle of delight. Ishmael pointed to the stain on his felted boot. "Look."

Mam sank down to examine it. Her finger traced the lacings down to the tip of his toes, where the strange light shouted its presence against the dustiness of the heavy felted wool.

"This is what keeps you from your chores? A grease stain?" she finally said, rubbing at the spot.

"That's no grease stain," he said.

She clucked her tongue and rose.

He captured the ribbon of light on his sleeve. "Can't you see this?"

"Of course. I see a beam of light on you," she said.

"It's not just a beam of light. Look at how it separates here." He pointed. "And here, too!"

He desperately wanted to share this wonder, this joy with Mam. She needed it even more than he did. He put his hand into hers. The skin was calloused from work, the nails short and broken. "Look again," he begged.

"There's work to be done. Market day is coming." She pulled her hand away and pointed to the row of pails hanging on the wall. Ishmael reluctantly turned from the glass without noticing that the bands of light had disappeared.

CHAPTER 3

Ishmael crossed to the springhouse to deliver the milk, walking past the unfinished well—a permanent reminder of Papa, and how Papa was gone, and how it was Ishmael's fault.

Ishmael and Papa had toiled for days on the half-excavated well, with Papa dredging and Ishmael dumping the filled buckets. That last day at the well haunted Ishmael with a series of images that repeated in his mind: the glint from the new glass in the barn door, the indentations from his own footprints in the grass, the muddy streak on the glass from his finger. The return to the well. The well itself, its uneven sides not nearly so deep as they had been before.

"Papa?" There had been no answer. Ishmael had leaned over the edge of the well, but there was no Papa, and there was no water. Only clods of dirt and stones squeezing the space where Papa had been.

Papa was gone.

Now the dirt and the stones pressed on Ishmael, morning and night, overwhelming him with guilt and grief, reminding him that he should have been there at the well. It had been Ishmael's duty as the next oldest to assist Papa since Luc had gone, but Ishmael hadn't been there when Papa needed him most. He had been beguiled by the glass in the barn door.

Now the glass beguiled him again.

All morning Ishmael thought about the span of light, this ghost he had seen, wishing he could give it a name. *Span? Light? Bands?*

All afternoon, he saw the image in his mind, and the bands of light danced over his grief and his guilt, brightening the dimness in his spirit.

Pattern? Ghost?

All night the stain on his boot tapped at his imagination, and he pictured the stain elsewhere: on the gray barn floor, the empty sky, the shorn and solemn sheep.

Beam? Wonder?

He tried to imagine the sky sharp and hot like the one end of the light, and his throat constricted at the smothering energy. To erase the image, he pictured the farm covered in that soft coolness from the center of the bands of light.

Splintered light? Yes, that was it. He would call it splintered light. As the name settled into place, each muscle relaxed. His breath slowed and he slept, and for the first time since Papa's death, his dreams were untroubled by darkness and falling stones and half-dug wells.

The next morning, he ran to the barn early, leaping nimbly over a stone in his path. He rushed, not to tend the sheep, but to see if the splintered light from the day before had returned. And indeed, when he entered the barn and shut the door, there it was. Ishmael's heart swelled at the sight.

It was so beautiful that his breath caught and his fingertips tingled, and again, he was overcome with the desire to share this beauty with someone. He wished he could show Luc, but in his absence, he ran back to the cottage and tugged Jerusha, his seven-year-old sister, to the barn. Perhaps she would do.

"Do you see that?" he asked. "Isn't it beautiful?"

"See what?"

"That there." He pointed to the splintered light.

"What are you talking about, Ishmael?" She looked around. "You're making fun of me, aren't you?" She left the barn in a huff.

As he watched her walk away, disappointment welled up inside. Jerusha could never replace Luc. Ishmael wished he could talk to Luc, that he could ask him what this all meant, but the truth was, Ishmael didn't know where to find him. Luc's disappearance had come after a period of peevishness, a time when Ishmael would catch him, strangely enough, staring into buckets of soapy water. Anytime Ishmael tried to ask him what he was doing, Luc silenced him with a look. Four long years had passed since the day he disappeared, with a birth and a death in their family. And Ishmael, caught in the middle, missed his older brother.

CHAPTER 4

Ishmael squatted by the splintered light. He wanted to touch the very heart of it—to stick his hands into its essence—but he didn't know how to get there. He was certain his fingers would simply graze the rough boards of the floor, rather than graze the sparkle of the light.

Ishmael studied each segment, each band, the places of sharpness and the places of softness, the heat at one end and the chill at the other, and he wished it were larger so that he could see what was at its core. He wished he could stretch it out, so its wonder would grace the whole drab barn from top to bottom. For that matter, he wished it could grace his whole drab life, from top to bottom.

As Ishmael studied it, the light grew stronger, but this time, rather than hesitating as he did before, he held his finger right out to it, reaching for the streak in the middle—the same one that stained his boot. It rose up to meet him and settled on his finger, heavy and humming in its lively way.

He wished once again that he could share this sight with someone. But since he couldn't, he would enjoy it on his own. Maybe he could use it to make the drab barn look different. The thought intrigued him.

Ishmael heaved his arm up, testing its weight. The splintered light soared in the air, and then dropped to his hand. The weight was too much, though, and the light fell to the floor leaving a large splotch. He knelt down and touched it. The effect of the strange light on the dusty boards was delightful, as much a mystery to him as the light itself. He couldn't wait to do it again.

He held his hand out to the bands once more, feeling the heft of the light before he let it sift through his fingers onto the floor. It was a simple game, but it filled him with delight. Again and again, he reached for the splintered light, staining the floorboards until that middle shade covered the floor in a grand sweep. The effect pleased him, and he wondered if he could do this with all the bands of light.

Ishmael reached for the next shade over, and found it as willing as the middle shade. He balanced its weight on the palm of his hand, then pitched it against the wall. It flew like an arrow, splattering on wall, ceiling, and rafters. Exhilarated, he kept going, reaching for a lighter shade and staining the beams. He added bits of all the hues to the animals' pens, the latches, even the door, until the inside of the barn was so full of splintered light, it no longer appeared to be a barn, but an odd, magical place.

He worked fast, for Mam was sure to come searching for the milk if he didn't bring it soon. His arms were sore but somehow stronger, as if the task required more than physical strength. It was as if he were flexing a muscle he hadn't known existed, and the stretch felt so satisfying.

When the light shifted and the bands faded, when the interior of the barn was nearly glowing, when his arms were too tired to lift and his hands tingled, he milked the sheep, then picked up the buckets feeling like all the good things in the world were his for the asking. It was a heady, powerful feeling, one that he wished he could bottle up and store. He smiled as he realized he didn't need to store it; he could replenish this feeling each morning in the barn.

His smile carried him toward the little springhouse. But when it came into sight, reality checked his euphoria. The grayness nullified the glory in the barn, and all good feelings drained out of him footstep by footstep. The door latch hung at an awkward angle, the roof sagged, and the retaining walls bulged in a foreboding way. Only the spring bubbled on, oblivious to the slow ruin happening overhead.

Whatever it was that had happened in the barn, whatever that light was, it had nothing to do with Ishmael's existence here. It had nothing to do with Papa's death or Mam's life or the animals' needs. It had nothing to do with how much he missed Luc, or what his duty was now that Luc was gone. It had nothing to do with him. Not now. Perhaps not ever.

He set the milk down and bent over, choked by the darkness and how very alone he felt. If Luc were here, Ishmael would be able to endure the bleakness that accumulated into minutes and hours and days and weeks.

But Luc was not here.

He needed to find Luc. Ishmael breathed in and out until he was calm again, thinking of how things would be easier if Luc were here. He picked up the bucket and entered the springhouse. He glanced at Mam as she pulled out a tray of ripening cheeses. Her mouth turned down in sadness, with the look she had worn for weeks.

"Mam?" He spoke her name, but his mouth was so dry, it came out as a whisper. He licked his lips and tried again. "Mam?" he said, a bit louder.

"What is it, Ishmael?" she said without looking at him, carefully putting the tray down. "I think these will be ready to sell next market day—and a good thing, too. I've got to start making smaller cheeses. I can't lift these the way your father could." She arched her back, stretching, and then began turning the cheeses.

But Ishmael didn't know how to say what he needed to say.

"What is it?" Mam said again.

"I want to find Luc." Ishmael pulled out another tray and set it down next to hers.

Mam stopped, a wheel of cheese frozen in mid-turn. The

heavy cheese slipped out of her hands and landed with a loud thud. "Luc?"

Ishmael grimaced at the sound in her voice. "He should know what happened to Papa. And I . . . miss him." He didn't say that if Luc were home again Mam wouldn't have to make smaller cheeses or that the door latch could be fixed or the roof might have a chance of being shored up. He didn't say that their struggles would be eased or that Simon might listen to Luc in a way he never listened to Ishmael. But he thought it.

Mam picked up the tray and returned it to the rack. She got out an empty tray and the tub of brine with yesterday's cheese soaking in it. But all she said was, "Luc's gone." Ishmael couldn't see her face, but her voice was tight, and it made him nervous.

Ishmael took a hook off a peg to retrieve the cheese from the brine. "But where is he? He can't have just disappeared."

"He did." She took the hook and splashed it into the brine with a little too much force. "You need to forget him."

"I can't. I don't know how you can, either." The words slipped out of Ishmael's mouth.

Mam's face struggled to contain sudden emotion. She lifted the new cheese from the brine, letting the salty water slide down the cheese like tears dropping into the tub, and then placed it on the tray. She turned back to the brine, her hand at her mouth.

He squeezed his eyes closed, shutting out everything. "I'm sorry, Mam. I just need to find him."

Mam turned and touched his eyelids with the tip of her

finger, one after the other, then let her hand drop. She sighed. "Open your eyes, Ishmael."

He opened them. Ishmael clasped his hands together instead, squeezing his knuckles hard as if that could keep his sorrow from leaking out. "If you know where he is, please tell me, Mam."

"Your father said you'd ask questions some day." She turned away, tapping her fingers on the table. "Of course, he was the one who urged Luc to go when the circumstances arose. Said he had more potential than to waste his life with sheep. I thought he was needed at home." She returned the hook to its peg on the wall and rubbed furiously at her face. "I've suffered too much loss this year." To Ishmael's eyes, she suddenly looked very scared, not like his Mam at all.

"Please, Mam. Can you just tell me where he is?"

She took a deep breath and straightened her shoulders. "Have you ever seen someone who is different here?"

Ishmael thought for a minute. "What sort of 'different' do you mean?"

"My mother used to tell me a story of a man who was different. They said he could talk to the stones he used in his trade, that they would obey his word. The villagers drove him out of town. It's said that the very next day the Commons appeared fully formed, right there on the hill, looking for all the world as if it had always been there."

Ishmael hadn't given much thought to the Commons since that day when he and Luc had rolled down the hill, the day he was taught to stay away from it.

"What does that have to do with Luc?"

Mam bent over and swished her hands in the water of the spring, drying them off on her apron. "That's where Luc is."

Her words jolted Ishmael. The Commons?

"Come," she said, reaching for the bucket of milk in the spring. Mam made her way to the cottage where she went directly to a chest in the corner of the kitchen. Buried deep in the chest was a large leather-bound book that she handed to Ishmael. "Perhaps this will help you understand."

He glanced at its title, *A History of the Commons*.

"Luc left this behind." Mam retrieved the bucket of milk and sloshed it into the cauldron set over the coals left from breakfast.

Confused, Ishmael set the book down on the table and opened the cover, pausing at the title page with its intricate loops and scrolls and letters: *A HISTORY OF THE COMMONS, from Its Inception*. On the next leaf was a map.

Ishmael scanned the map, following a heavy line around the edge of the page. It formed a large lopsided oval, an oval that appeared to represent the exterior wall of the Commons. Tiny dots led from the road to the wall, and where they met sat the gate.

Within the walls, there were sketches of dozens of tiny buildings, a confusing array of architectural shapes rising up: crenellated turrets, plunging rooflines, squat chimneys, domes, spires, and arches, as well as courtyards and cloisters. There were walkways large and small, and Ishmael saw what even looked like a bell tower.

He turned the page.

The table of contents listed sections with headings about seven different halls, but he became stuck in the meaning of the words. Hall of Shape, Hall of Motion—those were the only words he understood. He knew what shape was. He knew what motion was. He could imagine putting shape together with motion: the sheep, round with their wool just before shearing, moving through the pasture. But Hall of Scent? Hall of Hue? Hall of Gustation? What was scent? What was hue? What was gustation? And why was Luc there?

Ishmael turned back to the map and studied its lines, trying to imagine himself knocking on the massive door in the gate, walking those paths, finding his brother. But the thought of going to the Commons made him squirm inside. That whipping switch from so long ago had convinced him that he shouldn't go near there. Ever. But Mam would never ask him to get Luc, even if it was clear she wanted him to come home.

Days passed, filled with a mixture of wonder and grief and work and indecision. Each morning, Ishmael would see the light in the barn, which soaked him in a warm bath of joy. But come nightfall, he saw how tired Mam was from the never-ending work. Threaded through this was the certainty that Luc needed to know about Papa's death and the desire to ask Luc about the splintered light. The only way any of these things could happen was if Ishmael went to the Commons to fetch him home.

After nearly a week of this uncertainty, Ishmael made a decision. That night, he wrote Mam a note.

Dear Mam,

I am going to find Luc. I won't come back without him.

Love, Ishmael.

PART II

THE COMMONS

Glory be to God for dappled things—
For skies of couple-colour as a brinded cow;
For rose-moles all in stipple upon trout that swim.

Gerard Manley Hopkins, "Pied Beauty"

THE STONES

The walls surrounding the Commons were ancient stone walls, thick with history and mystery. Each stone could tell stories of time gone by yet there were few who listened, so the stones sat mute, encircling the turrets and towers and domes of the Commons. They kept their silence as time passed, and hunkered down against the other stones of the wall, until they were called upon for a higher purpose.

On this day, a higher purpose appeared. A boy stood before their gates. He carried a satchel slung over his shoulder, and he wore rough woolen breeches and a plain jersey. The stones drew themselves up, and fitted themselves together a bit more snugly to look their best.

Stumbling over an uneven spot in the path, the boy reached out to steady himself on the stone wall. As the whorls and swirls on the boy's fingers touched them, the stones read the story in the cracks and crevices of his skin and looked into his soul. What they saw there made them sag in disgrace.

This boy had been betrayed by their own kind, by dirt and sand and rock. In a moment of weakness, their unstable cousins had taken his father. Appalled, the stones in the wall wondered how they could make amends for the inconstancy of their kindred. They couldn't give him back his father, but perhaps they could make amends another way.

His hand told the story of another that he sought. His brother. They would begin their penance by leading him to his brother.

It wasn't much, but it was a place to start.

CHAPTER

5

I shmael stared at the huge wooden gate in front of him. On the left half of the gate was a plaque with The Commons carved in bold letters. Below it was carved Hall of Shape, Hall of Motion, Hall of Manufactory, Hall of Hue, Hall of Sound, Hall of Scent, Hall of Gustation. As he watched, the letters glowed more brightly, and the plaque shone with a patina he hadn't noticed before.

A small door set within the right side of the gate bore a shiny metal knocker and a barred window. Ishmael fingered the knocker. It was heavy, shaped like a teardrop, with the face of a man protruding from it. Underneath, in small letters were the words The Common Man.

Ishmael looked around, worried that the book was wrong, and he shouldn't be here. He rubbed his thumb over the filigrees, took a deep breath, and let the knocker fall. The reverberations rang out on the other side of the gate. A rumbling came from inside, a groaning and a creaking and a light pattering of pebbles, but no one came.

He lifted the knocker and let it fall again. Stretching as high as he could, he grasped the windowsill and pulled himself up to peek through. There was only a small, dull courtyard: gravel pathways, pale vines growing along the walls, an archway. He had expected something grand, not this very plain and very ordinary square. No one was there, and he saw nothing that could have made that rumbling noise. Dropping from the window, Ishmael tried the doorknob and found the door unlocked, so he pushed it open and stepped through.

"H-hello?" he called out, his voice wavering. He wouldn't do this if it weren't absolutely necessary—for Mam *and* for him.

Behind the door, the gravel pathways were raked, the hedges neatly trimmed and edged. The walls surrounding the small courtyard were covered in vines bearing tiny flowers. On a closer look, Ishmael realized they were all carved stone—each flower, each leaf, each vine. Cut into the wall was a single archway at his left.

There was no other way to go so Ishmael stepped toward the arch. A swirl and a flash came from behind the wall. He hesitated, then ducked inside and caught his breath at the glimmer of splintered light.

A meadow of aging light rolled into the distance, surrounded by stones that were no longer a soft, wise gray, but bright and brilliant. The air was sharp and clear. A small breeze ruffled his hair, and with a great rushing sound, it rolled through the grasses so that it seemed as if the meadow pulsed in a dance of sheer joy.

Ishmael filled himself with that vibrant air, all thoughts of finding Luc and returning home gone. Why had he been so nervous to come here? He wanted to soak up the light until he overflowed with it. His body tingled from the top of his head through his fingertips, and down to his toes. Gazing at the meadow from one end to the other, Ishmael realized it was smaller than the yard between the barn and their cottage back home, perhaps only an acre. He caught sight of someone at the far end of the meadow with his back turned toward him. His arm was raised and a flash of light sprang from it.

"Hello?" he called out.

His voice startled the person. A globe of splintered light spun on his finger, which wobbled and fell as he turned. In a split second, the young man's hand dived under it and he pulled it back up.

Something familiar about the gesture made Ishmael look closer. The boy glowed in a vibrant way, as if he couldn't contain the brilliance inside. It almost made Ishmael's eyes ache to look at him.

"Luc?"

The young man peered at Ishmael. "Ishmael?"

Ishmael nodded, grinning from ear to ear.

With a great whoop that echoed off the relieved stones of the surrounding wall, Luc charged toward him. "It *is* you!" He put his hands on Ishmael's shoulders, spun him around, and then bent over to hug him. "I hardly recognized you! What are you doing here?"

Ishmael's face fell, and the purpose of his trip rose up like a monster before him.

"What is it?" Luc asked.

"Papa's dead." Ishmael explained what had happened, about the well and his own neglect, and finished with, "Mam needs you. I told her I wouldn't come back without you." Ishmael shuffled his feet nervously, afraid that Luc would blame him as much as he blamed himself for what happened.

Luc's head bowed, and Ishmael could see disbelief and then grief settle into the lines and planes of Luc's face. He couldn't remember the last time he had seen Luc's tears, from either grief or pain. He reached for Luc's hand and squeezed it. Luc returned the squeeze, and they sat like that for some time. Luc finally wiped his eyes, and as he did so, his view shifted.

"What's that?" he said. "On your boot?"

Ishmael was taken aback. "You can see that?"

"Of course I see it. You have it, too?"

"Have what?"

"Color."

"What's color?"

Luc gave him a knowing look. "You saw something back home that nobody else saw, didn't you? A shifting of light maybe?"

Ishmael nodded cautiously, wondering how this conversation had turned so suddenly.

Luc smiled, then squeezed Ishmael's shoulder. "That's color. I'd better take you right to Color Master. She's going to want to test you."

"But what about Mam and the farm? We need to go back."

"I'm sorry about Papa, truly I am, and I'm sorry that Mam is struggling, but the stones wouldn't have allowed you to come in if you didn't belong here. You're going to be a color keeper, little brother."

"A what?"

Though Luc was still grief-stricken, he tried to smile. "A color keeper, like me. Color Master lectures about the duties of a color keeper the first day: *Color keepers seek harmony through the use of our skills by honoring each color and respecting its individuality. To do otherwise is forbidden.* You'll recite that every morning until the day you leave."

Ishmael looked at him blankly.

"What you saw back home?" Luc said. "That's color. What you have on your boot? That's color. What's all around us here? Color. And it's my color."

Ishmael looked at the color surrounding them.

Luc tapped the stone at his side. "I designed and worked on the color. This is my posticum."

"What's a posticum?"

Luc gestured to the meadow. "*This* is a posticum. Posticum

means 'back door.' It's a room for creation that opens up in the stone wall of the Commons. Back home is a posticum, too, but you'd never know it. Color Master told me it was one of the first. All the oldest posticums are worn out and run-down and only have oval sheep and round chickens. The sheep and chickens in the newer posticums are more refined. Plus, they have all kinds of other creatures as well. That's how you know the age of posticums."

Bewildered, Ishmael lifted the strap of his satchel over his head and let it slide down his arm. He didn't care what a posticum was; he just wanted to bring Luc home.

Luc misunderstood Ishmael's silence. "You don't understand, do you? That's all right—you don't have to worry about it for some time."

Ishmael frowned. "Can we go home now?"

"Ishmael, I . . . I can't. I've got to finish my work and attend the laurels ceremony. It wouldn't be fair to the others who have worked so hard here."

Not to be deterred, Ishmael said, "When can we go, then?"

"I don't know. But in the meantime, you can be tested and begin training as a color keeper. Then we'll see, all right?"

"I can't stay here."

"No, you can't stay here. You're not even supposed to be in here. Let's go see Color Master about testing."

"That's not what I mean. I can't stay here at the Commons."

"I know. But you also can't stay here in my posticum."

Luc twirled the handle of the glass instrument in his hand

and walked toward the arch. Ishmael pulled the strap of his satchel back over his shoulder, and tried to get a better look at what Luc held. How different it was from the pane of glass back home. At the thought of home, Ishmael had a sinking suspicion that this wasn't going to be as easy as he thought.

CHAPTER

6

W hen the two brothers left the posticum, Luc led Ishmael across the small courtyard to an archway. Ishmael stopped at its threshold, a bit unnerved. "This wasn't here before. There was only the entrance back there." He pointed to the arch leading to Luc's posticum.

Luc nodded, unsurprised. "The stones were at work."

Ishmael remembered the rumbling he had heard just before he opened the door. He touched the stone of the archway. It felt warm, but very solid. Ishmael shook his head, then passed through into a much larger courtyard. Again, this space was without color, but it seemed shinier than the smaller courtyard they had just exited.

"Papa's really gone?" Luc said.

Ishmael nodded.

"It's just hard to believe he's not there chasing the sheep or fixing a fence."

"It feels pretty empty without him. Of course, it's felt pretty empty ever since you left, too. Now it's just emptier."

As they walked, Luc pointed with half a heart. "This is the Great Courtyard," he said. Paved with slabs of stone, the space extended to a collection of buildings and walls. In the center, a fountain splashed.

At their left was a building with rounded windows and multiple chimneys. "That's the refectory. We eat there. That other building," he pointed to a large domed building on their right that had a bell tower adjoining it, "is Wright Hall. And that doorway over there," he pointed to one of the arched doorways in the wall opposite them, "is where we're headed. That's the entrance to the Hall of Hue. Come on—Color Master should be in her office."

They walked across the Great Courtyard and through the arched doorway. To the left and ahead of them were two matching squat buildings lined with dozens of windows.

"Dormitories," Luc said.

There was a tower at the end of the second dormitory, then a cloistered walkway leading to another arched doorway.

Luc led them through the arched doorway and down a hallway to a workroom. Ishmael stopped in his tracks. The room was easily three times the size of the barn back home, with light pouring through enormous leaded-glass windows. Around the perimeter of the room, single colors circulated through vials and tubes in complicated machinery. Directly in front of them were rows of workbenches. At the rear of the room, a large stone sink stood next to a doorway leading into another room. At their left, vials of color hung suspended from a rack, lined up neatly in the order Ishmael remembered from the splintered light in the barn. Empty vials dangled from another rack next to it. Stone jars stood in the back left corner.

Several bands of color hung in the air—some spinning slowly, some whirling in a centrifuge—each one projecting from a single prism stationed beneath. Ishmael edged closer to one of them to get a better look as the colors spun overhead. They flowed together, so that he couldn't tell where one band ended and another began.

He stood spellbound at the sight. Warm sweetness stretched through his arms and legs, momentarily releasing him from the worries of the farm and his family. Strangely, even though he couldn't have imagined such a place existed, he felt like he was home.

"Like it?" Luc asked.

Ishmael smiled. That was an understatement.

Just then a woman poked her head out of a doorway to their left. Though she, too, glowed in the same way Luc did, everything else about the woman bespoke disapproval, from the incline of her head to the hard light glinting off her spectacles to the stance of her tall, thin body. Even the color of her robe seemed to agree. It blazed ferociously.

"And who is this?" she said.

Luc steered Ishmael around to face her. "Color Master, this is my younger brother, Ishmael."

"Your brother?" The clipped words were just as disapproving. "And how did you come to be here, brother of Luc? Did someone let you in?" Suspicion showed in her eyes.

"No, ma'am," he said. "I knocked at the gate, but no one answered, so I tried the door and it was unlocked."

Her eyebrows rose, and she looked at Luc. "You brought him for testing, I presume?"

"Yes, ma'am." He smiled, but she didn't return the smile.

"The sight rarely shows up this early, and never in the same family line," Color Master said, shaking her head. "Certainly, in all my years as Hall master for the Hall of Hue, I've seen it only once."

This information was a strange relief to Ishmael. Perhaps he wouldn't have to be tested after all, and he could just persuade Luc to go home, though he would be sorry to leave this room of color.

"How old are you?" Color Master said.

"Eleven, last spring," Ishmael replied.

"Hmm." Color Master made a tent of her fingers and tapped her lips. She looked at Ishmael, sizing him up. Her eyes stopped at the large splotch of that brilliant hue on Ishmael's boot. Ishmael immediately slid the marked boot behind his other ankle. Color Master angled herself to study Ishmael's boot. She tilted her head and squinted behind her spectacles.

Ishmael slid his foot farther back.

Color Master picked up a large canvas bag. "Since the day is fine, we'll go outside. Would you care to join us, Luc? Normally, I test privately, but since you are family, I'll make an exception."

"But I don't want to be tested," Ishmael declared.

"Come, come, now. Just nerves, my boy."

Ishmael opened his mouth, but nothing came out. How could someone so very *tall* be so utterly wrong? And why wasn't Luc standing up for him? Luc knew he had to return home. He couldn't leave Mam alone on the farm.

And just like that, inspiration struck.

CHAPTER

7

They walked back outside to the colorless courtyard. Bending over like an awkward bird, Color Master pulled a large canvas cloth from her bag and spread it over the ground. She smoothed the wrinkles, then gestured for Ishmael to sit.

Ishmael glanced at Luc. Pride and excitement had pushed some of his grief away, and he grinned.

Color Master took a linen-covered bundle from her sack and unrolled it. Inside were dozens of sticks, each a different shade. Ishmael immediately ran his fingers across the sticks, wanting to line them up from lightest to darkest.

Color Master tipped her head, studying him.

The movement caught Ishmael's attention, and he remembered that if his plan were to work, he must not react. He took a deep breath and pulled his hand away from the colored jumble on the cloth. He needed to trick Color Master into thinking he couldn't see color.

A breeze blew, lifting the corner of the cloth.

"Pick one," Color Master said, watching Ishmael carefully.

Pick one? The task seemed simple, but which one should he pick? And why? Ishmael's eyes roved from one stick to the next. They were all enticing. It was hard enough trying to ignore the brightness of Color Master's robes. This was infinitely worse.

He looked from stick to stick to stick, hopeless. At the edge of the pile, he saw a stick that lacked color. It was pale, the color of nothingness. It was the color of *before*. It was the color of the linens after wash day, the color of newly shorn sheep, the color of fresh cream. Relief settled upon him. If he picked one of the colored sticks, Color Master would *know* he could see the color. This one might trick her. With a great deal of confidence, he presented this stick to Color Master.

"Hmm," Color Master said, nodding. "You're left-handed."

That wasn't what Ishmael had expected to hear. Deflated, he nodded with a guilty look. "Sorry. I forget sometimes to use my right hand."

"By all means use your left hand if you're more comfortable that way. Most of our apprentices do." Color Master waved the chosen stick in her hand. "Interesting choice. White."

"White?"

"That's its name. Why did you choose that one?"

"It . . . it looks—" Ishmael faltered, looking for an appropriate word. Bland? Flat? Different? Plain? "Clean," he finally said. "It looks clean."

Luc snickered.

"To be sure," Color Master murmured, peering at Ishmael until he squirmed under the scrutiny. "And none of that, Luc, or I'll have to ask you to leave."

She closed the notebook and placed the stick back with the others.

"Is that it?" Ishmael asked.

Color Master raised her eyebrows. "We're only just beginning," she said with a small smile. "Your observation is . . . unexpected."

Ishmael reached for the stick closest to him and rolled it in his hands. "How is it that one person can see something and another cannot?"

"My job right now is not to question *how* something exists, but to question if it exists at all. Are you ready for the next test?" Color Master asked. Without waiting for an answer,

Color Master pointed toward the pile of sticks jumbled up in front of Ishmael. "I'd like you to match these sticks. I will pick one stick, and I want you to find a stick that looks similar. Do you understand?"

"Yes, ma'am," Ishmael said. "But what if they all look the same?" He looked sideways at Color Master.

"Do the best you can," Color Master said. She picked up a stick the same color as the splotch on Ishmael's boot. "We'll begin with green. This is green."

Ishmael looked at it. "Green?" he asked, testing the word on his tongue.

That color spoke peace to him. He smiled, thinking of the floor of the barn—the hay and muck and dust—all covered by green. *Don't react*, he reminded himself, and let the smile sink downward until his face smoothed out.

"Go on," Color Master said.

There were several sticks scattered across the cloth in various shades of green. Ishmael slowly pulled a stick out from under the others and laid it on the cloth in front of him. It was the shade of energy, of heat and anger and courage—about as far as one could get from green, and it matched the color of Color Master's robes.

"Hmm. Could be a red-green imbalance," Color Master said under her breath, noting it in her book. She picked up a different one. "This is indigo. Please find an indigo stick."

Indigo. Ishmael had used that color for the ceiling of the barn. It was the color of wishes and wants, the color of luck. He wished for luck now as he perused the pile of sticks to find the opposite of indigo. He found a perfect color, raw and violent. He picked it up and laid it next to the indigo stick, seeing spots when he looked away.

"Ishmael! What are you doing?" Luc burst out.

Color Master silenced him with one look. "Orange? But the wavelength is so much longer than indigo," Color Master muttered. "Try this one," she said, sizing up Ishmael. "This is yellow."

Ishmael ran his fingers through his hair, pulling at the ends. Anxious to finish, he turned toward a peaceful color.

"Hmph." Color Master squinted at him. "Let's try something different. Match the sticks as quickly as you can, and I'll time you." She set out a new row of sticks to match.

Ishmael gulped the air and grabbed sticks in as random a pattern as he could, making sure he never matched colors. When he came to the final stick, he glanced up at Color Master, who watched Ishmael with a curious expression.

"I'm finished," Ishmael said.

"Yes, I see," Color Master said, pursing her lips.

"Is everything all right?" Ishmael asked after a few seconds.

"Everything is fine." A faint smile crossed her face.

The look made him nervous. More than anything, Ishmael wanted Color Master to say they were done so Ishmael could leave, return to his colorless world with Luc, return to normal. "Are we finished, then?" Ishmael asked.

Color Master tapped her chin with one long finger, giving first Luc, then Ishmael, a measured look. She shrugged, then lined up the edges of all the sticks. Rolling up the bundle, she tied it shut, and returned it to her sack before answering. "I have learned as much as I need to know."

"And . . .?" Luc said.

"He gives every indication that he sees nothing out of the ordinary."

The tension in Ishmael cracked, and he took a deep breath of the sweet air. He had done it, but he wasn't sure if he was pleased or disappointed.

Luc, on the other hand, looked disbelieving.

"This has been very enlightening for me," Color Master said. "Will you join us for our midday meal now, Ishmael? You are welcome to stay."

"Yes, please." Nerves had driven away Ishmael's hunger, but now that the testing was over, it was back in full force, and a loud grumble came from the depths of his stomach.

Color Master picked up her sack and folded the canvas they had sat upon. "What will become of you?"

"I'll return home and tend the sheep. Mam needs me."

"Ah. Familial duty. There are few things more important than one's family."

Ishmael shrugged.

"There are few, but there are some." Color Master took a twist of paper from a deep pocket of her robe and held it toward Ishmael.

"What's that?" Ishmael asked, taking the packet.

"Some seasoning you might enjoy at lunch. Many outsiders who visit the Hall of Hue find our meals somewhat . . . lacking. Just sprinkle the contents over the top of your food."

Ishmael regarded the twist of paper with curiosity.

Luc peeked over Ishmael's shoulder. "But that looks like—"

"Ah!" Color Master cut Luc off. "Let's allow Ishmael to enjoy his meal, yes?"

Luc looked doubtful. "If you say so."

"I do. Now, why don't you boys head to the refectory? I'll return this to my office, then follow."

"Thank you, Color Master," Luc murmured.

Ishmael echoed him, and they headed through the archway back into the Great Courtyard.

CHAPTER
8

W hat were you playing at, Ishmael?" Luc said.

"Nothing." Ishmael moved his feet faster, as if he could out-run Luc's question.

"Oh, come on. You could have matched those colored sticks!"

"I can't stay here. Even if I wanted to, I can't leave Mam on her own. Papa died because of me," Ishmael said, his voice catching on the words. "No one else can help Mam, because there is no one else. There's just you. And me. Jerusha and Simon are too young."

"Simon?"

"He was born after you left."

Luc stopped. "I have another brother?"

"Yes, he's—" But any further explanation he might have given was interrupted by the loud bong of a bell.

At the sound, dozens of apprentices converged on the courtyard and headed toward the refectory. Each of them carried the same brightness that Luc had, as if there were a spark kindled deep inside that caused them to glow. The wave of apprentices flowed around the two brothers as they stood rooted there—Luc surprised at the existence of another brother and Ishmael overwhelmed by the sheer number of apprentices, the sound of the bell, and the newness of the Commons.

Luc started moving toward the refectory again, joining the crowd of apprentices, and Ishmael trotted along behind him. "Clearly we have a lot of catching up to do. Can't you stay for a few days, little brother? You just got here."

Ishmael looked up to reply, a split second too late to notice the girl in front of him. Too late to see her standing still in the mass of shifting apprentices. Too late to stop his forward motion. Too late to do anything but collide with her and fall to the ground. The bump from him pushed her off-balance. She tripped over his legs, then landed on top of him in a tangle.

"Oof!" The air rushed out of Ishmael in one big whoosh. He tried to say something, but couldn't manage even the smallest squeak.

The girl pushed herself up, grinding Ishmael's knee into the stone pavers below him.

"Are you all right?" she asked him. "I'm sorry—I didn't see

you until . . . I—I was listening to the echo of the bell." She brushed off her hands and nervously twisted something she wore around her wrist while Ishmael got to his feet.

"The bell?" Ishmael said.

"Didn't you hear the way . . .?" She stopped at the uncomprehending look on Ishmael's face. "You're not . . .?" Confused, she looked at Luc, then back to Ishmael. "Sorry. Never mind." The girl cocked her head. "I'm Phoebe, by the way. Who are you?"

"Ishmael."

"Ishmael," she repeated, stringing the syllables of his name together in a melodious way. When the final sound faded, Phoebe backed away from them, then said, "See you later." She turned and ran toward the fountain. As he watched, the tails of the scarf around Phoebe's neck fluttered down into the water. She seemed vulnerable. The palest of pale colors. In fact, she didn't seem as vivid or as gleaming as the others. Pale skin, pale eyes.

"Novice from the Hall of Sound," Luc explained. "You can tell by the pitch pipe they wear around their wrists."

There were so many things in those sentences that Ishmael didn't understand. "What's a novice?"

"New student here. A first year. After a year of training, you become an apprentice. Once you're assigned a posticum, you're called an artisan, like me. When you finish your posticum, you're given a crown of laurels and you become—in our case—a color keeper." Luc lifted his chin toward the girl. "In her case, a sound keeper. The Hall of Sound novices arrived last week. They hear things."

Ishmael pulled his satchel higher on his shoulder. "Don't we all?"

"They hear more."

Ishmael looked back at Phoebe, wondering what things she heard that he didn't. She sat on the stones surrounding the fountain, oblivious to everything but the sound of people's feet shuffling along. She closed her eyes and lifted her head. One finger tapped out a rhythm.

Luc continued. "The Commons isn't made up of just the Hall of Hue. The rest of the Halls do other things. None of them can see color, though—they're all colorblind. Let me show you." He whipped out the glass instrument he used before. "Watch this!" he said with a wink.

In seconds, Luc threw globes of color into the air, one after another. They swirled above Phoebe and landed on her head, streaming down her long, dark hair. Color oozed onto her shoulders and down her back.

Several of the apprentices stopped to watch. One of them guffawed loudly, pointing at Phoebe.

"See? She's blind to it," Luc said.

Phoebe sat by the fountain, her hair streaked indigo and yellow and green. Oddly, the colors suited her, but something about it troubled Ishmael. He wasn't sure if it was because she was being ridiculed or because she didn't know it. It didn't seem fair or right. It didn't seem like Luc.

Ishmael wished he had the pane of glass from the barn with him so he could do something about the colors that draped over her—even if he had no idea what. He glanced at the instrument in Luc's hand.

"Can I see that?" Ishmael pointed to Luc's hand.

"My prism? Sure! Once you learn how to use it, you'll be able to do amazing—"

The moment it touched Ishmael's fingers, the splintered light coalesced above his head, colors appearing from nowhere—from nothing—as if they had simply been waiting for Ishmael's attention. Before he could say or do anything, a ray of green edged toward Phoebe.

Luc gaped upward, utterly speechless. He grabbed the prism, and the colors disintegrated.

Dozens of apprentices stared at Ishmael and at the place the color had been seconds ago. He might have fooled Color Master at the testing, but in one fell swoop, Ishmael had somehow paraded his gift with color in front of all the other color apprentices. He hadn't meant to; in fact, he hadn't realized he would be able to do anything. "I just wanted—"

But Luc didn't let him finish. A broad grin lit up his face. "I knew you weren't being honest before. How did you do that?"

Rattled, Ishmael said, "I didn't do anything." He wished he could hide.

Luc pulled him through a door into the refectory and prodded him up a flight of steps. The other color apprentices who had witnessed the spectacle followed, whispering and staring at Ishmael. They entered a large room filled with seven rows of long tables and benches.

"We'll talk more later," Luc said quietly. Louder, he said, "Shove over, Stephen. My brother is going to be the youngest master color keeper ever—mark my words—but first we need to eat!"

A tall boy at the end of the table moved, and Ishmael settled on the hard bench next to him. Luc sat opposite and said, "It's so good to see you."

Before anyone else could speak, a man stood at the lectern and raised his arms for attention. He was thin, and his balding head was crowned with a circle of cropped hair. Thick spectacles magnified his eyes so that they appeared larger than normal. The sounds of scuffling ceased.

"That's Head Master," Luc whispered.

"Soon we will indulge in this glorious meal, but first, please remember that the Hall of Hue novices will join our circle tomorrow. We look forward to welcoming them. Now, let's extend our appreciation to the Gustation apprentices who have prepared today's inspiring food."

At his words, everyone applauded, and groups of apprentices marched through the refectory carrying platters of sliced bread, meat pies, bowls of fruit, and steaming dishes of vegetables. They served the long table at the front first, then set platters and bowls, full to overflowing, on each of the other tables.

Stephen poured water into his mug and handed the pitcher to Ishmael. "So you came early, eh?"

"I'm not a nov—" he began, but Luc interrupted him.

"My brother is ahead of his time, in more ways than one. I can't wait to begin his training." He beamed at Ishmael.

A boy settled a meat pie in front of Luc. He cut into it and lifted a piece onto Ishmael's plate. Meals at home were mostly all porridge and cheese and mutton. Ishmael had never seen anything like this. In fact, he had never been at such a lively meal. Ever since Papa had died, meals had become progressively more silent, as if he had taken all the words with him, sucked down into the well. Here the amount of talk seemed limitless.

Ishmael picked up his fork in his right hand, but when he awkwardly stabbed at a piece of the crust, his elbow knocked Stephen's arm and the crust flew off his plate. Each apprentice at his table ate with his left hand. Though Mam wouldn't approve, he switched hands, relieved to finally be able to eat in a way that felt natural.

"Don't forget about what Color Master gave you," Luc said with a small smile.

"Oh. Right." Ishmael took the twist of paper from his pocket.

"What's that?" Stephen asked.

Luc shrugged, and then popped a bite of pie into his mouth while Ishmael untwisted the paper and opened the packet. It was filled with a very fine powder. He hesitated, so Luc reached over and tilted the contents onto Ishmael's food, and the meat pie turned a brilliant shade of violet.

Ishmael choked, coughing and sputtering. Stephen walloped him on the back, and Luc poured some water into a cup for him.

Just then, Color Master came up behind him. "Enjoying your food, Ishmael?"

"Something's wrong with the pie! Look at it! Can't you see—" He stopped speaking. Of course Color Master could see. So could everyone else sitting at his table. The twist of paper held color.

"You tricked me!" Ishmael rose, indignant.

Color Master smiled brightly and nodded. "Might I remind you, however, that I am not the only one guilty of trickery here?"

Ishmael turned away from the bizarre sight on his plate.

"Would you like a new serving?"

He closed his eyes and nodded. When he opened his eyes again, a clean plate sat in front of him with a fresh serving of the pie. Ishmael wasn't sure he could eat it now, with or without the color.

Color Master kept talking. "The novices will begin their training the day after tomorrow. I'd like you to be part of that group," she said.

Her words troubled Ishmael. He looked at Luc, proud older brother. The thought of being immersed in all that color was so enticing, but Ishmael hadn't journeyed here to become a color keeper. Mam needed him—*and* Luc—back at the farm.

"You think about it," Color Master said and returned to the table at the front.

CHAPTER 9

Once Color Master left, conversation carried on. Luc chatted, not noticing how quiet Ishmael was. Ishmael could neither talk nor eat. Instead, he pushed his food around on his plate with his fork, like he was herding the sheep. He almost wished he had never come.

When Luc finished eating, he went to speak to Color Master and returned after a few minutes. "I asked Color Master for permission to have you observe my work this afternoon to get a better sense of what we do here. Normally, no one gets to see the posticums until after the laurels ceremony, but considering you've already seen it *and* you're my brother, she said she'd make an exception for you."

The walk to the posticum took only a few minutes, during which Ishmael tried hard not to compare the crisp lines of the

Great Courtyard, the carved stone parapets, the bell tower, and the gabled windows to the packed dirt, ramshackle cottage, and slumping barn that was his home. It was hard not to; it was as if he were in a completely different world here.

When they reached the posticum, Luc walked directly toward the back, where he had been when Ishmael first saw him. He pointed to a swath of colorless plants fanning out from the side of the stone wall. Several different types grew, grouped together in clumps. All were long and straight, from the groundcover to the trees to the flowers. Everything pointed upward. "Today, I need to finish coloring the plants so Sound, Scent, and Gustation can do their part."

"How do you color them?"

Luc's eyes lit up. "That's the fun part. Watch this." Luc retrieved a stone jar from the edge of the plants and pulled out his prism. He opened the jar slightly, releasing a flash of light, and whirled his prism in a circle to splinter the light. When the colors were strong and clear, he rotated his prism until yellow began to rise from its place among the others and spin into a sphere. When the sphere was complete, Luc flicked the prism, releasing the globe. All the other colors drifted away while the sphere of yellow revolved, turning from light to dark until Luc found the hue that he wanted: a very pale golden color.

Luc lifted the prism, and the pale golden color rose upward in a stream, as if the globe of color were unwinding. He shifted his arm and the color followed its trajectory, drifting down on one clump of plants, sprinkling the leaves and stems and flowers.

"This isn't the final color," Luc said. "It needs time to mature."

Ishmael was fascinated by the sight. "What will it look like when it matures? How long will it take until it's done?" He knew he had no right to be curious about the process, but he couldn't help it.

"Oh, not too long. A couple of days, maybe. Why? You want to see it finished?" Luc grinned.

Ishmael shrugged, trying to be nonchalant. Even though he thought playing with the colors in the barn at home had been glorious, he had never dreamed how sophisticated color could be. Entranced, Ishmael watched as the minutes passed, happy to be at his brother's side once more. It would be so good to have Luc at home again.

When Luc worked color over the leaves of the last barren plant, he twisted the prism, releasing the pale golden ball. It hung in the air for a moment before fading away.

"How can you hold the color that long?" Ishmael asked. "It's so heavy."

Luc smiled. "You get used to it. Besides, there are no impurities, which makes it lighter. Ready for more?"

Of course Ishmael was ready for more. He could watch this all day.

Luc released a flash of light, lifted his prism again, and repeated the process until another yellow globe spun before him. This time, he drew a deeper golden shade upward and let it slink fluidly to the broad stem of one of the plants. The line wrapped itself around the stem, and immediately, the color began to seep into it, darkening it.

Ishmael never would have thought such a thing possible. He stood spellbound at the sight.

Before Luc could color another stem, Ishmael blurted out, "Can I try?"

Luc paused, holding the globe steady. "I wish I could let you, but I'm supposed to do all the work. Besides, this is pretty advanced stuff. What you did before—back in the courtyard—was pretty impressive for a novice, but it's taken me years to learn how to do this. Creation is no small matter, little brother. You'll get a chance soon enough." Luc sent more color out of the globe to a stem.

Ishmael tried not to feel disappointed as he watched the color swirl about, infusing the stalks with a lush glow. Nothing at the farm was even a fraction as brilliant as what was here. It filled Ishmael with a deep longing—before that day in the barn, he never even knew such beauty existed and now, seeing the skill and depth of his brother's work, he wanted nothing more than to be surrounded by it, always. And yet, he couldn't. Or at least, he shouldn't.

The golden glow of the afternoon lingered until the bell rang to call them to the refectory for supper.

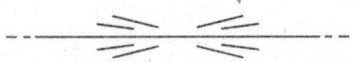

Thankfully, supper passed without any oddly colored foods, though Ishmael was surprised by the meal. Once again, it was nothing like the bland food they had back home. The food here seemed as if it were a secret he had known all along or a reward for something he had done. It was far better than anything at home even though Mam worked so hard. That realization made him strangely homesick.

When they finished eating, Ishmael followed Luc out of the refectory. He stopped at the workroom. "I want to show you something."

He strode over to the edge of the room and pointed to a series of plaques mounted on the wall. On each plaque were rows of names with simple descriptions next to them.

OBADIAH, son of Samuel and Ada. *Bold.*

SARIAH, daughter of Noah and Elisabeth. *Finest posticum in an age.*

GIDEON, son of Gad and Hannah. *Delicate and subtle.*

"These are the names of the color keepers that came before us. Once you're granted a posticum, your name goes up here with a description of it." He pointed to the very last name on the plaque: Luc, son of James and Talia.

"Why is there no description next to yours?"

"The description doesn't get added until later, when the posticum is finished."

Luc stood in silence, gazing up at the plaque, a slight smile on his face.

"What description will they give you?"

Luc's smile widened. "*Yellow*, I expect. But what I'd really like? *My color, my world.*"

Ishmael wanted to point out that there were others involved in the creation of his posticum, but Luc had already begun walking toward a flight of steps. Ishmael followed him up the stairs to a spacious room with windows flanking two walls. Across from the door, four cots lined the wall, each one separated from its neighbor by a small wooden cubby. To the right of the door were hooks and to the left, a large wardrobe.

"This is the novices' room," Luc said. "Since you're the first one to arrive, you get your pick of beds."

"I'm not a novice." It pained Ishmael to say this aloud, but he needed Luc to accept this before the misunderstanding went any further. He slowly sat on the cot at the far right, next to the window. "I'm just waiting for you to finish your work so we can go home to Mam."

"I know. But you need a place to sleep now, and this is the only open room. Get some rest, and we can talk more in the morning."

Ishmael ran his hand over the blanket covering the bed, so different from the one he left back home. He pictured Mam peacefully warming some milk for Simon and Jerusha and putting them to bed. More likely, she would be in the barn milking while Jerusha whined and Simon flung bits of fleece everywhere. She probably had several more hours of work to do before she could go to bed.

Ishmael pressed his lips together. "You must know how much Mam needs us. Will you please come with me?"

Luc ran his fingers through his hair, making it stand on end. "I can't. Not now."

"But maybe later?" Ishmael grabbed at any reason to hope.

"Maybe."

"Once you're done with your posticum?"

Luc turned away. "Yeah, maybe then." He opened the wardrobe, rifled through some things, and then tossed Ishmael a pair of pajamas. "Here. Go to sleep. I'll see you in the morning."

Luc turned to leave.

"Can I go to your posticum tomorrow, too?" Ishmael asked in a small voice.

Luc turned back around, ruffled Ishmael's hair, and smiled. "Sure, little brother. Now get some sleep."

Even though he was tired, Ishmael couldn't sleep. Too many things swirled around in his head. Mam. Color. Sheep. Posticum. Novice. He decided to go to the small courtyard to see if he could put his thoughts in order.

He shoved his feet into his boots and padded down the dark stairs and out of the Hall of Hue. Ishmael reached out, touching the wall as he walked into the courtyard, curious about the stones. He paused under the arch and sensed something, a sort of benevolence or protection. A belonging. The feeling settled deep into his core.

When he emerged on the other side, he saw a figure sitting on a bench to his left. It was Color Master.

"Seeking serenity?" she said.

"Yes, ma'am."

Color Master chuckled. "I did the same thing on my first day here. It's overwhelming, isn't it?"

"Yes, ma'am," he said again, mulling over all that had happened that day.

"Have a seat." Color Master made space for him on the bench, and then studied Ishmael. "You intrigue me," she said. "And not many people do." Color Master's eyes traveled downward, landing on Ishmael's boots, and a smile cracked her long face.

Even though it was dark, Ishmael fought the urge to hide his boot behind his ankle. "Can you tell me . . . what I mean is . . . how did that happen?"

"Transfer of color. Simple transfer of color, spectrum to object," Color Master said. "Undoubtedly you saw Luc doing the same thing in his posticum this afternoon. You'll learn much more about that in the coming months."

The words made Ishmael uncomfortable. He wouldn't be here long enough to learn about it.

A silence fell between them. Color Master put her hands together and tapped her fingertips on her nose. As if reading his mind, she said, "Ishmael, why did you come here?"

Ishmael couldn't lie, but he couldn't tell her the truth either, so he simply said, "I wanted to see Luc."

"And then you wanted to return home?"

Ishmael nodded, feeling an unexpected shame.

"It's not always easy to see that our contributions to the world are worth the personal sacrifice, even when they take us beyond what we see as our duty. Few people have the gift of seeing color. Fewer still are able to be its steward. It's a complicated matter." Color Master smoothed the hair above her forehead. "It requires a lifetime of study."

"If so few people can see color, what is the point of this place?"

"A valid question. As a novice, you begin by learning about color, but by the time you're an artisan," Color Master gestured toward the posticum opposite them, "you begin the work of creating. While we cannot permanently alter what has already been formed, like your village or any number of villages around, we *can* change what will come after. When we fill new posticums, we hope to create places that are full of color and sound and scent. Places full of joy."

"But there was no color back home."

"All places have a shadow of these gifts, even color. Your home is in one of the oldest posticums, created long before color distillation was stable. Its colors are weak, but you wouldn't have been able to see color there if it hadn't been there in the first place."

Ishmael chewed on that for a moment. "If there was color back home," he said slowly, "does that mean there were other things, too? Like the other Halls?"

"Your home has most of these things, but I think it predates the work of at least one of the other Halls. Gustation, maybe?"

"But then, why didn't I hear things the way I see color? Or smell things the way I see color?"

"Think of it this way: You see color where others only see light and dark. The Scent apprentices can smell the way you see color. What you smell is like light and dark—only a shadow of what the Scent apprentices smell."

Ishmael furrowed his eyebrows. What he smelled back home was all a variation of sheep smell. Sometimes it was a bad smell, like when the barn needed to be mucked out, and sometimes it was a good smell, like the smell of the mutton cooking. Sometimes those two blended together in a good-bad smell, like the smell of wet wool.

They sat quietly for a moment in the darkness.

The Commons seemed full of a hundred mysteries now.

"What happens to the posticums when they are finished?"

"The artisans settle there, and the posticum closes permanently. It continues as a world unto itself."

Ishmael reeled. "They . . . live in the posticum?"

"You lived in yours. That's one of the reasons I let you stay with Luc today. I figured you'd like as much time with him as you can get before the posticum closes. In fact, I think you should continue to observe Luc as much as you can, so you can learn from him. You'll have big shoes to fill, once he leaves. As I said, contributing to the world in a bigger way is worth the personal sacrifice. Now, though, I suggest you head back to bed."

Ishmael thought of the plaque in the Hall of Hue, of the description that would be added next to Luc's name once he finished the posticum and disappeared forever.

Speechless, Ishmael returned to his bed, but sleep did not come.

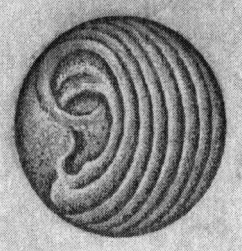

SOUND

Up in the trees and upon the rooftops and balustrades, the silence waited. In the almost holy stillness, an apprentice from the Hall of Sound came, his footsteps muffled by the weighty press of the predawn quiet. He opened the door to the bell tower, where he climbed 107 steps, winding around and around the circular stairs until he emerged in the dusty belfry. There, he shoved a wad of wool into each ear, and made his way to the center of the room where a rope as thick as his forearm hung from a pulley. The pulley was attached to a beam holding the bronze bell. When he hoisted himself up and let his weight pull the rope down, the silence shattered as the clapper struck the side of the bell.

Each morning, the apprentice confronted this mystery of sound. Though he had studied tones and frequencies and vibrations, acoustics and amplitude and echo, he still puzzled over the source and power of sound. Each morning, the bell ringer marveled anew at the privilege of having a daily appointment with the giant bronze bell instead of a daily appointment with his brothers' pummeling fists.

"Aaron! Listen to this!" they'd say, and he'd hear the whistling as their fists came at him. Sometimes he'd dodge their blows, but all too often, a sharp crack would follow the whistling as fist struck skin.

His home, his whole town, had been no place for anyone who had hypersensitive ears. He could hear sound, yes, but he could see it and taste it, too. He could smell it, feel it glide through him and wrap around him. Here, there were others like him, and for that, he was grateful.

When Aaron's task was finished, he pulled the wads of wool from his ears and left with music reverberating in his soul.

The peal of the bell ruffled across the Commons, touching first one sleeper, then another. By the time the bell ringer descended the steps of the tower, the sound had summoned all the apprentices from sweet sleep into wakefulness.

CHAPTER

10

Ishmael awoke with a vague sense of confusion. The light was different, and a bell bonged nearby.

Then he remembered.

He was not at home. He was at the Commons, and Color Master had said last night that Luc would stay in his posticum forever. He leaped up and dressed in his trousers and tunic.

He had to persuade Luc to return to the farm.

Today.

But when Ishmael met Luc at the top of the dormitory stairs, Luc left him no opening to talk about the farm, or to say anything at all. Instead, he rattled on about his posticum and what he still needed to do all through breakfast. So Ishmael bided his time, certain that he would have an opportunity once they were working, certain he could make Luc see how much they needed him at home and how staying in his posticum would be selfish.

At the entrance to the posticum, they were met by a petite young woman standing near four crates, a small tank filled with water, and another stone jar similar to the one Luc had yesterday.

"I thought Anna was supposed to give me the fauna?" Luc said to her.

"She was, but you're all behind schedule. Does Color Master know you're bringing people in here?" she asked, lifting her chin toward Ishmael.

"This is my younger brother, Ishmael, and yes, she knows." He turned to Ishmael. "This is Delilah. She's the Motion artisan for our posticum."

Delilah said, "Don't worry about the change in schedule—they should be easy enough to deal with."

"What about the land animal? I remember the teeth in the drawing," Luc said, tapping the largest crate.

Delilah rolled her eyes. "I suspended his motion until Gustation is done with him so you don't need to worry." She put her hands on the next two crates, both one-tenth the size of the first crate. "I didn't see the need to suspend the motion of the others. Just don't let them out of their crates. The taller crate is the fowl. The flat one is the reptile. The smallest one holds the creeper. And of course, the sea creature is in the tank. Any questions?"

Luc shook his head.

"It would help if you were timely with your work this week."

"Have I ever *not* been timely?"

Delilah raised an eyebrow.

After she departed, Luc turned to the crates. "This ought to be interesting." He ran his hand through his hair. "First, we need to inspect yesterday's work, before I can pass the flora to the Sound artisan, and then we can turn to the fauna after lunch." Luc led the way toward the back of the posticum. "Coloring the animals is the last assignment."

"So you'll be finished soon? Today, even?"

"Possibly. It depends on how much trouble these animals give me. I'm not used to working with quickened fauna."

"What does that mean, *quickened fauna?*"

"The Hall of Motion breathes movement into the animals, what we call the fauna. Once they do, the animals are quickened. They live. They move. They skitter away when you try to give them color."

Ishmael nodded, silent for a moment. "If you finish today or tomorrow, that means we could possibly be home in two or three days."

"Uh . . . not quite. *I* will finish in the next day or two, but the whole posticum won't be finished until Gustation, Scent, and Sound have their turn. And once the other Halls are done, Head Master holds the laurels ceremony. I've still got at least a week before my duties at the Commons are complete."

Ishmael stumbled over a large root. "And then what?"

"And then . . . you know. Ah! Here we are." Luc stopped in front of the clusters of plants he had colored the previous day and examined them one by one, checking leaves and stems for even coloring.

Frustrated that he couldn't pin Luc down, Ishmael stared at the plants. The stems and stalks were deep golden, while the leaves and flowers fluttered in a delicate yellow. Somehow Ishmael had thought it would be more complex. As he studied the effect of the whole swath of plants, something bothered him. It took him a moment to figure out why. "Aren't you using any other colors?"

A look of delight lit Luc's face. "I've hidden them," he said, lifting up a golden stone by the wall. Streaks of blue ran across its underside. "Posticums require all the primary colors."

Ishmael touched the blue, tracing its path with his fingertip. "It's a beautiful shade," he said. His brow furrowed as he looked up at Luc. "I don't understand why you'd want to hide it."

"It's not that I'm ashamed of it as much as I want everything golden here."

Ishmael frowned, thinking of the glorious jumble of Color Master's sticks. It seemed a shame to show only one color when there was so much beauty in all of them. In fact, it seemed not very different from back home where everything was colorless. "But I still don't understand why."

Luc dropped the stone back into place. "Do you remember that day we rolled down the hill of the Commons? When we got into so much trouble?"

Ishmael nodded.

"Do you remember the feeling before we got caught? That

feeling of flying, of euphoria, of joy? Yellow gives me that feeling."

Ishmael knew that sensation well. It had been his constant companion since he first saw color, but the exhilaration came from all the colors, all together. "Don't you get that feeling with other colors, too?"

Luc shook his head. "My color, my world."

There was that phrase again. "You said that before, *my color, my world*. But doesn't a posticum require more than one creator?"

"This is *my* posticum, and I want my color here." Luc said. "Whatever anyone else does is irrelevant."

If that was truly Luc's feeling, then persuading him to return home was going to be the challenge of his life.

CHAPTER

11

When Luc finished his lengthy inspection of the color—stem by stem, leaf by leaf, flower by flower—he notified the Sound artisan, who pulled a tiny bell, a large coil of wire, and a set of matching wooden sticks from a pouch at her side. Before Ishmael could see what she would do with those baffling items, Luc had turned to the fauna at the front of the posticum.

"What's she going to do?" Ishmael asked, pointing back at the Sound artisan and hurrying to keep up with his older brother's long stride.

"I don't know," Luc said without curiosity, "but let's hope it will be worthy of the color."

In the distance, the bell tolled, signaling lunch.

"Lunch already?" Ishmael said, surprised at how the time had flown.

"Good thing the Gustation apprentices bring lunch to the artisans when a posticum is in process." Luc pointed toward a large basket just inside the door.

He opened the basket and pulled out a small pot, a knife, and wedges of bread cut from what must have been an enormous loaf. "Looks like some kind of spread. You want to try some?" Luc held the knife and spread out to Ishmael.

Ishmael scooped a bit out, smoothed it on a wedge of the bread, and took a bite. The flavor exploded on Ishmael's tongue. He closed his eyes as he chewed. Colors flashed into the darkness, reds and oranges and yellows.

"What are you doing?" Luc interrupted.

Ishmael opened his eyes and saw the plain wedge of bread slathered with the plain spread. "Seeing the colors in my mind. Don't you see colors when you eat?" Ishmael took another bite and again, his vision was peppered with red and orange.

Luc took a swig from a jar of water. "Let me try." He bit into a piece of the slathered bread and closed his eyes. After chewing and swallowing, he shook his head and laughed. "I'm beginning to think you belong here more than I do." The words should have unsettled Ishmael, but he was too occupied with the bursts of red and orange in his mind.

They finished eating quickly and returned to the fauna. Luc pulled out his prism and loosened the lid on the jar. He let a flash of light escape from the jar, pulled a spectrum from it, and once again, separated a globe of yellow. When he found the shade of yellow he wanted, he opened the smallest crate and let the color drip onto the many-legged creeper. Dots of yellow speckled it. "You don't need much for such a small creature. Besides, the color will even out as he moves around." He shut the lid tight and said with a wink, "I hope."

He repeated the process for the sea creature. As the color sank into the water, wisps of yellow reached out like fingers into the clear water. "This will take time to disperse," he said and moved off to color the fowl.

Mesmerized, Ishmael stared at the sea creature as it swam in and out of the ribbons of descending color. Yellow striped its sides, crisscrossing it in random patterns.

"This is amazing!" Ishmael grabbed Luc's sleeve and pulled him back to the tank.

Luc yelped as the bird that had been in his grip fluttered away and perched on a low branch of a nearby tree. Wild-eyed, Luc shook his head in disbelief. "Tell me you did not just grab my arm and make me lose that fowl."

Frozen with horror, Ishmael couldn't speak. Nor could he take his eyes off the bird, nearly invisible in the golden leaves, but for one bright streak of yellow at the crown of her head.

Luc ran his fingers through his hair and began pacing. "Climb the tree and catch it? But with what? Ask Delilah for assistance? She knows its motion. She might be able to help. No, I can't ask her. I'd never live it down."

Ishmael broke into Luc's monologue. "It's got some color on it already. Won't the color spread to the rest of it?"

Luc turned to him, as if seeing him for the first time. "You need to leave. Now." He charged toward Ishmael. "Go!"

Ishmael didn't need any prompting. The expression on his brother's face drove him toward the archway in a stumbling run.

CHAPTER

12

When Ishmael dived through the archway into the court-yard, he nearly ran into a tall boy with tightly curled hair—wiry, springy coils that stuck out all over his head. The boy swallowed nervously, and the lump in his throat bobbed up and down. "*The naked man insists that a belt is not useful without pants*," he said. "I hope that I'll be as useful as pants while I'm here. Or a belt."

Ishmael wasn't sure how to respond to this boy's strange words. "Um . . . I hope so, too?" He looked over his shoulder to see if Luc had followed him out of the posticum, but of course, he hadn't. Luc was more concerned with catching the bird than catching Ishmael.

The boy tugged at his left sleeve, trying to cover a bony wrist. "Sorry, that wasn't the right one. I'd practiced two—in fact, I had decided to use the other one, *The new lamb is always welcomed to the fold, especially by predators*, but then at the last moment, I didn't like the bit about the predators, so I decided to use the belt and pants one, but that one didn't come out right, either." The boy let out a heavy sigh. *"Better to stumble than make a slip of the tongue.* I'm Thomas. I collect proverbs."

Ishmael really looked at the boy now. There was something different about him, but he couldn't put his finger on it. He wore well-made clothes, though they were somewhat threadbare and a little short at wrist and ankle. Thomas stood still while Ishmael scrutinized him.

"I hope I haven't ruined your first impression of me," Thomas said. He really looked nervous now. "You're not Color Master, are you?"

"No, I am." And there was Color Master, her red robes blazing through the Great Courtyard archway. "This is Ishmael," she said to the newcomer.

Ishmael tried to smile, but failed to produce more than a nervous grimace.

"Why aren't you in Luc's posticum?" Color Master asked.

"Um." Ishmael didn't know what to say. Because he accidentally let one of the animals loose? Because Luc was really angry? Because he had no business being at the Commons to begin with? All were appropriate answers, though none were suitable to tell Color Master.

Luckily Color Master didn't have the patience to wait for an answer. "If Luc has no use for you," she said, "stay here and wait for the other Hue novices to arrive. I need to test each of them individually. Matthew, Jacob, and Rebekah are already here, so we just need Hannah and Lilith." With that, she led Thomas out of the courtyard toward the Hall of Hue.

Ishmael sank down on the stone bench opposite Luc's posticum. From here he could see both the large gate at the entrance to the Commons, as well as the archway to the posticum. One entry led to home. The other led to Luc. Should he go straight home? Should he go to Luc first and then go home? But how would he make amends to Luc? And how could he go home when he promised Mam that he wouldn't return without Luc?

Ishmael pulled his legs up to his chest and hugged them, resting his chin on his knees. Glancing down, he was surprised to see part of the green splotch on his boot crumbling off. He picked at it a bit, and a large section disintegrated in his hand, turning into a colorless dust. How could he have wreaked so much havoc in a mere day?

"Stupid, stupid, stupid," he berated himself.

"What's stupid?" a voice asked.

Ishmael looked up. Standing before him was a girl with kind eyes, a broad nose, and thick hair. And suddenly he knew what had made Thomas different, because this girl was different in the same way. He had gotten used to the gleaming light of the apprentices inside the Commons. Thomas and this girl looked like him: drab and dull in comparison to the others here, but their eyes shone brightly, as if they held all of the brightness that their bodies lacked.

"What's stupid?" she repeated.

"Me. *I'm* stupid."

She sat down next to him. "I doubt that," she said, looping a twist of hair around a finger. "You look rather intelligent to me. Here's what I see. You're much too young to be a laborer, which means you must be here as an apprentice, and if you're here as an apprentice, you must be gifted—because you're young. Therefore, you can't be stupid."

When Ishmael finally untangled her logic, he ducked his head, a little bit embarrassed by her deductions and a little bit pleased, but mostly astonished at how perceptive she was.

"So, are you an apprentice?" she asked.

"I'm not sure."

She shifted her whole body to face him. "Well, you're here, aren't you?"

"Yes, but I came here mostly to fetch my brother and bring him back home. Our father died, and my mam needs help running the farm."

"You came here *mostly* to fetch your brother? But not entirely?"

Ishmael began to think she might be too perceptive. "Well, I had some questions, too."

She smiled at the surprised look on his face. "Me, too. So it sounds like you *could* be an apprentice, if you wanted to."

Ishmael tipped his head. "What do you think I should do?"

"I couldn't say. It's not like one choice is right and the other is wrong. You just need to decide which path you want to take: stay here or go home."

If only it were as simple as she made it seem. He tried to smile. "Thanks. I'm Ishmael, by the way."

"Nice to meet you, Ishmael. I'm Hannah. I hope you decide to stay here."

Ishmael saw a flash of red through the archway. "Color Master's on her way to come collect you."

Hannah threw a worried look over her shoulder.

"Don't worry—the testing's easy."

The two stood as Color Master walked toward them.

"And you are?" Color Master asked, gazing down her long nose at Hannah.

"Hannah."

"Very good. Let's go."

Hannah waved and said, "See you later, Ishmael."

Color Master continued talking. "We'll test first, then . . ." Her voice trailed off as she and Hannah went through the archway.

Color Master came back fifteen minutes later. "Lilith hasn't arrived?"

"No, ma'am."

"Keep waiting, then. If she comes, bring her to my office. If she's not here by supper, go to the refectory."

Ishmael waited an hour. Then another. No one else came.

MANUFACTORY

The late afternoon light loved to swim over chimney and rooftop, flowing through the windows of workrooms, settling like a blanket of comfort on all surfaces. It brushed by one particular Manufactory apprentice, Michael, who had paused in his motion only long enough to wet his sharpening stone and push his chisel against the rough surface.

His hands were busy, but his mind was even busier, dashing through twists and turns of possibilities. When his assigned projects from Manufactory Master were done for the day, Michael unleashed his imagination, letting it dart through the land of invention, pushing the carving and chiseling and sanding he did each day further. He wanted to create something far greater than the sum of its parts. He wanted to make something grand.

When Michael first arrived at the Commons two years ago, he brought samples of things he had built—joinings, carvings, gears, gadgets—along with page after page of detailed designs he had drawn while planning their construction. Manufactory Master had tossed the plans onto his desk without a glance, and instead, twisted the gadgets, turned the gears, ran a finger along the carvings, studied the joinings.

What Michael hadn't known then was that design work was the sole responsibility of the Hall of Shape. Members of the Hall of Manufactory were meant only to build things. After a few weeks, Michael saw why. The designs from the Hall of Shape were complex compared to the simple plans he had made. But, oh, how he would like to join forces with the Hall of Shape apprentices!

He thought his chance had come earlier that day when a set of plans arrived from the Hall of Shape that appeared incomplete. He brought them to Manufactory Master expecting him to be full of gratitude for his perception and willingness to collaborate with Shape. Instead, Manufactory Master waved his plump hand, saying, "They're always like that, giving us their inferior plans. Now at least I've got fair warning they'll come complaining."

"But—" Michael started to say.

Manufactory Master had turned away, dismissing him.

So Michael honed the surface of the metal chisel, drawing it one last time against the grit of the stone, making sure he and his tools would be prepared for tomorrow. He wiped the chisel on a sturdy leather strop and placed it into its slot in the wooden block. Then he began gathering the materials he would need. He would complete that set of plans himself.

CHAPTER

13

W hen the supper bell rang, Ishmael looked for Luc. He was desperate to apologize and somehow persuade him to come home.

But Luc didn't leave his posticum.

And Ishmael was hungry.

So he walked to the refectory by himself. Places were set at the tables as before, and seats were filling fast.

Color Master stood at the entrance to the hall. "No Lilith? No Luc?"

"No."

Ishmael waited for Color Master to ask for details about Luc, but all she said was, "Very well. Go sit with the other novices." She pointed to the front of the Hue table, where Hannah and Thomas sat with a few other newcomers.

"Come join us," Hannah said.

Thomas smiled a welcome, too, though he looked a bit sheepish. "Can I try again? No predators or pants this time. How about, *The appetite comes during a meal?*"

Ishmael tried to smile back, but without Luc at his side, he felt very alone. It was as if Ishmael really were a novice, not just a visitor. As he walked to an empty seat next to Hannah, he noticed that all of the faces at this table looked subdued and flat in comparison to the dozens of other apprentices surrounding them. That must be how all novices arrived at the Commons.

He sat down, knocking the fork at the side of his plate, and as he straightened the fork, he noticed that his hand wasn't as drab as Hannah's. He didn't glow in the same way that Luc or Color Master did, but maybe the more time a person spent here, the brighter he or she became. Maybe he was beginning to shine, too.

Ishmael tried to think of something to say. "How did the testing go?" he finally said. He looked from Hannah to Thomas, and glanced at the others sitting at the table.

Thomas bobbed his head. "*He who has a boat floats down the stream with ease.*"

"Do you always do that?" the girl sitting across from Ishmael asked Thomas with genuine curiosity.

"What?"

"Speak in proverbs."

"Yes. Pretty much." His vigorous nods set his curls bouncing.

The girl smiled and said, "What an interesting way to approach life." She turned to Ishmael. "I'm Rebekah."

"I'm Ishmael."

She had very light, wispy, chin-length hair with extreme bangs cut just above her eyebrows. Her chin was round, her nose was narrow, and her eyes shone with good cheer. Ishmael immediately liked her.

"The testing was no problem," Hannah said. "Just like you said."

Before Ishmael could respond, Head Master arose and stood at the lectern. The room hushed. "The work of creation is a privilege and a joy, and it is my great delight to be with you as you increase in knowledge and skill. The work you perform—no matter how small or how grand—is a vital contribution to what we do here."

The apprentices clapped.

Head Master kept talking. "Often, unfortunately, the things that we do begin to feel ordinary because we see them every day, and we lose our wonder for the marvels around us. In order to rectify this, once every fifty years we celebrate a jubilee year—a year of instruction and meditation, a year to see the wonder in our work. This is our Jubilee Year. The celebration will continue all year."

A loud whoop sounded from some of the more boisterous apprentices.

"While a jubilee *is* a year of celebration, it is also a time to return to the foundations of our history and remember who we are. We are here because of Godfrey Wright."

"A wise man is remembered by word and deed," Thomas muttered. "But who is he?"

No one answered him.

Head Master gazed at the apprentices before him. "The towns you each come from are ancient places. Many of these early posticums functioned as they were meant to, but some did not. Those that did not became places of darkness, places where the abilities of their creators faded. However, once the light of creation has graced a place, it is rarely extinguished completely.

"Our founder, Godfrey Wright, left a gateway to the Commons to give sanctuary to those who still carry the light of creation within them. It is through this gate that each of us has come, for we are heirs of that light.

"You would do well, all of you, to study the works of Godfrey Wright. He loved all things, each individual part of creation, each color, each shape, each flavor, each gear, each note, each movement, each scent. Consider his compassion and attempt to emulate him. I do."

"Hear, hear!" one of the men sitting behind the lectern called out.

"We have a series of events, lectures, and challenges in light of this reflection, culminating in a special contest, which we'll announce later. Without further ado, let me extend my sincere welcome to our Hue novices, and let us give thanks to the Gustation apprentices for their diligence."

The room erupted into applause as food was brought out. Platters and bowls were passed around as the apprentices filled their plates, chattering. Ishmael looked at the others sitting with him and allowed himself a moment to wonder what it might be like if he were to stay.

"How long have you been able to see color?" Thomas asked Ishmael.

Though it seemed like an innocent question, Ishmael paused. He took a serving of mashed vegetables from a wide bowl and passed it to Hannah at his right.

He wasn't sure how much he wanted to tell them. Hannah had said he had a choice—stay here and be an apprentice or go home and run the farm. If he really did have a choice, then what he said now could have a greater effect than he realized. If he said the right thing, would he make the right impression? And if he said the wrong thing, well, would his path—right *or* wrong—be set forevermore?

He was thinking too much. All he could do was tell the truth. "A couple of weeks," he said with a shrug.

"A couple of weeks!" Thomas looked stunned.

Ishmael knew immediately that was an unexpected answer, but he didn't know if it was right or wrong. "How long have you seen color?"

"About a year."

Ishmael looked at Hannah. "How about you?"

"Off and on for a year."

"I've seen color for the past two or three years," Rebekah offered, passing a basket of bread to Ishmael. "But I was always in trouble for one thing or another, and no one believed me. That's why I didn't come earlier."

He pulled at a loose thread on his breeches and a small hole opened up in the weave. He wiggled the edge of his fingernail into the hole, uncomfortable. What else could he have said? It *was* the truth.

"How did you end up here if you haven't seen a lot of color?" Thomas asked. "I mean, it's a bit unusual."

Ishmael hesitated. Another moment, another question, another chance to set an impression. Instinct told him that the truth would be an unexpected answer yet again. He looked at the faces surrounding the table. Besides Hannah, Thomas, and Rebekah, there were two other boys, both older than him.

The first boy had stopped eating, placed his fork down, and turned his full attention to Ishmael. He had long fingers, a quiet manner, and intense dark eyes.

When Ishmael looked at the second boy, the word that came to mind was "bold." There was nothing soft or uncertain about him, nothing quiet or unassuming. Pale scalp showed through hair cut short. His eyebrows ran in two thick straight lines. His posture was distinct, even while sitting. His body gave off the impression of tightly coiled energy waiting to spring. He looked at Ishmael expectantly.

Ishmael considered his options. He decided that he didn't want to tell them about the dismal farm at home, or about venturing here to find Luc, or about going back home himself. These were just regular novices. If he pretended to be just a regular novice, what would he say?

"Well? How did you end up here?" Thomas repeated, his long, thin neck stretched forward as if the proverbs stuck inside him were trying to unfurl and escape their confines inside his head.

"There was a pane of glass in our barn," Ishmael began slowly. Yes, if he were a regular novice, he would talk about color. "I was playing with the colors that came from it, and I colored my boot."

The second boy's fork clattered on the table. "You *colored your boot?*"

Ishmael winced. He was glad his boots were hidden under the table. He nodded, embarrassed.

"Most novices don't know how to do that," Hannah said. "That's really advanced."

"It is?"

Thomas nodded. *"Greatness proceeds from simple things."*

"But you've both seen color for so long, you must have done something like that." He looked from one to the other.

They shook their heads, so he turned to Rebekah and the other two boys.

Rebekah's light hair swished around her chin as she shook her head.

The second boy said, "Never. I'm Jacob, by the way."

Ishmael acknowledged him and turned to the first boy. "Nor I," he said. "I'm Matthew. You're . . . Ishmael?"

Ishmael nodded.

"*Seeing* color is enough to be invited here," Hannah said. "But to actually *move* color? That's impressive."

"I don't even know how I did it."

"That's even more impressive," Hannah said.

Though Ishmael was surprised at their reaction, he was even more surprised to find how it made him glow inside, how a flush of pleasure rolled through him at the thought that he might be good at this strange new beauty. Even as he registered his delight, Hannah's words about his choice lay before him, a choice that led down two very different paths, and he still wasn't sure which one he should take.

SHAPE

A certain apprentice from the Hall of Shape always took the most worn-down part of the bench at the refectory table, the place no one else wanted because it was too sunken. She found its curves and its smoothness comforting, as if generations of Shape apprentices had made it just for her. Ironically, it must have been the most desirable seat at one time. Its worn state attested to that. She understood why. The view took in the entirety of the room, from the Masters' table at the front to the Hall of Hue table at the rear. If she sat up tall, she could even see out of the arched windows along the opposite side of the room. All that was visible was the bell tower and the sky, but it gave her a sense of security, as if she were a shape (a cylinder) within a shape (the cube of the refectory) within a shape (the great dome of heaven).

The other Shape apprentices ate their supper, but she was caught in Head Master's words and the name of Godfrey Wright. A name with beauty in the shape of its letters, so full of lines and curves.

In the early years of her apprenticeship here, she had studied variations of the straight line. You take a dot and connect it to another dot and you get a straight line: one dimension to two dimensions. You take the end point of that straight line and connect it to a third dot and you get an arrow. You connect those two straight lines with a third straight line and you get a triangle, the simplest of shapes.

The square, the parallelogram, the rhombus, the cube, the pyramid, the dodecahedron, even. Dozens of shapes, two-dimensional and three-dimensional, all from dots and lines. This was her work. She dealt in dimensions, and discovering how to make those dimensions useful. But dimensions all began with a dot and a straight line. Even the alphabet began with a dot and a straight line.

Her own name—Dora—began with a *D*, a letter with line and curve, a letter that aspired to be a dot, but only made it halfway there. While she didn't have a dot in her name, the circle of the o was close. But the name Godfrey Wright—well, that had it all: a name beginning with a curve, ending with a straight line, with both a circle and a dot in the middle. She knew already that he must have been someone who understood.

CHAPTER

14

Have you picked cots yet?" Ishmael asked the other boys. Before he finished speaking the words, he could see the answer in front of him. He gazed at a crumpled comforter askew on the third cot, clothes on the floor, and the cubby spilling its contents.

"*A messy house invites unexpected guests,*" Thomas said.

Jacob flung himself onto the bed. "Unexpected guests are always welcome. The more, the merrier!"

Matthew moved to the cot at the other side of Jacob's and retrieved a pair of pajamas from his cubby.

"*And its neighbors suffer silently.*" Thomas leaned over to see if Matthew agreed.

Matthew hiccupped.

"Or not so silently."

"It's not that bad, is it? Most of the time you're in here, your eyes will be closed anyway," Jacob said. He flashed a brilliant smile, and Matthew hiccupped again.

"Sorry," Matthew said. "This happens a lot when I'm nervous."

"What do you have to be nervous about?" Jacob stood up and went to the wardrobe. "Do you have a uniform yet?" he asked Ishmael, who had settled on his cot.

"No." Up until now, Ishmael had been adamant about *not* having a uniform since he planned to go home. But home felt farther away than ever.

"Color Master got our uniforms from here," Jacob said, shuffling around in the wardrobe. "Ah! Here's one." He pulled out a pair of breeches and a tunic and held them out to Ishmael. "This looks like the smallest pair, but they might be a little long."

"I doubt they'll be too long," Thomas said. When Jacob gave him a quizzical look, he said, "Do yours fit?"

"Perfectly," Jacob said. "As if they were made for me."

Thomas turned toward Matthew. "And you?"

Matthew hiccupped and nodded.

Thomas continued, "If there was a uniform here that precisely fits each of us—including my long legs—then there will be a uniform to fit Ishmael. This place is special. It's as if we belong here, like we're meant to be here."

Ishmael took the uniform and held it against himself. Even though he was so much younger and smaller than the other novices, the uniform *did* seem the right size—as if someone had been expecting him and had prepared a perfectly fitting uniform.

He slipped off his pants and jersey and donned the uniform. The trousers and tunic were soft—much softer than anything he had ever worn before. The sleeves fit to the edge of his wrists, the length of the pants exactly to his ankles. He had never had anything that fit him so perfectly. "This doesn't feel like wool."

Thomas looked up. "It's linen. Well-worn linen."

"Now what about pajamas?" Jacob asked.

Ishmael went to his bed and retrieved the pajamas he had worn the night before. "I already have some."

"If you're all set, then we'd better get to bed. I'm sure we've got a lot of work ahead of us tomorrow." With that, Jacob threw on his nightshirt, blew out his candle, and hopped into bed. "Besides, you won't see my mess in the dark." He was asleep in moments.

"*All beasts are gray at night,*" Thomas said. "Good night."

"Good night," Matthew said, with one last hiccup.

Ishmael quickly changed into his pajamas, which he realized also fit him exactly. He eased himself under the comforter, wishing things had gone differently that day, wishing he could have told Luc how sorry he was. Ishmael wondered if he was still in the posticum, chasing the bird.

Another night in this curious place. Another night away

from the farm. He let his thoughts wander through the paths at home—from cottage to barn, from barn to pasture, from pasture to road, from road to cottage again. Before he knew it, he was fast asleep.

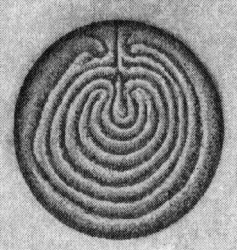

GUSTATION

An apprentice from the Hall of Gustation stumbled down to the kitchens. When he opened the door, his elbow banged into a tower of large bowls someone had left out for the morning's experiments. They clattered to the floor. He rubbed his arm, a premonition of what this morning would hold.

The Gustation apprentice was named Gabriel, and he had a picture in his mind, an elevation map of sorts, where each of the seven flavors occupied a part of the body. Floating at eye level were clouds of sweetness. At neck level was sour. Salty was in the chest, then came bland in the gut, meaty in the abdomen, richness in the legs, and bitter at the feet.

This was how he had always thought of flavor. Level by level with the favored flavors up high and the shunned flavors down low. But on a day that began with a blow to his elbow, his elevation map told him "bland" would be forthcoming. Not like yesterday when he woke with a fluttery feeling in his head and neck and chest. He made a salty, sweet, and tangy spread to be eaten on bland bread. He had thought his creation was a masterpiece. Luckily, so did Gustation Master. *That* was a good workday.

Gabriel picked up the bowls that were still spinning on the floor, and set them on the long worktable. When there was order again, he returned to the entrance of the workroom where Gustation Master had posted a chart of the assigned flavor profiles for their experiments that week.

Sure enough, this morning's flavor assignment was bland. Sometimes he really hated being right, and now was one of those times. He hated beginning the day with bland. It sat in his gut, an immobile stone, unimaginative, uninspired. Boring. He preferred flavors with a zing or a jolt or a bang, especially in the morning, but there were too many complaints from the other Halls, those ignoramuses, when he did breakfast with a zing, which was probably why Gustation Master had assigned him bland.

Why were flavors such a strong sensation for him and not for the apprentices from the other Halls? He had asked Gustation Master that once before, back when he was a novice, but all Gustation Master said was, "Be satisfied with your gift." It wasn't *his* gift that was in question; it was the lack in other people.

Gabriel glanced at the shelves. Lots of bread left from yesterday. Toast and porridge it would be, then. Curds and whey, too. Hard-boiled eggs? Sure, why not? It didn't get any more bland than that.

He took down one of the knives and a cutting board, thinking about all the apprentices who would eat this bland toast, all the hands that would touch it, all the teeth that would chew it, all the mouths that would taste it—or not taste it, as the case would be. Bland. Blaugh.

SCENT

A Scent apprentice woke from a dream, fragments of it floating around in her memory. She had held a child in her arms, so small and so new. He weighed scarcely more than a loaf of bread from her papa's bakery back home. She lifted a corner of the swaddling. His hair was fine and dark and plentiful for a newborn. His eyes were closed, and he slept. She held her finger out to his soft, downy skin, and he wiggled in her arms, his small mouth opening and closing as if to suckle. She didn't know whose child he was, or why she held him, but holding him was sweet, and she liked it.

She bent down to kiss his head, and the scent of the newly born babe overcame her—a scent of perfection and divinity and freshness and something else, though she couldn't quite place her finger on it. She cuddled the child in her arms until she realized what that final scent was: possibility. She inhaled deeply, and when she awoke, it was with the fresh smell of this child in her mind.

Where did he come from? Was he real—existing somewhere in some posticum? Was he some memory caught in the deep places of her mind? Or was he some sort of inspiration that slipped through the open window during the night? Keturah couldn't tell. Wherever the inspiration came from, she was thankful for it.

She would create the scent of that child today. It wasn't often that she came in contact with such a dry ethereal scent, but the promise of it intrigued her. The apprentice threw the crisp sheets off her cot, and ran over to the row of windows. She stuck her head outside and inhaled deeply before turning to her preparations for the day.

CHAPTER

15

Much like the previous morning, Ishmael awoke to the sound of a bell ringing, the herald of a new day in this different place. He dressed quickly, made his cot, and hurried out the door. For good or bad, he had to find Luc and face what came. When he arrived at the refectory, warmth and bright lights met him. Luc stood at the doorway, chatting with another Hue apprentice.

"Luc, I—" Ishmael began, but Luc interrupted him with a laugh.

"I finally caught that bird, but you wouldn't believe what I had to do to catch her. And just in the nick of time, too. Color Master is giving you novices a tour of my posticum this afternoon."

"Am I forgiven?" Ishmael asked.

"Of course you're forgiven, little brother." Luc put his arm around Ishmael, and the simple gesture filled Ishmael with relief.

Head Master rose from his place at the front of the room, the light reflecting off his thick spectacles, and they quickly took their seats. "This evening, we will be treated to our first All-Commons Challenge, hosted by the Hall of Hue. It will be a fine exposition of creation for our novices by apprentices chosen from each Hall. The challenge Hue has issued is 'order and chaos.' And now, your bellies are empty, and there is much work to be done. Let us have gratitude for the food that fuels the work of the Commons, for our creative powers, and for the founder of the Commons, Godfrey Wright." He nodded at the apprentices from the Hall of Gustation who brought platters of toast and eggs and bowls of porridge and curds with whey to the long tables.

"Fruit for the belly is fruit for the soul," Thomas said, dishing up a large helping of porridge.

Rebekah spun her plate, giggling. "That's not fruit."

He shrugged, his mouth already full. "I didn't mean it literally."

A slim girl passed a bowl of eggs to Ishmael. She had dark eyes shaped in a way that Ishmael had never seen before, and truly, she was the most appealing person Ishmael had ever observed. He couldn't help but stare. "I didn't have a chance to meet you yesterday," she said. "I'm Lilith." She sat straight and tall with her left hand gently reaching for her napkin. Her thick dark hair was pulled back, and her uniform draped neatly from her shoulders. Nothing was out of place. There was not a smudge, nor a speck on her. His own uniform already had porridge on the sleeve, though he had no idea how it had gotten there.

"I'm Ishmael. When did you arrive?" He put an egg onto his plate and passed the bowl to Thomas.

"Yesterday evening. My chaperone delayed me. She wanted me to pack all kinds of useless things, like matching spoons, even when I told her I wouldn't need any of them here."

Ishmael couldn't imagine what Lilith's life must have been like if her chaperone thought matching spoons were essential for her journey.

"What did you do at home?" Hannah asked.

"Manners," Lilith said.

Thomas picked at his teeth with his fork. "Manners?"

"Yes, manners. Lessons in poise, polish, and grace." Lilith lifted her chin. "More useless things."

Hannah leaned toward Lilith. "I wish they had grace lessons where I'm from. I'm an oaf next to you."

Lilith's lips turned down. "What good is grace when there are important things to be done? There's injustice out there—people are suffering, at war, starving—and my parents made me learn how to sit up straight and how to converse and how to manage a household."

Jacob took another piece of toast. "Is there anything wrong with learning how to sit up straight or converse or manage a household?"

"There is when you've been in a drought for the past fifteen years. There is when the drought has caused a famine, and the famine has caused a war."

"What's a war?" Ishmael asked.

Matthew leaned in. "It's when groups of people fight each other until they all die or until one side gets what they want and the other side surrenders."

Horrified, Rebekah said, "But why would they do that?"

Matthew set his fork down. "Often, it boils down to greed of some kind or a difference of opinion. Usually, the two sides believe different things, like, one way of thinking is better than another way of thinking. Or they want the same things, like land—or in Lilith's case, water. Sometimes people go to war to protect a weaker group of people. It's a complicated business."

Jacob turned to Lilith. "But that's not your fault. You didn't cause the drought."

"No, I didn't cause the drought, but with all the resources my family had, I could have done so much. I could have shared their suffering if it meant there would be less suffering for them to bear. But instead, I learned how to walk gracefully—the most useless of all useless skills." The depth of her emotion ambushed them.

Matthew poured her some juice. Gratefully, she took the glass and sipped from it until she regained her composure.

"You have a great deal of compassion," Matthew said with a quiet kindness.

"How can I not have compassion?" Lilith said. "But compassion doesn't feed starving people."

Matthew leaned forward. "Compassion is the first step to solving problems. It's the first step to approaching—and opening—boundaries, to building bridges, to compromise. If you have compassion for the people suffering around you, you find a way to do what needs to be done."

"Perhaps." Lilith placed her glass on the table. "But there's not much I can do with my compassion now—it doesn't solve the problems for the people back home." She looked around at the others, embarrassed. "So much for poise."

The egg slowly slid down Ishmael's throat. His compassion *here* didn't solve Mam's problems *there*. Not witnessing the decline of their farm didn't make it less real.

"You're here now, though." Jacob smiled at Lilith, trying to lighten the mood.

Hannah patted Lilith's shoulder. "Some things are not easy to forget."

"And some things are not meant to be forgotten," Lilith countered.

"We can't change where we come from," Matthew said, "but we can change where we go. We can learn from the problems in the past and avoid them in what we create. We're here to create, right?"

They nodded, all but Ishmael.

"So we create newness in our color. We make things different."

Rebekah nudged Lilith. "We just need to learn how."

Lilith gave her a weak smile. "Thank you—all of you. I'm glad I'm here."

Matthew smiled. "So am I."

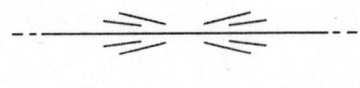

Following breakfast, the novices walked back to the Hall of Hue workroom in a cluster. Ishmael followed along, standing at the edge of the room next to Hannah. Color Master emerged from her office, and when the chatter quieted, she said "Apprentices, you know your tasks for the day. Novices, follow me."

The older apprentices scattered while Color Master led the way through the rear door of the workroom into a much smaller room. Though Ishmael didn't consider himself a novice, everyone else did, so for now, he trailed after the others. He took a seat with them at a long, central table streaked with color.

"I suspect many of the things we do here will seem peculiar to you. There is no fabric to be fashioned into garments, no gardens to weed, no wild beasts to hunt, no sheep to tend, no children to watch, no lessons in comportment, nor games of martial strategy."

"Martial strategy?" Lilith said. "How awful!"

"It is an important skill for those who serve as diplomats. Right, Matthew?"

Matthew hiccupped.

"You were supposed to be a diplomat?" Jacob leaned toward Matthew.

Matthew closed his eyes and inhaled deeply. "Yes," he said, then hiccupped again.

"You don't much look like a diplomat," Jacob said.

"You've seen many diplomats?" Lilith asked.

"No," Jacob said. "But I will admit that he sure sounded like one at breakfast."

"I was no good at diplomacy," Matthew said, with a hiccup.

"I'm sure you were better than you think," Lilith said. Another hiccup. Matthew pinched his nose.

Color Master tutted. "From now on, you must think of yourselves as color keepers in training. You are here to study color, and ultimately, to produce color for a posticum."

"What's a posticum?" asked Hannah.

"You will understand them better when we visit Luc's posticum this afternoon. For now, think of it as a blank space that you will layer with color." She passed out pieces of thick paper, and then set pots of color and brushes on the table. "We begin our studies with the first law of color: *All color is contained in pure light.* When light passes through a prism, the colors separate, and we see the spectrum." Color Master demonstrated by holding up her prism and angling it until it captured a beam of light. One moment, there was nothing and the next, a brilliant spectrum swayed in the air.

The colors that were so enticing to Ishmael in the barn were even more radiant here. Ishmael scooted forward on the bench. How could such a mystery be so simple? There must be more to it, or else how could he be so deeply attached to something so *intangible?*

Color Master moved the prism from one hand to the other to allow each of them to see the spectrum. Without thinking, Ishmael reached out, feeling the tug of the colors, the familiar weight, as the splintered light—no, the *spectrum*—edged closer. He lifted his pointer finger and a green swathe leaped toward him.

Ishmael didn't notice the other novices staring at him. He didn't hear Color Master call his name. He was oblivious to everything but the color as it tugged at him.

"Ishmael?" Color Master said again. "Ishmael!"

This time Ishmael heard her and jerked away from the splintered light, suddenly aware that no one else had reached for the color. No one else had connected with the color. No one else had become lost in the colors. He ducked his head. "Sorry," he muttered, embarrassed.

"On the contrary!" Color Master said. "Well done! You're the first novice I've seen who has had an immediate connection with the spectrum. Bodes well for this group." She beamed at the novices gathered around the table.

"Why is that?" Lilith asked.

"There are seven of you and seven colors. Each of you represents a color. Just as the seven colors make a spectrum, the seven of you together make a spectrum." She patted Ishmael's shoulder. "You will have a strong anchor with Ishmael, as his color is clearly green. He rests squarely in the middle and will provide stability for the rest of you. So the question now is, what are your colors?"

Rebekah shifted in her seat. "What if we have no idea?"

"It is a rare novice who comes to me already knowing his or her color." Color Master held up a circle split into three equal sections, each section a different color. "We discover our colors with a simple exercise. Color circles."

While she instructed them on how to make a red-yellow-blue color circle, Ishmael, still embarrassed, watched Rebekah begin her color circle with yellow. She filled the section quickly, added a final touch of yellow, then took a quill and outlined the hue with a steady, straight line of black ink.

"Why did you do that?" Jacob asked her.

Rebekah's hair slid from behind her ear. "It makes me happy. The hue stands out more. See?"

Color Master looked over her shoulder. "Ah, but a black line separates the hues, making it difficult to see their relationship to each other."

Rebekah frowned at the circle.

"Never mind," Color Master said. "We'll be making at least a dozen color circles, so a black outline on this one won't matter. Ishmael, are you going to join us? Even though you already know your color, you still need to make the color circles," Color Master said.

Ishmael's paper sat empty in front of him. He reached for a brush and sketched out a circle, but it seemed dishonest to him to do work that he would abandon. He found, though, as he began, that nothing felt more honest in the world to him—nothing felt truer than these colors before him.

Color Master walked around the table, inspecting their circles. "All novices begin," she said, "with a red-yellow-blue color circle. These are known as the primary colors. When you blend any two of the primary colors, you get a secondary color—orange, green, or violet. That's when you begin to see the relationships among the colors. Primary colors have more influence on their surroundings. Secondary colors follow."

The meticulous color circle in front of Jacob bore no trace of the slovenly state of his space in the dormitory. The three sections were equidistant, and the boundaries between the colors were neat.

Color Master spun Jacob's circle under her finger. It slowed, then stopped spinning with the red section at the top. "It takes one to know one," she murmured, eyeing Jacob. "You are red," she said to Jacob, decisively. Her brilliant red robes flashed as she straightened.

"The nature of red is to stand out in the spectrum. Red is a spirited color."

Jacob looked pleased.

"But you must be wise, because others will inevitably follow your lead," Color Master warned. "Rebekah's color wheel speaks loudly in favor of yellow, and not just because she outlined it in black. Yellow is a cheerful color, full of joy. Your optimism and good cheer will be vital during dark days."

Rebekah smiled, pleased to find her place so quickly in spite of the black lines she drew to separate the colors.

"Now for blue." Color Master touched Hannah's circle, looking closer at it. She looked at Hannah with eyebrows raised.

"Me?" she squeaked.

"Yes, you have the temperament of a blue, the calmness of a blue, the kindness of a blue. You have the capacity to influence others, to bring calmness and kindness to situations, which is perhaps the most significant role of all among the primary colors. Let's see about the rest of you." She passed out new circles and requested that they repeat the exercise, blending the primary colors to create secondary colors. It quickly became apparent that the enthusiasm of orange fit Thomas quite well, while Matthew's personality was entirely suited to soothing violet.

"What about me?" Lilith said.

"You are indigo, and not just because the process of elimination tells us so. Indigo is a tertiary color not included on the more simplistic color wheels," Color Master pointed out. "It's a complex color, just as you are a complex person."

Lilith took that as a compliment.

"The colors have special relationships with each other. Likewise, you will, too. You are a spectrum. Just as your individual colors have a particular bond with the colors on either side of it in the color wheel, so, too, will you have a particular bond with your neighboring novices. In color theory, we call these color harmonies."

"Are all the rest of the apprentices in spectrums?" Jacob asked.

"Yes, with the exception of the most senior spectrum—Luc's group. A few members of his spectrum have already moved on to their posticums. Now, I'd like you to find similarities with your analogous brothers and sisters. You are a group and you'll be working together for many years to come. You will progress much faster if you become unified quickly."

They chattered until they found connections with their neighbors. By the end of the morning, each novice had settled into his or her part in the spectrum, and the stones in the walls of the Hall of Hue sighed in relief.

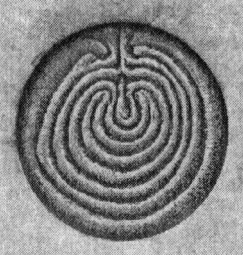

GUSTATION

Bushel baskets of stone fruit lined the long central table. Gabriel contemplated the sheer number of them. Hundreds, maybe even thousands. He had spent the better part of the past year perfecting their flavor in experimental creations, and this was the first harvest of what he hoped would be the finished fruit.

He picked one out of the basket in front of him and let the weight of it roll around in his palm. They weren't much to look at, their skin all fuzzy and their shape not quite symmetrical, but that was the Hall of Shape's doing, not his. Besides, the way they looked wouldn't match the way they tasted. He took a knife in his hand and sliced around its perimeter, then twisted the halves until one side loosened from the pit. He popped the pit out of the other half with a flick of his wrist, and gazed at the interior.

What an odd thing this fruit was.

No matter. He was interested only in its flavor. He sliced off a piece and tossed it into his mouth. Brilliant. Sublime. It was the perfect example of *sweet*, and the flavor floated up around his eyes. Sweet, with a bit of zip.

He sighed with a short-lived pleasure. Yes, it was good, but maybe it was too sweet? Maybe it wasn't complex enough to be *sublime?* Yesterday's spread had been complex—the combination of sweet, sour, and salty—but not sublime. Maybe a sublime taste came with the combination of opposite flavor profiles?

Gabriel would have to think about this. And in the meantime, he would have to figure out something to do with all this fruit.

CHAPTER
16

After lunch—a meal Ishmael classified as leaning toward *orange*—the novices gathered by the fountain in the courtyard. The water droplets reflected Color Master's red robe. "It's time to tour Luc's posticum. You will see in detail the end result of what we accomplish here."

"But I still don't understand what a posticum *is*," Hannah said.

"It is a place. It is infinity. It is a vastness of space. It is an expanse of immensity. It is nothingness."

"Well, that clears it up," Jacob said, dryly.

"That is," Color Master continued, looking at Jacob with vexation, "It is nothingness until we begin creating. Once each of the Halls begins their work, that *nothing* is turned into *something*."

She turned and led the way to Luc's posticum.

Luc stood at the entrance with a wide smile on his face.

"Ready to show us your work?" Color Master said.

"Yes, ma'am." He stepped back from the doorway and allowed them to enter.

"You're finished, then?" Ishmael whispered to him.

Luc smiled broadly and nodded.

Ishmael wanted to be happy for him, but he couldn't quite muster the emotion, not when it came at the cost of Mam's happiness. All he could do was say a simple, "Congratulations."

Thomas was the first one through. He took three steps and stopped. Matthew walked into him, and Hannah bumped into Matthew. Matthew hiccupped.

"Not again," Color Master muttered.

"Hey! Why'd you stop?" Jacob shoved his way through the others, emerging next to Matthew. He stared at the landscape before him.

Hannah drew up next to Jacob. "It's . . . not what I expected."

"*A stone that emerges from a seed will always be a surprise,*" said Thomas.

"I think it's glorious," Rebekah said. "Yellow must be your color, then?" Her face was aglow at the thought of sharing the same color with Luc.

He nodded.

Ishmael took in the view of the posticum, already so familiar to him. The leaves of the plants were light yellow. Their stalks were a few shades darker. The sky above them glowed yellow, and the clouds shimmered in the light. A deep yellow bird flitted over a pond so pale yellow that it was nearly colorless. This was the place that Luc would spend the rest of his days—unless Ishmael could persuade him that Mam's need was greater.

"What do you mean it's not what you expected?" Luc asked.

"It's all the same color," Hannah said, looking from one side to another.

"It's not," Luc said, defensive. "The differences are subtle, probably too subtle for your inexperienced eyes to see."

"Luc, I confess, I am surprised," Color Master said. "This doesn't match your representative palette. Where are the other primary colors?"

A self-satisfied smile stole over Luc's face. "Here," he said, flipping over one of the narrow-leafed plants at their feet. The veins of the plants were clearly outlined in red. "And here." He lifted a blue-streaked stone by the wall.

"Clever, indeed," Color Master said, her mouth wrapped tightly around the words. "Why don't you tell the novices more about your process from the very beginning so they can understand the work of a posticum?"

Luc settled the stone back by the wall and stood up. "I began with a palette," he said. "As you can see, yellow was my base color. I used as many variations of yellow as I could. Then," he glanced at Color Master, "I included red and blue because each posticum must contain all of the primary colors."

"Usually there is a greater balance of those colors within a posticum," Color Master added.

Luc smiled, clearly pleased with himself. "I wanted nothing to stand out, though."

Color Master frowned. "Continue."

"Since a posticum is created with apprentices from the other Halls, there is a standard order of work—from the primitive to the sublime." He reached down and scooped up a handful of dirt, letting it sift through his fingers. "In other words, age before beauty. The oldest Halls—Shape and Manufactory—begin the work. A Shape apprentice designs everything first, from the foundation to the flora and fauna."

Luc brushed off his hands. "Naomi was the Shape apprentice who designed this." He knocked his knuckles against the stone hiding the streaks of blue. "And this." He ran his palm over a tuft of some low-growing plant. "And this." He pointed toward a creature flickering through the waters of the pond.

"Once the designs from the Hall of Shape are complete, Manufactory begins construction. When a posticum opens, there is nothing here but empty space," Luc explained. "Manufactory puts the ground under our feet."

Lilith looked at Color Master and tapped the ground with the toe of her shoe. "That's what you meant? None of this was here?"

"Not a single thing."

Lilith stopped tapping her foot. "Is it safe?"

"It's completely safe," Color Master said. "The Manufactory apprentices are highly trained in the uses of their raw materials."

Luc jumped up and down to demonstrate. "See? Solid. Once Manufactory is done with the foundation, then Motion comes in to stir up the pot. Often, though, Motion waits until the other Halls—Hue, Sound, Scent, Gustation—are done with the fun stuff."

"How did you actually color this?" Rebekah asked.

Luc's mouth opened, ready to respond, when Color Master interrupted. "We'll discuss methods of moving color in the coming days," she said. "At this stage, you only need a basic understanding of the posticums." She turned to Luc. "Thank you for letting us visit."

"But—" Luc stepped in front of her. "I wanted to show you some of the highlights."

Color Master sidestepped him. "You can't give away all your secrets. Otherwise, their posticums will look like yours, and it would be a pity to influence anyone else's creative vision, wouldn't it? Come, novices." She pivoted and left the posticum.

Jacob, Thomas, Lilith, and Hannah followed.

"I think the posticum is really wonderful," Rebekah said, before turning around to follow the others.

"Yes, it's great," Matthew said.

Luc regarded the novices and Color Master as they departed. "Thank you for visiting," he said in a dull tone. Ishmael touched Luc's arm, but Luc shook it off, so he followed the others, taking one last look at his brother. Whether it was because of the oppressive shades of yellow or the knowledge that this was meant to be Luc's home forevermore, Ishmael could not leave the posticum fast enough.

MANUFACTORY

A prototype of a magnificent animal stood before Michael. He had done it: his first full prototype. It was the perfect opportunity to exhibit his skills to the Hall of Shape, and he wanted this prototype to be extraordinary.

While many of the Manufactory apprentices used materials for their creations that were prepared in advance by the novices—fabric, wire, sheets of metal, nails, glue—Michael had decided that he would start at the very beginning, making his materials from a vast quantity of motes of stardust collected from the House of Æther.

He had taken the greatest care in sifting the stardust three times for consistency and quality. From there, he made hard objects and soft objects and wiry objects to give shape to the beast, packing the powdery stardust into molds to harden into solid parts, mixing water into some of the stardust until he could knead it and shape it into internal supports, heating some until it liquefied and he could draw long wiry strands out. He even spun some of the stardust into gossamer filaments for fine detail work.

Michael had worked nonstop last night, preparing the materials. Today, he molded, stitched, stretched, glued, and stuffed. He climbed up and down a ladder to reach the high spots and bent under the belly to reach the low spots.

He circled it, studying its form, sharpened chisel in hand for last minute adjustments. It was dazzling, if he did say so himself. It stood taller than a man and had four cloven hooves, just like the Hall of Shape had requested. He had included the lever, incline plane, and gears within the curvature of the body and the length of legs. Impressive though it was, the best part of it was Michael's bold addition: the glorious swirling horn emerging from its forehead.

The incomplete plans from Shape had been easy to alter. The beast needed a tool of some kind besides the nearly useless cloven hooves, so Michael had added the great horn.

Now *that* was a useful tool. Besides, it looked spectacular.

Michael couldn't wait to show it to somebody, but first, he wanted to double-check the security of the magnificent horn's joinings so no one could treat it with contempt for technical reasons. He climbed back up the ladder when Luc, the Hall of Hue artisan, stalked past his window.

Michael wondered where he could be going this time of the day. Even if he wasn't working on a specific project, he should have been in his Hall or at his posticum. Luc went beyond Michael's line of vision, so he leaned closer to the window to satisfy his curiosity.

But Michael forgot that he was on the ladder. His arms flew

up and around as he lost his balance and hit the floor. Pain ripped through his left arm all the way up to his shoulder.

It was only much later after he was bandaged that he caught sight of his prototype, a large broken horn hanging from what had once been a magnificent spiral.

CHAPTER
17

The apprentices gathered that evening in Wright Hall to witness the first challenge. Wright Hall was the oldest standing structure in the Commons, far older than the Hall of Hue or any of the other Halls. Ishmael stopped in the middle of the large arched doors set in the center of the building. Inside, the ceiling rose high above, displaying ribbed vaults interlaced in intricate patterns. Just ahead, a large room—larger even than the refectory—opened up. Windows cut through great arches running the length of the walls, letting in the last light of the waning day.

A raised platform stood at the front of the room with a table at its center and a large chalkboard next to it. Around the sides of the room were graduated benches, cordoned off into seven sections. Patterned mosaics lined the floor.

Ishmael breathed out in amazement, and followed Thomas

and Hannah around groups of apprentices, some talking, some shuffling into the rows of benches. Behind them, woven tapestries hung from brass bars.

Ishmael took a seat next to his brother. "Luc, I don't know how much longer I can stay."

"Why? You don't like it here?"

"No, I like it too much. I'm afraid I won't have the will to go home if I don't leave soon. The only reason I came here was to get you, and if you won't go home, then I shouldn't be here, either. Mam really needs our help."

Hannah, who sat on the other side of Ishmael, hadn't heard them and innocently interrupted their conversation, saying, "I wish I knew something about who is competing tonight. Do you know them, Luc?"

A group of apprentices had gathered on the stand, three boys and three girls. One girl was dreamy-eyed and the other was dainty with small, perfect features. The third was tall and seemed very self-assured. Of the three boys, one was serious-looking with a generously bandaged arm, the second had wild hair and looked around expectantly, and the third had his arms crossed and seemed bored.

Luc pointed to the dreamy-eyed girl. "The girl at the far left is Dora. Hall of Shape. The small, dark-haired girl is Keturah. She's from Scent. The last girl is Anna, the artisan from Sound."

Hannah nodded. "And the others?"

"Thaddeus is the one with the wild hair. He's from Motion. Then there's Gabriel. He's from Gustation. I don't think he much likes apprentices from any of the other Halls. The one with the bandage is Michael. He's a funny apprentice. So earnest about everything."

"Earnest isn't bad," Thomas said. He sat on the other side of Luc.

The bell tolled and the sound echoed in the cavernous hall. A hush settled over the crowd. The apprentices who were milling around found seats, excited to see the challenge.

Head Master approached the lectern at the front. He introduced the apprentices to loud cheers, then said, "The challenge issued by the Hall of Hue is to create order and chaos. I am most eager to see what you make. Dora, you may begin."

The apprentice named Dora stood and smoothed her hands over her skirt. She took a piece of chalk and wrote "Order and Chaos" at the top of the large slate. So many lovely curves in those words! She sighed with pleasure, then turned her thoughts to what form she would design. All day, she had tried to plan something, but her mind would not settle on a structure, no matter how much effort she put into it. Around midday, she decided to stop worrying and just improvise. So she started with the only place she could start, a dot. Most Shape apprentices would move right into a line, but Dora drew another dot. Then another. She drew six dots.

Dora loved the dot more than the line, but if she had to include both order and chaos, she might as well have lines. She connected the dots with lines to form a hexagon, then put the chalk down and stood back to examine her work. It was just a shape. It didn't do anything, but she was pleased with its simplicity, with the order of its lines and the chaos of its dots. She turned to Michael, who had been studying each of her movements.

"I'm finished," she said, in a silvery, sweet voice.

He looked at her with disbelief. "Finished?"

"Yes," she said. "Finished."

Michael couldn't believe his luck. It was as if the Shape apprentice had opened a door for him that had slammed shut when he ruined the horn on his prototype earlier. And Manufactory Master had said he should skip the challenge because of his injured arm! Hah!

Michael stood and tripped over his case on the way to the table. He flushed, and pulled out a large circular panel, a bag, and three small vials with his uninjured arm. From deep inside the bag, he retrieved what looked like a tiny clear tablet of pressed stardust, no bigger than a teardrop. He set the tablet in the middle of the panel, then pulled some thin metal pins from one of the vials. Michael pushed six pins evenly around it, mimicking the shape Dora had produced. He paused and looked at the Shape apprentice. "This'll be good. You'll like it," he said. "Er, not this," he added, pointing to the pins. "This is just the temporary framework. I mean you'll like what comes from it."

Her eyebrows rose at the strange ways of this eager boy, though she appreciated the circle of the panel.

Michael opened another vial, took one more glance at Dora, then poured six drops onto the tablet. This wouldn't be like the horn on his prototype since he didn't have time to make a proper mold, but he still thought it could be spectacular. The tablet grew, stretching outward, forming itself into a flat hexagon with sharp edges and abrupt points, taking its shape from the metal pins surrounding it. "Symmetry," Michael said.

Dora, the Shape apprentice, smiled, happy that the Manufactory apprentice understood what she wanted to communicate in her simple shape. Order and chaos.

But Michael wasn't finished with it yet. He turned back to the flat hexagon, as it continued to expand around the pins, its six points extending into rays. When he was satisfied with the length of the rays, he pushed six more pins right in the center of the rays and dropped more of the liquid onto the growing structure. The six rays multiplied into twelve rays.

Dora frowned. Her hexagon was now adorned with lines that sprouted from the original six dots, with more lines coming from them. Far too many lines.

He continued pinning the object and adding drops from the vial until the structure was so intricate and so elegant, so delicate and so enchanting that when he lifted the panel up to show the watching apprentices, they gave an audible gasp. Michael sprinkled some powder—more stardust—from the last vial over the crystalline structure, and it hardened instantly. He deftly removed the pins and held the flat crystalline figure out to Thaddeus, the Motion representative.

Thaddeus let it rest in his hands. It looked fragile, but he suspected it was stronger than it seemed. He balanced the center of it on the tip of his index finger and then spun it, trying to sense what would be the right motion. It slowed and stopped. Spinning had order to it, but not enough chaos.

A wave had both order and chaos, but this structure didn't lend itself to the motion of a wave. He thought for a moment, unwilling to leave the wave behind. Perhaps he could combine the two: a fluid spin and a rhythmic wave.

He held the structure high, took a deep breath to mingle with the air already circling inside his lungs. When he couldn't take any more air in, he sent it charging toward the structure in his hand. The powerful gust gave the figure loft, and it went whirling upward, spinning end over end before it gradually descended to land back in his hands. He took another deep gulp, filling his whole self with breath and blew three times in succession, a wave of air, sending the figure upward spinning and swirling and swooshing, before it floated gently down in a slow topsy-turvy dance. Spinning order. Chaotic wave. The form fell lightly onto the head of Gabriel, the Gustation apprentice.

"All yours, my friend," Thaddeus said, and sat down.

Gabriel balanced it on his head, the site of his favorite flavor profile on his elevation map of tastes. "Sweet!" he declared loudly. The gathered apprentices laughed, and this annoyed Gabriel. They didn't know about his elevation map of flavors. He tipped the structure off his head and into his waiting hands, making a snap decision that he would not squander the best flavor profile on this bunch of ignorant apprentices, even if it meant the Hall of Gustation would lose this challenge.

He'd hand it off without taste to the Scent apprentice if the other Gustation apprentices wouldn't throttle him. But they would, so he decided to feature a bland flavor instead, just for spite. Gabriel pulled a small container from a bag at his feet, twisted it open, and sprinkled a fine white powder over the intricate structure. When he was satisfied, he presented it to the next apprentice. What was meant to be sweet was bland instead.

Keturah, the Scent apprentice, took the structure in her hands, holding it gently and studying the structure's delicate arms. It looked nothing like the baby she had dreamed of, the scent she was hoping to use. It looked nothing like anything she had ever seen before. Of course, she had been trained to add scents to all sorts of things that were beyond her imagination. This structure at least had a beauty about it. She balanced it lightly on the palm of her hand and dabbed a thick salve on the very center of it. "Ethereal," she said. Then she grabbed a small bottle from a partitioned tray and misted the entire thing. When the mist rose to her nose, she frowned and lifted the bottle. It was labeled Cold. Cold? Where did that come from? She had meant to use Warm. The newborn babe spoke of warmth to her, not cold.

She inhaled deeply, disappointed. There was nothing she could do about it now, so she passed the figure to Anna, the Sound artisan.

Her lips moved silently. It looked like she was whispering "chaos" and "order" over and over. And, in fact, she was. She regretted having entered her name in the competition, because now that her work was done in the posticum, it seemed as if she was all out of ideas. She could have just spent these final days relaxing. Instead, she was up here with everyone's eyes glued on her and, worse yet, everyone's ears wide open with not a single idea of how to use sound to show order and chaos.

What to do? Order. Chaos. Chaos, order. She bit her thumbnail while staring at this object—this *thing*—before her. The Sound artisan looked up to see the watching apprentices shifting in their seats, growing restless with her inaction.

This thing looked chaotic enough on its own, a far cry from the simple figure the Shape apprentice had designed. So, she began with order. She tapped each of the six points with a fingernail, making a soft clicking sound, so that when any of its points touched anything, it would give forth a dull sound. When its points touched anything in succession, there would be a light patter. A simple sound: order. A random rhythm: chaos.

The Sound artisan let out her breath in a whoosh of relief. She picked up the figure and handed it to Head Master. "Here is order," she said. "And here is chaos." Then she sat down, her ears ringing.

Head Master looked amused. "Order and chaos: a creation to be remembered, thanks to the Hall of Hue. My congratulations to the competitors. The winner of this round is Michael, Hall of Manufactory, for building such ordered chaos." Head Master's eyes twinkled as he handed the figure to Michael. Dumbstruck, Michael took it, amazed not only that he had been allowed to tinker so much with the shape, but that his tinkering was actually appreciated. What a strange day it had been.

Head Master continued, "The Hall of Manufactory will host the challenge tomorrow evening. This challenge will be open to all apprentices, including novices." His gaze took in the novices, settling on Ishmael. He winked, then dismissed them into the night.

THE STONES

The stones always knew when something was afoot. And something was definitely afoot. Deep down, something stirred. Something pushed against boundaries, fatigued and needing to stretch.

It was always this way, always this deep-down disturbance, all along the wall, the miles of it stretching around the perimeter of the Commons. Over generations, it had happened time and time again, and it could only mean one thing: relief was on its way. A posticum would be closing soon.

CHAPTER
18

I shmael lay in bed that night, thinking. Nothing had gone well since he had arrived at the Commons. He tried to tell himself that it didn't matter, but it *did* matter. Not only was he no closer to bringing Luc home, the guilt he felt from Papa's death was compounded with the guilt he felt at leaving Mam. On top of that, he found himself more deeply entrenched here, part of a spectrum. He'd never felt part of anything so complete, and worse yet, it made him want to stay.

He wiggled out of his covers and tiptoed down the stairs into the night. Ishmael headed toward the fountain in the middle of the Great Courtyard and sat on its edge. The water splashed down in tinkling arcs, and he held his hand to the mist—a ghostly water that he felt but couldn't see.

Three days ago, he didn't even know this place existed. Now, it was as if the very stones owned him, as if the colors that were here had wrapped themselves around him binding him to a future made of color. He belonged here. But he belonged back home, too. The sheep owned him as much as anything else did, and the needs of Mam and Jerusha and Simon had wrapped themselves around him first. He was being strangled, but he wasn't sure who was strangling him. He put his head in his hands and groaned.

"Ishmael?"

Ishmael jumped. Hannah stood halfway between the entrance to the Hall of Hue and the fountain.

"Are you all right?" she asked.

"Can't sleep."

"Same." She walked over and sat down next to him. "When I couldn't sleep, my mother used to tell me stories," Hannah said, her voice low. "Do you miss home?"

Did he miss home? Funny how he had been thinking about home, but it hadn't occurred to him to miss it. The place in his memory was not the home that existed. The sagging laundry line, the broken door latch, the slumping stone wall, and the weedy kitchen garden were no longer tempered by Papa's sturdy presence, no longer lessened by Luc's cheer. The thought of home as it was now—with Mam and her tired eyes and rough hands, Jerusha with her twists of yarn, and Simon underfoot—seemed less like a safe haven and more like a sad habitat. There was work and there was responsibility and there were empty bellies. And there was guilt.

"That's a hard question to answer," he said. "Home isn't really home anymore."

"Because your father's gone?"

"Yes, but it's more than that." He told Hannah the full story about digging the well, about leaving Papa to look at the glass in the barn and the well's collapse, about the colors and the sheep, about the work and the want. "Papa's gone, yes, but everything else has changed, too, and it's my fault. The only thing I can do to fix it is to bring Luc back. But I'm not certain he'll come." He twisted the fabric of his nightclothes around his fingers, remembering what Color Master had said about apprentices entering their posticum.

Hannah put her hand gently on his shoulder. "Would his presence really make that big of a difference? He can't bring your father back. He might take a share of the work, but would things really change?"

Hannah's words ruffled Ishmael. "You don't understand," he said.

"No," she said, "I don't. I can't, because I haven't been there, but it's possible that Luc might not make as big an impact as you think he would. I'm afraid you expect him to come home and save everything. I don't think he can."

Ishmael stood up, indignant. "You don't know Luc."

"Of course I don't—not like you do. But neither of you can make things go back to the way they were."

Ishmael sank back down onto the edge of the fountain. "It's

not that I want to go back to the way things were. It's just that I feel responsible . . . if I had been there—"

Hannah interrupted him. "If you had been there, what would you have done? What *could* you have done?"

"I could have dug Papa out. I could have gone for help. I could have—"

"Maybe. But so often we only see what we might have done in hindsight. It's just as possible that you couldn't have changed the end result at all. Luc might not be able to change the end result, either." She looked back toward the Hall of Hue archway and yawned.

"You go ahead. I'll be on my way in a minute," he said.

"All right. You're sure?"

He nodded, so she stood and left him sitting by the fountain.

CHAPTER

19

The bell came far too early the following morning—at least according to Ishmael. He rolled over to see Thomas already up and dressed, though his springy hair stood out every which way.

Thomas poked him. *"He who slumbers late, tempts fate.* Besides, Head Master is going to announce the next challenge. Better get moving or you'll miss the announcement."

Ishmael groaned and sat up.

Beyond Thomas, he saw Jacob already up and dressed, too. "I'm entering the challenge," he said.

"But we haven't learned anything about coloration yet," Matthew said.

"Luc told me I'd have no trouble—that I just needed to get a few vials of color and sprinkle it onto whatever was given to me."

Ishmael stretched, noting that Luc hadn't told *him* to enter. He threw on his uniform and followed the others out the door.

One hour later, he retraced his steps from the refectory back to the Hall of Hue.

"The substance of that which is insubstantial? It sounds like the beginning of a bad proverb. How can that be the next challenge?" Thomas faced Jacob and Matthew as they walked into the Hall of Hue. "What does that even mean?"

Ishmael shrugged. Right after Head Master announced the challenge, each Hall master drew names for participants. When Jacob's name was announced as the Hall of Hue representative, he looked as if he had choked on his courage. He still looked that way. Ishmael couldn't blame him.

Matthew patted Jacob's shoulder. "Manufactory was just trying to be clever because they won't be participating in the challenge since they're hosting it. I wouldn't worry, Jacob. Like Luc said, you just need to color whatever they give you."

Jacob gave a weak smile to Matthew as they walked into the smaller room in the back. There, they found Luc at the table with a crate at his side.

Once everyone was seated, he said, "Color Master asked if I would begin your training with light and prisms since my work is done in the posticum." Luc withdrew a long, triangular piece of glass with a wooden handle from a crate on the table and handed it to Jacob. He passed one to Ishmael and the others.

Ishmael ran his finger along the smooth edge. He lifted it

level with his face and saw his reflection in it. Dark hair, light eyes. Small nose. He wished he could recognize what it was that made him see differently, but the prism didn't show that.

When Luc finished handing out prisms, he said, "Prisms are your tools, but they only work if they are clean and if you have light. Without light, your prism is just a piece of glass. But with light you can create marvels." Luc caught a ray of light and formed a spectrum. "Prisms up!" He directed them to raise their prisms. Ishmael was the first one to form a spectrum. Hannah was next, then Rebekah. As each novice caught a ray of light, the room became a wild riot of spectrums, colors bouncing off every surface.

Ishmael blinked, dizzy with the overload of color.

Luc let the unruly colors ricochet for a few moments before he said, "Prisms down!"

"Do we have to?" Jacob asked. "I just got my spectrum."

"You'll have plenty of time to form spectrums later."

The novices reluctantly put their prisms down and the spectrums dissipated.

Luc patted a stone jar on the table. It had a wide lid and a spout that rose straight up from its side. "First law of color: *All color is contained in pure light.* This jar contains pure light given to us by the astronomae from the House of Light. It is precious and rare, very difficult to collect. They siphon it directly from the stars and give it to us with the understanding that what we create in the posticums will bring more light. *Light begets light,* they say."

"This is the light we use for color in the posticums." He

unstoppered the spout on the jar and released a tiny bit of light, then angled his prism to catch the light, and in an instant, the brightness transfigured into a spectrum so brilliant that Ishmael squinted in the sudden illumination.

Lilith held her hand up to shade her eyes. "Why is this so much brighter than regular light?"

Luc picked up another prism and caught an ordinary ray of light coming in the window. Another spectrum sprang up, but it paled in comparison to the spectrum hovering at his other side. "Regular light is ancient. It's softened by the refining touch of millennia. It's diffused and won't provide the color we need when we're creating a posticum. Light from the astronomae is new and incredibly powerful, as you can see."

Lilith nodded.

Luc released the first spectrum. It was so strong that it held steady by Luc's side. "Second law of color: *In the presence of the complete spectrum, a color will always take its place among like kind.* Let me show you."

Luc lowered the spectrum of regular light. He separated yellow and formed a ball with it, just like he had in his posticum. The novices watched as he let the other colors in the spectrum fade. When there was nothing left but the yellow ball, Luc heaved it upward, hurling it toward the ceiling. It rose, spinning through the air, a golden glow radiating through the room. As soon as it began its descent, the yellow ball zipped into its rightful place between orange and green in the brilliant spectrum, leaving no trace.

The spectrum pulsed next to Luc. "You may be wondering about the origins of the color in the workroom since pure light is so difficult to obtain."

Lilith nodded. "I *was*, actually."

"We distill that color from regular light. This gives us processed color, which isn't as true as color from pure light, but it's close enough for learning purposes."

"So that's what all those machines are in there," Jacob said, pointing behind him to the workroom.

"Exactly. We form a spectrum, separate the colors, and distill each color to remove impurities. The distillation process takes a few weeks, so this, too, is a lengthy process. A word to the wise, Color Master has no tolerance for wasted color."

"No, she does not," Color Master said, entering the back of the room. "Thank you, Luc. I'll take it from here. While I have no tolerance for wasted color, no color is wasted if it is used to help you learn."

She settled a large bag on the table. "Since you will be representing the Hall of Hue tonight at the challenge, Jacob, and I'd hate for you to go in unprepared, I'm going to show you all some rudimentary methods of color transfer. This afternoon I'll work directly with you while the others can observe the work of the more senior apprentices."

Color Master pulled from the bag an assortment of brushes, a large feather quill, several twigs with their ends wrapped in strips of linen, a pouch made of fine netting, a tube the size of

Ishmael's forearm, a vial of red, a vial of orange, and four clear, flat boards.

She held up the brushes. "You already know how to use these so I won't say anything else about them, except that they are the easiest form of direct application. This is a swab," she said, holding up one of the twigs. She handed the swab to Jacob to examine while she uncapped a vial and reached for another swab.

She dipped the swab into the vial, and then lightly blew the color over the board. A fine powder sifted down, sprinkling the surface with red. The speckles of red grew into spots, which grew into patches until the whole surface was solid red. "Swabs are useful for coloring areas that don't have much detail to them.

"When you have detail work that requires an exact transfer, you can use this." She held up the feather. "This is a quill, and it works like a regular writing quill. Dip it in liquid color, let the reservoir fill, and then transfer it directly onto what you're coloring." Color Master dropped the quill into Ishmael's hand.

Ishmael inspected the quill from its pointed end to its stiff tip. "This isn't what Luc did in his posticum."

Color Master laughed. "No, indeed. These are the oldest and most basic methods of color transfer that we have." She uncapped the vial of orange, reached for the quill, and dipped it in, holding it there while the color moved fluidly into the reservoir. "We transfer color directly from the spectrum now—it's much more sophisticated and accurate. But this is the foundation of current color transfer theory and so you must learn it."

When the quill was full, Color Master wrote neatly on one of the boards. Immediately, the color began to creep from the words outward.

Ishmael stood spellbound at the sight. The other novices had also gathered close, watching the transformation.

"Can I try that?" Rebekah asked.

"I'll give you each a chance to try all of these methods once I'm finished demonstrating. Now, this is a sifter," she said, holding up the pouch. "You put powdered color inside and tap it like this." She tipped some of the red powder into the netting and tapped it until a fine sprinkling of red descended onto the third board. "This is similar to using a swab, but this gives you more control."

Color Master set the sifter down and grasped the tube, picking at the edge of it until a corner came loose and she unrolled what it held. "This is color wrap. You can cut pieces and attach it to whatever you want colored. The color will sink through the wrap into the object, like so." She cut a piece of the yellow wrap and massaged it onto the surface of the fourth board. Again, the color seeped into it and spread.

"This is a quick demonstration, but these methods aren't difficult. They just require some practice, and so that's what you'll do now," she said as she passed out swabs and quills to each of them.

One of the upper apprentices popped his head in the door. "Color Master, there's a problem with one of the distillation machines."

"Again?" She placed the rest of the swabs and quills in the center of the table. "Practice these methods," she said to the novices. "I'll be back as soon as I can."

They settled in to explore the new instruments, but as soon as Color Master was out the door, Jacob pulled out his prism and summoned a spectrum. "Anyone up for a spectrum duel?"

"Jacob! We're supposed to be practicing," Lilith said. "You need to get ready for tonight."

Jacob tossed his spectrum up in the air. "I'll be fine. This stuff is so easy."

Lilith pursed her lips and dunked her quill in the vial of orange with a look of disapproval.

"Anyone?" Jacob asked again.

Rebekah's prism flashed as she pulled it out and formed a spectrum. Jacob's spectrum charged toward hers, but Rebekah flicked her prism so her spectrum formed an arch and tumbled end over end around the room. Jacob moved his spectrum to chase after it, but always seemed to be a step behind.

"Come on!" Thomas called out, cheering on Jacob, but the red-heavy spectrum couldn't seem to keep up with the antics of Rebekah's spectrum as it flashed and tumbled. Hannah clapped and even Lilith laughed at the twirling and looping spectrum.

Ishmael's fingers itched. He watched the colors zooming around, and when he couldn't resist anymore, he reached for the handle of his prism. Immediately a spectrum sprang up. He cast some green at Rebekah's spectrum, but couldn't catch it, and the green splatted on the wall. Jacob whooped, so Ishmael hurled some blue toward Jacob's spectrum. It landed dead center, but instead of covering the colors as Ishmael expected, the blue funneled itself back into blue.

Realizing he had just shown the second law of color, Ishmael hurtled his entire spectrum toward the ceiling. When the spectrum met the solid surface, color exploded outward, splintering and shimmering above them, encasing the two other spectrums in a glowing light.

Lilith and Hannah held their faces up to the light, looks of wonder overcoming them as bits of color rained down. Thomas cheered loudly, arms up. Matthew held out his hands as if he could catch every smidgen of violet that drifted by. The air held a sparkly glow as Jacob's spectrum raced after Rebekah's. Ishmael laughed in delight.

Until Color Master poked her head inside the door.

"What in the blazes is going on in here?" she said. "I believe I told you to practice."

Rebekah let her spectrum fade. Jacob's spectrum was high in the air, weaving through the tendrils of Ishmael's color explosion. He pocketed his prism sheepishly.

"*A bird may be known by its flight*," Thomas said. "And a Hue novice by his color."

"Swabs. Quills. Sifters. Now," she said, glaring at Thomas.

CHAPTER
20

After lunch, the novices were paired with an upper apprentice to observe their work, so Jacob could practice coloration methods with Color Master. Being brothers, Ishmael was assigned to Luc.

"Let's go to the tower room," Luc said. "We won't bother anyone else there."

Ishmael followed Luc through the cloister and up the tower stairs. When they reached the top, Ishmael was immediately drawn to the view out the windows. From this vantage point, he could see the Hall of Hue and the Great Courtyard beyond. Farther out lay the other Halls, the refectory, and the entrance to the Commons surrounded by the stone walls and the gate. Where his town should have been visible, he could only see mist and fog. He looked up at the sky, but it was clear above. He looked back down again. Foggy. He turned toward Luc's posticum, and that too, seemed fuzzy and out of focus.

While Ishmael studied the landscape, Luc had pulled a couple of barrels over to the south window and settled a crate between them. "Have a seat."

Ishmael turned his attention to the room. It was not big, only about eight feet by eight feet, but it had a vaulted ceiling and light poured through the windows.

Luc summoned a spectrum and began flicking tiny specks of color at the wall opposite him. He made small patches of red and orange and violet, and patches of green and blue and yellow.

"What are you doing?"

"I'm making an image."

It didn't look like an image. It looked like nothing more than patches of color, an uneven spectrum. "Why?"

Luc laughed. "It's just habit. Color Master will make you do hundreds and hundreds of these practice sessions once you finish learning some of the more rudimentary methods of coloring. You'll do so many that whenever you sit down with a bit of free time, you'll begin creating an image."

"It doesn't look like anything."

"Have some patience, little brother. Watch and learn."

So Ishmael settled himself on the barrel next to Luc and watched as Luc flicked beads of color onto the walls. He found himself entranced by the color zipping by, appearing suddenly on the wall in front of them.

Areas of shadow began to form where Luc had crowded dots of violet and blue and red together. It made the areas of yellow and green and orange stand out in highlight. A line seemed to settle and then a curve and suddenly the rhythm of specks began to merge together in what appeared to be a continuation of the view from the windows.

Ishmael was smitten. "It's the sky," he said. "And the clouds. And the refectory!"

"Correct! This is one of the more direct ways we transfer color now."

Ishmael took a step back to look at the wall from farther away and marveled at the combination and placement of colors. It was so beautiful with all the colors gathered together. He wondered why Luc hadn't done something like this in his posticum, but he was afraid to ask, certain that Luc would misconstrue his words as criticism. "You've put so many colors in the clouds."

"Color Master claims this exercise trains our eye." Luc grinned. He flicked another speck of color on the wall. "You're a quick study. You should try this—it's advanced stuff, but you'll be able to do it."

Ishmael watched as Luc held the spectrum up with one hand, and with the other, flicked a particular spot on the spectrum, aiming it at the wall in front of him. It looked hard, compared to what Ishmael had done in the barn at home, flinging color around with little dexterity and absolutely no grace. "How do you get such small specks?"

"You'd think it would come from the finger, but really it's all in the wrist. Like this." Luc flicked his fingers, shooting forward from the wrist.

Ishmael practiced the motion a few times, and then pulled out his prism. When a spectrum appeared, he watched Luc once again, and mimicked his movement. A large glob of green spattered against the wall.

Luc took Ishmael's wrist and gently moved it in circles. "Make your wrist looser. Make it floppy, but keep your fingers sharp."

Ishmael tried again, but with little effect. Another shapeless splat of green landed next to the first.

"Keep practicing. You'll get it. And when you have some control, you can begin to do some of the shadows and highlights."

The thought of joining Luc—of being able to make such an image—thrilled Ishmael to his very center. He concentrated on keeping his wrist loose and his fingers sharp and made an attempt at controlling the color. Gradually, the size of the globs became smaller and rounder, as he practiced. Within a short amount of time, Ishmael's specks were nearly indistinguishable from Luc's.

"Now you've got it," Luc said. "Come join me." He made progress on the wall while Ishmael had been practicing. Silhouettes of the clouds were filling with color, saturated in a way that was completely unexpected, reds and yellows and purples. And the stone refectory seemed as solid on the interior wall of the tower room as it was outside the window.

"Go on," Luc said.

But Ishmael looked at the wall, then looked at Luc, and

lowered his prism. With a scared smile, he said, "I'm kind of . . . overwhelmed. I don't know what to do."

Luc lowered his prism, too, and let his spectrum fade. "What do you mean? Your specks are nearly flawless."

"I'm afraid I'm going to do the wrong thing," Ishmael said. "Pick the wrong color, or put it in the wrong place."

"There is no right or wrong with color in here. We're just playing."

"But how did you pick the colors? How did you know where to put them? How did you make this wall look like a bank of clouds?"

"Practice. I told you, Color Master makes us practice these until we can do them in our sleep. It's not always easy to imagine color where you've never seen it, especially when you come from a place where there is none. You're used to seeing the everyday nothingness. So you see the everyday nothingness."

Even though Luc meant to be helpful, Ishmael was stricken at the thought of the everyday nothingness back home and the contrast of the everyday fullness here. But he could do the same thing on the walls of the barn when he returned home. He could make the same kind of beauty there. It wouldn't be exactly the same, but it would have some semblance of the beauty of the colors here.

"The longer you're here, the more you're able to pick out colors for the everyday things around you. Follow your instincts."

Luc's assumption that Ishmael would be here for a long time nettled him, and Ishmael jumped down from the barrel. "But

Luc! I'm not going to be here. I have to go home." Ishmael shoved the barrel and walked to one of the windows. He put his hand on the stone windowsill and leaned out, taking a deep gulp of the chill air. He felt like a cloud himself, misty and blurred, and liable to begin raining great teardrops if he thought too hard about what was to come.

Luc climbed down from his barrel and joined Ishmael at the window. He paused, and then said, "I can't go back." He breathed deeply as if it took all his energy to say the words.

Ishmael tried to walk past him, but Luc grabbed his arm. "This is a higher calling, Ishmael. You should see that by now."

"I do see that, but Papa is gone and—"

"Even Papa saw that this was a higher calling, and he couldn't see color. You *can* see color and you have been chosen for that same calling if you've got the courage to accept it."

"Wait. What did Papa tell you?" Ishmael was suddenly greedy for Papa's words, starved for one of his thoughts, anxious to spend a few minutes back in his presence, even if it came secondhand through Luc's memory.

"Didn't you hear everything that night? Mam didn't even attempt to keep her voice down."

"I heard Mam crying and Papa rumbling, but none of it made sense to me. And then, in the morning, you were gone."

Luc looked up, stunned. "You mean this whole time you didn't know where I was?"

Ishmael shook his head. "You just disappeared."

"How did you find me, then?"

"I told Mam that you needed to know about Papa. She gave me that book—*A History of the Commons*—and said you were here."

"And she just let you go?"

"Not exactly." A twinge of guilt poked Ishmael. "I left her a note."

Luc ran his fingers through his hair.

"What happened that night you left?" Ishmael pressed.

"I had seen color in the soap bubbles," he began. "I told Papa about it. He didn't know what it was, but he asked around in town next market day. Someone gave him that book about the Commons. Every time I opened it, I felt drawn here, even though I couldn't understand half of what I read. Papa said I needed to go, said this was a higher calling, and he gave me his blessing."

Papa knew he came here. Papa *encouraged* Luc to come here. Ishmael couldn't look at Luc.

"Mam didn't see things the same way. That night, she was . . . well, I've never seen her so angry. She beat on Papa's chest, asking how he could let me go to such a place. He just held her by her shoulders and said everything would be fine."

Everything was not fine. Papa could not have been more wrong, but he couldn't have foreseen that the well would collapse, and that Ishmael would, of necessity, have to step into Papa's shoes. It was his fault that Papa was gone. It was Papa's fault that Luc was here. It was Luc's fault that Mam was so unhappy. What was Mam's fault? Bringing the glass home that went into the barn? Asking Luc to wash the fleece in the soapy water? None of this was Mam's fault, but she was the one who was suffering.

Ishmael shifted his prism from one hand to the other, feeling its weight and the power it held. He wanted to stay. He had to go.

"You're not going to say anything?" Luc asked.

"What's there to say?"

Luc held his hands up in surrender. "Forgive me for stating the obvious, but not only do you see color, color responds to you in a way I've never seen."

"You're only saying that because you're my brother."

"I mean it, Ishmael. From your first day here when you took my prism after I lobbed color onto that Sound novice? And that streak of green bolted out of the spectrum when you touched my prism? Do you know how long it took me to learn how to flick specks of color?"

Ishmael shrugged, not trusting himself to speak.

"It took me two years. It took you *twenty minutes*. You've been here less than one week and look what you've done. Imagine what you could do with more time." Luc paused. "Ishmael, I'm not going back. You know that, don't you?"

Ishmael realized he *did* know that. He had known from the minute Color Master told him that artisans stay in their posticums.

Luc continued, "But it's not my future that is at stake here; it's yours. This is no longer about me, about whether or not I'll go back. This is about you, about whether or not you will stay."

Ishmael felt Luc's eyes boring into him, but he wouldn't meet his gaze.

"I have to go back. In fact, I should have already left. Mam's probably worried sick." Ishmael steeled himself. He would leave tomorrow. He would pack up tonight and leave first thing. He felt the sting of sacrifice with this decision—the same sacrifice he had asked of Luc. But if Luc wouldn't go home, then Ishmael would have to, and in returning home, he would always mourn what wasn't and what would never be.

The decision made, Ishmael turned around to gaze at the masterpiece on the wall, the colorful swirls of clouds stuck between heaven and earth. Always reaching for heaven, but always falling to earth. Ishmael lifted his prism and flicked a perfectly round speck of green onto the wall.

They spent the rest of the afternoon flicking color onto the walls of the upper room, not speaking, but forming a delicate mural of the heaven surrounding them.

CHAPTER

21

After a dinner that tasted predominantly of green—a comforting flavor for Ishmael—he decided to go for a walk. Mam used to say that walking makes everything clear, and he badly needed some clarity, even if it meant skipping the challenge that evening.

Luc's words had stuck with Ishmael—*It's not my future that is at stake here; it's yours.* Ishmael thought about life on the farm and life here at the Commons. How he would miss the air here, the wonder of this place, and the strangeness that surrounded him. He would miss being woken by the bell each morning and tasting the colors in the food and watching apprentices create.

He would miss his new friends—his spectrum. He would miss Thomas's strange proverbs, Hannah's kindness, Rebekah's enthusiasm, Lilith's sense of justice, Jacob's boldness. He'd even miss Matthew's hiccups. He'd never had friends like them before. He never really had friends. He only had brothers and a sister. And sheep.

But he had to go back.

Didn't he?

Just outside the refectory doors, he considered where he could walk. Situated around the perimeter of the Great Courtyard were entrances to the other Halls. He needed someplace small, someplace quiet, or else someplace he could become hopelessly lost to let his mind wander over and under and around the problem at hand. He didn't know if such a place existed here.

Ishmael made his way to the fountain in the center of the courtyard and faced the Hall of Hue. From this perspective, he could see the entrances to a few of the other Halls and a small archway just past the entrance to the Hall of Manufactory. He didn't know where the archway led, so he headed that way, ducked inside, and found himself in an alleyway with high walls.

He walked until the path branched into three separate ways, each marked with a carved stone. One stone had a series of rays extending outward from a central point. Another stone was marked with a simple leaf. A series of graduated ovals carved one on top of the other marked the third stone.

As he stood there, the stone with the oval symbols seemed to wink at him.

"Fine," Ishmael said. "Have it your way." He took that path, twisting and turning around boulders the size of a man. Ishmael scrambled up and over smaller rocks, until the path spit him out on a vast hillside littered with even more stone.

Ishmael had never seen a more perfect place. It was like an odd overgrown garden of stones, more tangled even than the thoughts in his head. Here and there, misshapen and enormous boulders were scattered about with stacks of smaller stones piled up around them. As he took a step, his foot slipped out from under him, and he knocked a small pile of pebbles over, sending them skittering down the pathway.

A face appeared around the side of a particularly large stone. It was the Manufactory apprentice who had won the first challenge, order and chaos, the apprentice Luc had said was earnest and needed to lighten up.

Ishmael flushed. "Sorry."

"No need to apologize. It's hard to walk around in here without kicking over some stones."

"What is this place?" Ishmael asked.

"The Cairns. It's the original quarry for the Commons. I'm Michael, by the way. Hall of Manufactory."

Ishmael nodded. "I remember you from the challenge. I'm Ishmael. Hall of Hue. Is it all right for me to be here? I was just looking for a place to think."

"You're in the perfect place, then. The Cairns is a place of epiphany. People come here when they have a decision to make or need answers. It's tradition to add a stone to one of the piles when you visit. After you do, the first thing that comes to your mind—the first memory that you have—is supposed to relate to your current need. It's considered an epiphany. An echo of sorts, or a manifestation, even."

Ishmael had walked down to where Michael was. "Does it work?"

Michael sat, and Ishmael joined him, leaning against the solid cool stone.

"It's uncanny how your memories from the past can fit the present so well. Makes you realize the answers you're looking for are already there, somewhere inside you," Michael said. "Go ahead. Grab a stone."

Ishmael picked up a pebble and rolled it between his hands. "You must have a decision then, too?"

Michael held up the stone in his hands. "I'm looking for some guidance."

Ishmael nodded, not wanting to pry.

Michael stood up. "Well, good luck."

"Thanks." They went in opposite directions and Ishmael heard the skittering of stones as Michael made his way down a path. He found a small cairn nearby and set his pebble on the top of it. Should he stay? Should he leave? He waited for the promised epiphany, but all that came to mind was the image of the barn at home, colored from top to bottom.

He looked out over the stones and was reminded of home. There was a wildness here and a lack of color—just like home— and the overall effect was bleak. It was in complete contrast with the tower room that he and Luc had colored earlier.

Was that supposed to be his answer? If it was, it wasn't much of an answer. Ishmael turned around to go back but spotted something so strange that he did a double take.

A tuft of green emerged from between two stones. He blinked his eyes. Green. He peered closer. Yes, that was definitely green. Not a trick of some sort.

He sat on a rock staring at the green. He looked away, then looked back at it. Still green. One lone spot of green in the midst of a colorless world. He knew what *that* felt like, he thought, and then caught his breath. If he returned home, he would be the lone green, the only spot of color, just like this tuft of green in the field of stone.

Michael returned while Ishmael was pondering this. "Did you get your answer?"

"I think I did, though I'm not sure that I like it." Ishmael stood up and brushed off his hands. "It's just made a hard choice even harder. Did you find your answer?"

Michael smiled. "Yes. I believe I did."

They began walking up the hill to the path.

"Can I ask you something?" Ishmael said. "The only place I've ever seen color here is in the Hall of Hue—until now. I see a small bit of color—there."

Michael glanced where Ishmael pointed even though he couldn't see the color. "Do you? That's not surprising. The Cairns reflects what's already inside you. When I come here, I see the seven simple machines in the stones—a lever or a pulley usually, though sometimes I've even seen gears. It's the only place outside of the Hall of Manufactory that I see them."

"Really?"

Michael nodded. "Sometimes I see shapes, too, though." His lips clamped together, as if they were unhappy that he had said so much.

Ishmael followed Michael up the hill to the path. "But you're not a Shape apprentice."

"No," Michael said, but he didn't elaborate.

They walked along the trail back toward the Great Courtyard. When they reached the juncture of paths marked with symbols, Ishmael asked, "Where do these other paths go?"

"They lead to the House of Æther and the House of Light. Everything we use to create comes from these places—the elements, the air, the light."

At the mention of light, Ishmael's thoughts turned to the small tuft of green poking out amid the towers of stones, and he wondered where it came from, if not from a distilled spectrum. Was it just in his mind? If so, that one lone bit of green made him feel very forlorn.

They reached the Great Courtyard. "Thanks," Ishmael said.

"Sure. I'll see you around," said Michael, and they each returned to their Halls, accompanied only by their epiphanies from the Cairns.

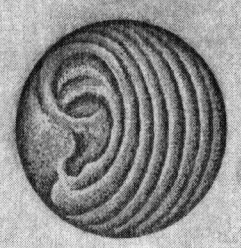

SOUND

The bell ringer opened the door of the bell tower and walked to the first step. He wondered, as he often did, who built these steps, all 107 of them. Who was the first person to climb them? And the person after that? And the next one? A great procession of bell ringers preceded him, climbing step after step, and undoubtedly, there would be a great procession of bell ringers who followed him. He felt honored to be a link in that chain.

Aaron reached the rope, and imagined the sound waves rippling outward, spreading through the air, touching the stone of the buildings, then the windows, then the furniture, and then the people before moving on. One building, then another, and another—the circle from the bell growing larger and larger until it encompassed everything, the whole Commons and beyond. Truly the Hall of Sound was the one Hall that touched all things.

He knew, though, that the other Halls felt the same way. While the older Halls—Shape, Manufactory, and Motion—had some justification, he didn't completely understand the other younger Halls, even though he had listened with all his might during the Hall Appreciation nights. He wondered if the other Halls' apprentices could smell or taste the sound wave. Did they see it differently? Did it descend like a blanket upon the Commons, or sprinkle like salt?

He shook his head. He'd never know how they experienced sound. To him, it was glory and sweetness and power all wrapped up into one experience. It was connection: one bell ringer linked to the next, one sound wave touching another, one note reaching out to all the notes surrounding it.

The bell ringer liked that thought. He wadded some wool into his ears so he wouldn't be overwhelmed by the imminent sound wave, took a deep breath, and pulled the rope.

CHAPTER

22

W here were you last night?" Hannah asked Ishmael at breakfast.

"I got lost."

Thomas picked up a spoon, breathed on it, and wiped it until it shone. "*The lost coin never gets spent.* You missed a great challenge."

"Jacob was superb," Rebekah said.

Jacob beamed at the praise.

Ishmael smiled ruefully. "Sorry, Jacob. Wish I could have been there."

"It's all right," Jacob said. "There will be other challenges."

But there wouldn't be other challenges for Ishmael. Regardless of what he had felt at the Cairns last night, today was the day. His things were packed. He had left Mam with the full intention of returning, and now it was time to follow through. He looked around at each of his friends, trying to memorize their faces and their mannerisms and their smiles so he could recall them when he was home. He would conjure up their memories while he was milking the sheep or turning the cheese or fixing the fence, and it would be like they were there with him, almost.

His thoughts were interrupted by Head Master. He stood at the lectern for the day's announcements. "Good morning, all. We have a very important—and may I add, delightful—change in the schedule today. Lessons will be postponed until this afternoon. Josias finished his work in the posticum last night, so—"

Cheers rang out, interrupting him.

Head Master raised his hands to quiet them. "Yes, yes, that means that directly after breakfast, we shall have our laurels ceremony!"

The refectory rang with applause. The Sound apprentices whistled and the Motion apprentices raised their hands high in the air and shook them. Closer to Ishmael, Hue apprentices slapped Luc on the back. Ishmael looked at his brother with a bittersweet pride. One more delay couldn't hurt.

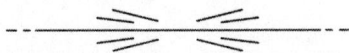

After breakfast, everyone paraded to Wright Hall. As the apprentices piled in, the room echoed with the lush sound of joy.

"You must be so proud of Luc," Rebekah said, taking her seat.

Ishmael wanted to be happy for his brother. He wanted to feel the celebratory sizzle in the air, but he only felt impending loss.

Before he could respond, Head Master stood, and everyone settled into their seats. "Today we honor seven: Naomi, Bartholomew, Delilah, Luc, Anna, Miriam, and Josias. Their task was to create a landscape with shape, form, motion, color, sound, scent, and taste. The result is masterful. We celebrate with the gift of the laurel crown, the symbol of the master."

The artisans glowed with pride up on the stand. Each Hall master stood and took their places at the front, a laurel crown in hand.

"Artisans, please take your places."

Luc stood and joined Color Master. He clasped his hands together behind him, then let them dangle from his sides, then laced them together in front. Jerusha, Ishmael's younger sister, used to do the same thing. When she walked, she clasped her hands behind her. When she stood, she clutched them in front. The recognition gave Ishmael a pinprick of sadness.

Head Master spoke. "We present to you the laurel crown, symbol of the level of master."

Color Master stood in front of Luc, her robes blazing in brilliant red. Lifting the laurel crown high, she placed it upon his head. Luc's hair curled around the woven branches, as if welcoming the leaves. A huge smile split his face.

This was a moment that Ishmael would never forget. It would be emblazoned on his memory for the remainder of time: Luc's glorious moment of triumph overlaid by his own stinging sorrow. He was about to lose his brother, once again.

CHAPTER
23

I shmael hadn't planned to stay for lunch, but there wouldn't be much food at home—only the meager mutton and porridge and cheese—and it would have to stretch to feed all of them. Rather than add to the hardship at home, he figured he might as well eat here. Besides, he wanted to get one last glimpse of color in his mind while he ate. The celebratory lunch, though filling, tasted like darkness.

Ishmael returned to the workroom to pick up his satchel, knowing the time had come no matter how much he dreaded it. He pulled out his prism, careful to hold it by its handle for fear of smudging the glass. He knew he should return it when he said goodbye to Luc. He took one last look around the workroom—at the vials and the spectrums and the worktables—and tried to be happy for having been in this magical place, even if it had been for such a short while, and then he walked outside.

Luc stood just inside the courtyard.

Ishmael headed his way. "I guess this is it," he said.

One of the laurel leaves from Luc's crown fluttered to the ground. "You're really leaving?"

"Yes." Ishmael still held the prism in his left hand, but found himself unwilling to place it back in its case and give it to Luc.

"You can't wait? Even a few more days?" Luc asked.

"No," Ishmael said with a rueful smile. "Now that you've been laureled, there's no need for me to stay." He popped the prism into the case and cinched it tight. He knew that if he waited even a few days, he would be lost—lost in the colors here, lost to Mam, lost to his purpose. This *was* a higher calling, and he knew it, but he had promised Mam he would come back. If he stayed one more minute, he would never go home. It would be too hard. He handed the case with the prism back to Luc.

Luc looked back at the workroom full of spinning color before turning his gaze to Ishmael. "You're really going to leave all this?"

Ishmael couldn't meet his eye. "I have to."

"You're wasting what has been given to you."

Ishmael looked at him then and recognized the hurt in Luc's eyes. It was identical to his own.

A muscle in Luc's jaw twitched. "If your decision is made,

then let's go." He pivoted and headed toward the entry. "I'll walk you to the gate."

When they arrived in the small courtyard, Ishmael dropped his satchel, as if it contained the weight of all of his mixed emotions. "I wish things were different."

Luc smiled wryly. "Yeah, me, too."

"Will you tell the other novices that I said goodbye?"

"You should have told them yourself."

Ishmael picked up the strap of his satchel and put his hand on the latch of the gate. "Well. Goodbye, then."

He turned the knob, but before he could pull the door open, a rumble sounded, crackling with energy along the wall. It was the same rumble he had heard when he first arrived, but it was magnitudes louder.

Luc whipped around toward the entry to his posticum. The rumble stopped at the entry, and a puff of dust sputtered from the cracks between the stones.

"The posticum is closing!" He wore a look of naked panic. "My bag is on my worktable. All of my tools are there! I have to get final directions from Color Master!"

Without thinking, Ishmael said, "I'll get it and meet you back here." He ran, retracing his steps through the courtyard, back to the Hall of Hue, back to the workroom, knowing how much this meant to Luc.

He could hear shouts from the courtyard. "The posticum is closing! Get the others!"

Scanning the room for a bag, Ishmael saw a canvas one lying

on one of the worktables. Another bag—felted wool—slumped at the side of another table. Then Ishmael saw bag after bag, propped against tables and benches, leaning on the walls, settled on the floor. One of them had to be Luc's, but he didn't know which one. Ishmael had never seen Luc with a bag, just his prism. Only novices and lower apprentices carried their bags around, since they still needed the swabs and sifters and other instruments as they learned the rudimentary methods of coloring.

As he looked at all the bags, a thought wiggled into his mind. If he didn't get Luc's bag, would Luc be able to stay in his posticum? Or would he return home?

No. Ishmael would not even think that. No matter what choices Luc made, Ishmael could not do that to him.

Ishmael studied the canvas bag on the worktable, unsure about it. His first instinct was to grab the slumped woolen bag because everything they had back home was made out of wool, but this bag wasn't on the worktable. Luc said his bag was on the worktable. He looked at the canvas bag again. Maybe he had traded a wool bag for a canvas bag with one of the other apprentices?

Life here would be so much easier with no reminders of the run-down farm and the constant recollection of responsibilities at home. He saw Mam in his mind, her hands rough and hardened by work. He saw the farm in all of its dilapidation, the ugly angular sheep, his needy brother and sister. Luc would have distanced himself from that, he was sure of it. He would only want to be surrounded by light and color and creation. Ishmael wouldn't blame him. He'd do the same thing himself.

He grabbed the canvas one off the table and ran for the small courtyard, pushing through the crowds of chattering apprentices.

When he got to the courtyard, only a narrow slit remained where the grand archway used to be. Luc stood half in and half out of the posticum.

"Luc!" Ishmael cried out, pushing his way to the front. "Here's your bag!" Ishmael shoved the bag toward him.

A look of horror crossed Luc's face. "That's not my bag!" He pushed the bag back at Ishmael. "You idiot! That's not my bag! I can't go without my tools. Head Master! You've got to hold the posticum! I don't have my tools."

"You know I can't do that, Luc," Head Master said, his voice somewhat reproachful. "The wall obeys no one."

The stones creaked. What to do? What to do? They knew the boy had come for his brother. They knew he had been about to leave the Commons, and once gone, he'd be gone forever. No penance would be served. Impetuously, they had begun closing the posticum because it was the only way to grab the boy's attention—to stop him from leaving—the only hope they had at being able to make amends.

Too late they realized the inevitable consequence of this: his brother should be within this very posticum, and if his brother were *inside* the posticum, the boy wouldn't have gotten what he had come for. They needed time to think what to do, but the pushing and shoving from the other stones was too strong, the release from the crushing pressure forced upon them was an uncontrollable flood, a chain reaction. They couldn't stop, but they still needed to repair the breach. Oh, this was hard. This was very hard, indeed. If they closed without the brother, would amends be made? Would their penance be done? Would the brother return with the boy?

Luc looked over his shoulder inside the posticum at the others who waited for him.

One of them waved him inside. "Leave your—"

But Luc pushed his way past the crowding apprentices. "Get out of my way!" Everyone scattered, and Luc ran toward the Hall of Hue.

They all waited, knowing that the wall would close in its own time. One stone shifted, then another. Minutes passed, and the stones had come to no conclusion about what they should do. In the very beginning, they were charged with creating space for posticums. They were commissioned to protect each posticum's inhabitants. That meant they should wait for Luc. But the boy! What about the boy and his father? What about their penance? Was that a higher commission than creation and protection?

The gathered apprentices nervously shuffled their feet.

"Hurry, Luc!" one of the Hue apprentices called out.

"He's coming," someone else said.

Ishmael held his breath. How could he have been so stupid? Of course the wool one would have been Luc's. Maybe Luc would make it back, and Ishmael's anxiety would be for naught.

Then Luc's feet were pounding the stone courtyard, and he appeared, the slumped woolen bag in hand, a huge smile on his face. The apprentices stood back, giving him room to make his way to the posticum.

Ishmael breathed out a jumble of mixed feelings.

"My color, my wor—" Luc began, and before he could finish his sentence, the wall closed, looking as if nothing had ever been there.

CHAPTER

24

N o!" Luc pushed against the wall where the posticum had been just moments ago. He stared in disbelief. The apprentices stood in stunned silence. Even Head Master seemed at a loss, his large eyes blinking from behind the thick spectacles.

Luc threw himself at the wall, banging at the stones with his fists and his bag. When his knuckles were bloody and it was clear the posticum would not open again, he stopped, with his forehead resting on the stones and his chest heaving.

"Luc," Color Master said quietly. "I am so very sorry. I know how special your posticum was to you. I'm sure we can make arrangements for another one."

"Another posticum?" Luc turned around, looking bewildered. "My own? Or someone else's?"

"I'm not sure. This has never happened before."

Ishmael heard a voice behind him whisper, *"A man should paddle his own boat."*

Luc glanced toward Thomas, but his sight focused on Ishmael, wrong bag at his feet. "This is your fault! You got the wrong bag on purpose!" He lunged toward Ishmael.

Ishmael was completely numb, his jaw slack at what had just happened. He couldn't even speak to defend himself.

Some of the other apprentices caught Luc and pinned his arms down.

"Easy, now," Color Master said. "Let's go to my office, and we'll sort this all out." Luc shook off the arms that held him and pushed past Ishmael, out of the courtyard.

In the silence, Matthew hiccupped loudly.

"Well, that was unexpected," Jacob said. He nudged Ishmael.

Ishmael shook himself, surprised to find that his body was still able to move. "I didn't know which bag was his," Ishmael said in a small voice.

"How could anyone *not* know which bag was his?" someone else said. He grabbed the strap of the offending bag and picked it up. "This one is mine."

The apprentices turned away, heading back to their Halls.

Thomas and Hannah stood next to Ishmael. *"A mistake maketh the maker quake."* Thomas patted Ishmael's shoulder and began walking back toward the Hall of Hue. "Come on," he called to Ishmael and Hannah. Ishmael looked at the gate to the Commons. On the other side lay Mam and the farm and his responsibilities. But on this side was his brother, furious and grief-stricken. On this side was his heart, sick and guilt-ridden. Surely Luc's pain was more urgent than Mam's burdens day in and day out? Not knowing what else to do, Ishmael returned to the Hall of Hue, trudging after Thomas.

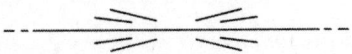

Before supper that night, Head Master rose, his ring of pale hair glinting in the candlelight. "There are often mixed feelings at the closing of a posticum. In order to make those feelings more sweet than bitter, I have two announcements. First, as part of our Jubilee celebration, the Hall of Scent will install fragrance globes around the Commons. Scent Master said these globes will give an aroma that will remind us of the gift of protection we have here, the gift that we can create without fear, thanks to Godfrey Wright. Even those who are not in the Hall of Scent will be able to perceive this.

"Second, we are sponsoring a contest in honor of the Jubilee." He paused, making sure he had everyone's attention. All eyes were on him.

His face glowed with excitement and his eyes twinkled. "A grand posticum."

Whispers broke out around the refectory, and heads swiveled looking for Luc. He was noticeably absent.

"Smart of them," Jacob said. "Under the circumstances."

"Maybe he won't hate you now," Rebekah said. She didn't sound very convincing.

"Oh, come on. I'm sure he doesn't hate you." Hannah arranged her silverware, then looked up into their disbelieving faces. "I didn't say he wasn't angry."

Head Master continued. "Our founder, Godfrey Wright, built Wright Hall and this refectory as a sanctuary for creative souls. Over the years, others have added to the Commons to accommodate the growing number of apprentices, for this is the only place of its kind. Though the Commons have expanded, our purpose has remained the same: to create. This Jubilee posticum is meant to honor Godfrey Wright. Because of the scope of this project, preliminary plans will be due in two days to the masters of your respective Halls. Hall masters will choose the winning entrants, and work will commence as soon as the wall provides us with a posticum. The contest is open to everyone, including novices."

"Except Hall of Hue novices," Jacob said. "This is clearly meant for Luc." He glanced at Ishmael.

"A good thing, too," Thomas said, shaking his head. "*You cannot break through a wall with your forehead.* I'm not ready for such a project."

A warm thread of hope wound its way through Ishmael. Here was a possibility. Here was a way forward. He would stay long enough to make sure Luc won the contest, to make sure Luc was happy, and *then* he would go. He would just have to hold on to the very last bit of strength he had to leave when the time came.

PART III

CREATION

Fresh-firecoal chestnut-falls; finches' wings;
Landscape plotted and pieced—fold, fallow, and plough;
And áll trádes, their gear and tackle and trim.

Gerard Manley Hopkins, "Pied Beauty"

CHAPTER
25

Ishmael tried to speak with Luc the next morning, but Luc wouldn't look at him, let alone talk to him. His noble thoughts last night at dinner about making sure Luc won the contest had drifted away, and he wished he had left when he had the chance yesterday. He wished he had let Luc deal with the posticum closing on his own. No doubt, all would have worked out for him. But now Luc was stuck here and so was Ishmael—neither of them were where they were supposed to be—and nobody was happy.

After breakfast, Hannah, Thomas, and Ishmael returned to the Hall of Hue, where a flurry of whispers met him when he walked into the workroom.

"Don't worry about them," Hannah said, her round cheeks earnest. "It was an honest mistake."

Ishmael cringed. It *was* a mistake, but it was a mistake he shouldn't have made. He should have known the woolen bag was Luc's, or he should have brought both bags, or at the very least, he should have checked what was inside of them. But to grab the wrong bag? That shouldn't have happened. He knew it, Luc knew it, and everyone else knew it, too.

They took a seat at the back of the room near the other novices as Color Master appeared.

"The first business of the day is to remind you about the Jubilee contest," Color Master said. "Yesterday, Head Master suggested that everyone enter. I, however, am requiring it."

Ishmael jerked his head up.

"What did I say about breaking through a wall with a forehead last night?" Thomas muttered. "I sense a great headache coming on."

"That's not very practical," Lilith said.

Matthew immediately hiccupped.

Color Master glared at him.

"Sorry!" Matthew plugged his nose to hold his breath.

"But what about Luc?" Jacob called out.

"What happened with Luc is an unfortunate incident and should be a cautionary tale to the rest of you," Color Master continued. "However, this posticum has been planned for many months as part of our Jubilee celebration." She nodded toward Lilith. "Whether you consider it practical or not, I want all of you to enter. The contest is not biased toward those who have a greater understanding of theory. This is an opportunity to think about color in a way that most apprentices do not get to until they prepare for their posticum. Each of you has instincts regarding color—insights and intuition about color harmony. Let this guide your plan. So, the rules:

1. **One entry per person. All entries deemed unfit according to the standards of color keepers will be disqualified.**

2. **Entries should include color schemes for the following base components: water, air, and foundation. Additionally, entries should include color schemes for flora and fauna for each of those base components, i.e., water plants, air plants, and land plants, and water animals, air animals, and land animals. Entries must be general enough to accommodate the work of the other Halls.**

3. **Each primary color must be represented in the entries. Additionally, no structures can remain uncolored.**

4. **Judging will commence immediately. Each entry will be blindly read, so names should be written on the back of the entry at the bottom. I will select one winner based on the following criteria: (a) originality, (b) creativity, and (c) feasibility.**

5. The chosen artisan will be announced at the all-Commons assembly when judging is complete.

6. The chosen artisan will work with the other members of his or her spectrum who will aid in the coloration of the posticum.

7. Those who are chosen as artisans have the option of remaining in the posticum.

"These rules will be posted in the Hall for your reference, and entries will be collected here." She pointed to a box next to her door. "They are due in two days' time."

The novices made their way back to the supply room, a look of disbelief on their faces, Matthew still hiccupping.

"Really?" Rebekah lowered herself into her chair, her usual enthusiasm wiped away.

"Luc's going to win whether we enter the contest or not," Jacob said with a sideways look at Ishmael.

"But Color Master said—" Lilith began.

"This is entirely for Luc since he got yoked with such a brother." Jacob laughed and punched Ishmael's shoulder, but Ishmael didn't think it was funny.

Lilith shook her head, not convinced.

Rebekah said, "Well, if I have to do this, I'm going to use lots of yellow." She hadn't noticed Color Master walk in behind her.

"Like Luc did?" Color Master said.

Rebekah flushed. "Is Luc coming today?"

Color Master carefully folded her hands together. "No, Luc needs some time to himself."

"Why is he so upset?" Thomas said. "The thought of being walled into a posticum makes me twitchy."

Color Master chose her words carefully. "During creation, each posticum becomes a special place for the artisans, almost sacred. It becomes the place where they are most comfortable, because it represents the best that is within those apprentices. The posticum calls to them, and becomes their heart's desire."

"I see. *As you cooked the porridge, so must you eat it,*" Thomas said.

"But what do the artisans do once they go into their posticums?" Matthew asked.

Lilith's nose crinkled. "It's awfully small to spend the rest of your life there, isn't it?"

Color Master walked to the far side of the table. "They go on creating there, but in a slightly different way. They live their lives. They get married. They have children. Their posticum grows and matures, as they grow and mature."

"But how does it grow, when the wall surrounds it? Do they take down the wall and rebuild it?" Ishmael asked.

"Godfrey Wright designed the wall to expand when there is need. The posticums only close so each creation remains separate from other creations."

Ishmael couldn't begin to understand how a wall could enlarge on its own, but he wished he could bring one of those walls back to the farm to replace the crumbling ones awaiting his return. That is, if he returned.

"Hasn't anyone ever stayed in the Commons?" Hannah asked.

Color Master shook her head. "Each apprentice is given a posticum. The wall knows how many apprentices are here; it knows when each apprentice is ready to become an artisan and how many posticums to open. That is the natural order here."

"You got to stay," Jacob pointed out.

"My presence here is entirely different from Luc's situation. The posticums are a special place for each artisan. It is their creation, even though, to an outsider, they seem like just another place."

"What about going home?" Ishmael asked. "Does anyone ever go home?"

"Returning to one's home is a dangerous thing." Color Master's long face was grim. "There are certain risks, certain . . . dangers involved. The danger is not necessarily one of physical harm, though the potential for violence still bubbles in some of the surrounding posticums. No, once someone has been a part of the Commons, it is difficult to go back to what was before."

Ishmael thought about that day in the tower with Luc, about what he'd seen so far, and compared it to the farm. He feared Color Master was correct.

"When a person sees more than others but can do nothing with that sight, they become susceptible to a certain type of madness. I've seen it happen more than once."

Liquid guilt poured through Ishmael. How could he have

expected Luc to return home to help Mam run the farm again? How could *he* expect to return home?

"Enough chatter," Color Master said. "We have work to do."

While she demonstrated how to make a swab, another apprentice stuck his head in the door. "Color Master, the rear distillation machine isn't working again."

Color Master pursed her lips in irritation. "I want you to practice making swabs. Materials are up here. And no nonsense like the other day." Color Master pointed to a basket of twigs and a crate of linen strips at the front of the room, and left with the apprentice.

"Have you thought about your entry yet?" Thomas asked Ishmael as they each took a handful of twigs and several strips of linen.

Ishmael made a sound of derision. "My entry doesn't matter. Luc needs to win."

Thomas nodded sagely. *"Give a person a head start and he will win the race."*

"You need to stop blaming yourself, Ishmael," Hannah said. "It was a mistake. Anyone could have done it."

"I should have known which bag was his. I should have chosen the right one." Ishmael almost wished a posticum would open up right there so he could crawl into it and disappear into its nothingness. He walked to the window and settled his hand on the stone sill.

Thomas made a loop out of a linen strip and tied a twig to it. "Don't be so hard on yourself. Mistakes happen."

"That's not much of a proverb, Thomas," Ishmael said.

"It wasn't meant to be a proverb. Mistakes *do* happen."

"That was one mistake that shouldn't have happened. And now Luc won't even talk to me. I have to make sure that he wins this Jubilee contest."

Hannah gently asked, "Why? I mean, it's likely that he'll win anyway, but I thought you wanted him to go home."

"I did. But he's my brother. I can't have him think I've sabotaged him."

"You didn't, did you?"

"No!" Ishmael was wounded that Hannah would think that.

"It's just . . . it's easy to see how you might have thought he would go home with you."

"But I didn't!" Well, he *had* thought it, but he had discarded the thought as soon as it entered his mind.

"What do you mean, Luc would go home with you?" Rebekah said. She looked confused and hurt and accusatory all at once.

Ishmael looked at each of the faces surrounding him—the faces of people that he belonged with—and he knew he had to tell them why he had really come to the Commons. He knew, also, that in doing so, the sense of camaraderie they held as a spectrum would change irreparably. He sighed, and began, "My father died this past year. He was digging a new well, and it caved in on him." The words were still difficult to say, and he paused to catch his breath at the sudden ache inside. "That left

Mam with everything—the two flocks of sheep, milch and wool. The half-dug well. The pasture fences that were falling apart. The leaking roof. The broken latch on the springhouse." Ishmael felt the words drip out of him into a steady flood. He finished with, "I came to the Commons to beg Luc to come home with me, to help Mam, to help all of us."

Thomas's eyebrows puckered. "But you see color." His voice took on a note of hurt. "You belong here. With us."

Ishmael nodded. "I know. But I also belong at home. As soon as Luc is chosen for this posticum, I've got to return home."

With her gaze on Ishmael, Rebekah spoke, her voice sad. "There are seven colors and seven novices. What happens to the spectrum when one of us is missing?"

Ishmael ran his finger along the edges of the stones in the wall under the window.

"We need you, Ishmael," Hannah said.

"You're the backbone of our spectrum," Lilith added. "If you're not around, we won't have balance."

"Jacob can become the center of the spectrum, and it will be as if I were never here," Ishmael said.

Jacob straddled a seat. "You can't just erase yourself from our spectrum."

"It doesn't work that way," Matthew said.

"Nothing would be the same if you weren't here," Rebekah said.

Thomas's straight eyebrows puckered. "*Where something is thin, that's where it tears.*"

"I'm sorry," Ishmael said. "Really, I am." There didn't seem to be anything more he could say.

His remorse wasn't satisfactory for anyone, though, and the novices each drifted back to their work leaving Ishmael standing by the window.

Ishmael picked over their words. He had never felt quite so special. And he had never felt quite so awful. With his hand still on the stone windowsill, Ishmael whispered, "I hope Luc does win. I really do. And then I wish the Jubilee posticum would open so Luc could have his new posticum and this misery will be over."

THE STONES

The stones quivered. They had thought their penance was served. Hadn't they led the boy to his brother? Hadn't they shut the brother out of his posticum? Wasn't that penance enough? They had thought so, but they were mistaken—they read it in the palm of the boy's hand. Closing the posticum without the brother inside had only made things worse.

The novice, the one who had been betrayed by dirt and rock, had asked for a posticum. He had wished for a posticum, clear as anything. Perhaps if the stones gave him this posticum, his problem would be solved and they would be absolved from the shame and the dishonor of a moment of weakness at a half-dug well. Maybe it would make things better with the brother. They sighed. They didn't want to—not so soon.

Opening a posticum was painful, and the grinding against the other stones rubbed away bits and pieces of their edges. But that wasn't the worst part. The worst was enduring that position for such a long time. You might think that holding still would come naturally to a stone, but even stones get restless. Each opening was a sacrifice. Each creative period was a sacrifice. But they knew their sacrifices were absolutely necessary—for new worlds, new domains, new possibilities, new life—especially now, if they wanted to serve their penance. Otherwise, they would have ignored such a request. After all, they were the stones. They didn't take orders from *anyone.* But this request was different. This was a sacrifice they must willingly make. There was no other way.

Still, this would take a very long time, this opening. A very long time.

The stones felt that twinge again. They had barely gotten comfortable from the closing of the last posticum, and now, once again came that pinch, that deep-down pushing, the struggling, as each stone was forced closer and closer to its neighbor. This was their penance. They accepted it, but that didn't mean they enjoyed it. No, sir, they didn't like it one bit. But this time, they would be stronger.

CHAPTER

26

On the morning of the day that the contest entries were due, Ishmael sat at a worktable while the other apprentices buzzed around the Hall, busy at their work. Their activity flowed around him while he sat unmoving, numb, thinking about his new friends, thinking about Luc, thinking about Mam, thinking about what he must do now.

The stone of the worktable was smooth, though it was left unpolished. Ishmael was glad, for he had no desire to see his face reflecting in it. All he really wanted was to lay his cheek down on the coolness of it and sense the solidity underneath him.

Instead, he pressed his fingertips into the stone and watched their shade change with the pressure. The contrast against the stone was startling. The stone was brilliant and alive, though not living. Ishmael, who was alive but colored only in shades of gray, looked pale in comparison. He looked dull next to the brilliant apprentices who had spent more time here. He forced himself to relax his hands, and placed them palm down on the table.

A constant flow of apprentices streamed to and from the box just outside Color Master's door. Even if the contest wasn't solely for putting Luc into a posticum of his own, he had to win. That was the only way Ishmael could part ways with his brother in peace.

Lilith leaned her elbows on Ishmael's table, balancing her chin on her hands. "Hi."

"Hi." Ishmael pulled out one of the color circles he had made with the other novices, held it down with an index finger, and spun it, waiting until it slowed to a stop. He told himself that the color that stopped directly under his finger would be the color he would use as the main color in his entry.

The wheel slowed, and then stopped at orange. Lilith stared at the orange. "Tell me you're not going to base your entry on orange."

"That's probably what Thomas did."

He spun again.

Blue.

"That's better—not that I'm biased, even though it *is* closer to my color," Lilith said and smiled.

"I don't think that will work, either."

"Well, you could always use your color and the colors on either side. That's what I did—indigo, blue, and violet."

Lilith sounded so confident, so sure of herself. Ishmael

supposed that came from her years of comportment lessons. She might have been dismissive of them, but they probably helped her more than she knew.

"You're not really going home, are you?" Lilith asked.

Ishmael sighed. "I feel like I have to, but I don't want to leave until I know Luc is happy."

Lilith stood up. "Other people's happiness is not always in our control, even if we want it to be. I know you want Luc to be happy, but I think you have to let him find his own happiness—and you need to find your own. I don't think I have to say that I hope your happiness keeps you here." She smiled and touched Ishmael's shoulder. "I'm heading over to the refectory. Want me to save you a seat?"

"Thanks."

Ishmael kept spinning his color wheel, but now he spun it randomly, with no expectation that it would give him a color scheme for his entry. Red, orange, indigo, red again. He pushed the color circle away in frustration. Ishmael wanted to pin it back up on the wall and go join the others, but he felt compelled to submit something. It seemed wrong not to.

If Ishmael could do anything he wanted in this posticum, he would do exactly what he and Luc had done in the tower room. He would dapple everything. Color upon color upon color. *That* would be glorious—in fact, the idea was so glorious that he was certain Luc would use that on his entry, so Ishmael immediately dismissed the idea. It was a winning idea, and Luc needed to win.

Ishmael stood up to retrieve a sheet of parchment, a brush, a quill, and several pots of processed color. On the return to the worktable, he wistfully thought of the first time he saw color, back when he had different problems, back when he didn't understand the importance of what he had seen, back when he could just enjoy the color for the simple joy it brought him.

The bell rang for lunch and the room emptied. He sat at his desk, staring at the blank page. Just write something, he thought. *Anything.*

Make it artless. Make it *simple.* Something simple would never be chosen.

Color Master had spoken about instincts and intuition, but Ishmael didn't even know where to start. He felt as frozen as he had in the tower room, frozen by all the possibility. He looked at the pots of color lined up in front of him. His eyes were drawn immediately toward green. That was his color. That was what had first called to him in the barn back home.

In the barn back home.

Of course! His contest entry could be the way he had colored the barn. Basic. Plain. Artless. Simple. Green and blue, with bits of the other colors here and there. He quickly put his vision on paper. When Ishmael finished, he dropped his entry in the box outside of Color Master's office, where it landed, artless and simple, nestled against dozens of others.

MOTION

Thaddeus, an apprentice from the Hall of Motion, stood in a small room in an upper floor of Wright Hall. How still it was up here. Their workroom was full of models, spinning and rotating, moving up and down, vibrating and rolling. Things were in constant motion so the apprentices could see the seven types of movement, as well as velocity, momentum, action, and reaction.

Motion Master had suggested that Thaddeus come up here to get a bird's-eye view of the motion of the other apprentices as they walked to the refectory. Just as valuable, Thaddeus thought, was this rare moment of stillness. Nothing moved, and the contrast to the normal state of the Motion workroom was startling.

Soon enough, one apprentice, then two, then dozens of apprentices flowed out of their Halls scattered across the grounds of the Commons.

They came together in the Great Courtyard below him, all converging on the refectory in one massive wave gathering strength and then crashing at the doors—all forward movement. There was so much beauty in the way all the apprentices came together in their individual Halls—and then in the way the groups of Halls came together. Is that what Motion Master meant for him to see? He tugged at his hair. Was it the motion? Was it the coming together? Was it the natural flow? The sight made him feel something inside, something he couldn't explain.

He remembered watching the crowds gathering at the market back home. He would stand at the top of the hill, looking down at the smooth movement, and it disturbed him, for every motion was dictated. Each gesture was choreographed. Each step was rhythmic. Groups of people lined up in neat rows. Each row advanced in an orderly fashion. It was very obvious if one person stepped out of line or advanced too soon, and there were consequences.

He had learned that the hard way. Thaddeus had always been a curious child, and on his first trip to the market, his eye had been caught by a movement at his left. He couldn't see around a rather stout man, so he moved away from his mother to get a closer look. The movement came from a caged bird, flapping its wings against the structure enclosing it.

Oh, how Thaddeus had wanted to open the cage, pick that bird up, and send it soaring! Watch its wings! See its flight! But as he reached to unlatch the door of the cage, two people stepped forward on either side of him. They each took one of his arms and paraded him up to the town square where he was made to sit very still all afternoon. Thereafter, he had to march up and down the square, matching the rhythm of the other villagers for hours and hours each day until the movement of the town had been bludgeoned into his being.

He had hated every second of it.

Thinking of it made his throat go tight.

He watched the courtyard while the mass of apprentices grew smaller and smaller as they entered the refectory, until there were only a handful of stragglers rushing for their lunch.

There were no blocks of people, no lines, no rhythm to their movement. Just groups of apprentices heading into a building. And it was beautiful.

His stomach growled, and he knew he must join the others in the refectory. As he turned away, one final apprentice from the Hall of Hue hurried to the courtyard. Thaddeus paused, watching his approach. Even that was beautiful, the speed and the flow of movement, as the late apprentice cut across the courtyard in a straight line, making for the refectory.

CHAPTER

27

The Hall of Hue apprentices sat at the long tables during lunch discussing the Jubilee contest.

"I don't know why you're getting yourselves all worked up," Jacob said. "I keep telling you, Luc's winning is a foregone conclusion."

"If Luc is going to win, why did Color Master require all of us to enter the contest?" Hannah asked.

"Isn't it obvious?" Jacob said. "She's just making it look like there's a real contest." He helped himself to a large serving of barley and vegetables.

"Color Master wouldn't do that," Hannah said.

"You're being dense."

"I'm not being dense!" Hannah's voice rose. Her eyebrows

became darts of anger, and her rounded cheeks flamed. "It's not obvious, it's not true, and it's certainly not fair."

"Why else would she do it? She had to give Luc a place to go. Besides, none of us could possibly oversee such a project."

"Not us, but what about the older apprentices? They've been here longer. They know more." Hannah ripped a piece of bread apart.

Thomas waved his fork back and forth. "*The fat man is not always the best cook.*"

The bickering was unbearable, and the glum look on Matthew's face cast a pall over the meal. Undoubtedly, he'd begin hiccupping soon. Ishmael tried to block out their quarrel by visualizing colors that matched the food, but he couldn't concentrate. "I'm going outside," he said and grabbed a piece of bread as he left the table.

"I'll join you." Hannah took a piece of bread, too, and followed him out the door. The noises of the refectory left them behind as they headed toward the shade of the cloister wall.

"All the talk about this Jubilee posticum is making me crazy," Hannah said. The two sat down with their backs against the wall.

Ishmael, who was afraid to turn Hannah's wrath toward him, took a bite of bread, chewed, and then swallowed. "I'll be happy just seeing the finished product."

"I thought you were going home."

"I was. I *am*. I just need to see Luc through this, so I can tell Mam what he's done. Where he is. What he'll be doing." He pulled off another bit of bread. He couldn't bring himself to meet Hannah's eyes. Was that really why he wanted to stay? "I can't leave knowing he's angry with me. I don't think I could bear it."

The raucous laughter of apprentices crossing the cloister sounded, and they both turned.

Hannah popped the final bite of bread into her mouth. "If Luc wins the contest, you'll find a way to fix this."

Ishmael stood up, brushed himself off, and they walked over to the fountain. He cupped his hands together and scooped up the water, drinking deeply. The cold water roused him. "I hope so."

They walked through the courtyard and passed an apprentice from the Hall of Scent with a large glass orb in his hands. Another Scent apprentice perched on a ladder. It was the diminutive dark-haired girl who had competed in the challenge. Three glass orbs were attached to the corner of the courtyard wall, and she reached down for the fourth.

Ishmael caught the slightest whiff of a scent, and he remembered the announcement about the orbs of fragrance from the Hall of Scent. He breathed it in, trying to remember what they were supposed to represent. Protection? Something like that. He couldn't put his finger on what the scent was. It puzzled him. "Is this what protection is supposed to smell like?" He glanced at Hannah.

She sniffed the air. "You smell something?"

"Don't you?"

Hannah shrugged. "I guess so. If you were to put a color to 'protection,' what color would you choose?"

They ducked into the courtyard in the Hall of Hue.

"Probably green."

Hannah laughed and shoved him. "Of course you would!"

"No, I'm serious. It's right in the middle of the spectrum, protected by the other colors."

"Ah. You do have a point. But I'd still choose blue."

When they walked through the archway into the workroom, any feeling of protection was obliterated by the chaotic sight that met them.

Color lay thick on the floor. Drifts of it spread, seeping into the cracks between the flagstones, curling in eddies around the columns, piling up in corners. The pure light that hadn't been separated into color swirled around in brilliant flashes, bouncing from wall to wall, from floor to ceiling.

Ishmael opened his mouth, then closed it in disbelief. All that color—ruined. All that pure light—escaped. Hannah made a noise of despair.

The sound of her voice startled a girl in the corner who had been unscrewing a jar. Her hair reflected the mixed color swirling all around, and in between flashes of light, Ishmael realized it was Phoebe from the Hall of Sound.

"What are you doing?" Ishmael catapulted across the room and shook her. She squeaked, and her hair bobbled on her head with each shake. The color floating around them wafted in the breeze he stirred, and a ray of light flashed.

"What's going on here?" Color Master walked into the workroom.

Ishmael released Phoebe. She backed away from all three of them, twisting the pitch pipe she wore on her wrist. The planes of her face looked monstrous in the flashing light.

"He told me that one of the jars contained something I'd want to hear, some new sound that would impress Sound Master. But I couldn't remember if he said the third jar from the left or the third jar from the right. The jar I opened had no distinct sound—it only blinded me with bright light." She dodged a ray of light that ricocheted off the floor. It highlighted her nose, which was turning a splotchy red. "So I opened another jar to see if that was the right one, but more light came out. I tried to catch it, but it just kept bouncing around, so I opened another jar, hoping it would go back into it. I gave up on catching it and decided to see if I could find the sound instead."

Ishmael groaned.

"You have released our supply of pure light," Color Master said, each word chopped into its smallest possible sound. "And from the looks of it, most of our color!"

Phoebe's face paled. "But he said the jars were empty." She looked around blindly, but Ishmael knew as well as she did that she wouldn't be able to see the color swirling around at their feet.

Color Master turned to Ishmael and Hannah. "Summon the other apprentices. As for you," she said to Phoebe, "go back to your Hall. I'll speak to you later. Your name?"

"Phoebe," she whispered.

Ishmael gave Phoebe a dark look, and she scuttled out of the Hall as he rushed toward the refectory.

When Ishmael returned with the other novices and the apprentices, the room looked much dimmer. Within seconds, Ishmael saw why: when the rays of light hit the floor or the ceiling or the walls, they bounced. When they hit the window, the light passed through and was lost. Color Master was at the top of a ladder tacking up some kind of opaque material over the windows to prevent that.

"Thomas!" she called. "Over here." Thomas traded places with her, and Color Master directed the rest of them to team up with a partner to collect their individual colors. "You upper apprentices— chase the light."

Used to the chaotic and expansive habits of pure light, the older apprentices quickly spread out in a circle holding swathes of black cloth to try to contain the light that was left. They inched closer and closer, but the light kept slipping through holes. Over and over again, they surrounded the light only to have it sneak out of their grasp. It was a thankless task, and one that was nearly pointless considering how much of the light had already been lost.

Meanwhile, the younger apprentices danced around them pursuing the liberated color. Like chasing puffs of dust, the color swirled away as soon as anyone got close enough to touch it. After much frustration, Ishmael got a thin sheet of mica and fanned the color into jars held by his partner, a girl a few years ahead of him. Hannah and her partner rolled up a sheet of parchment and blew through it to send their color into jars.

By the end of the night, only a fraction of the pure light that had been in the great holding jars from the last light harvest was recaptured, and some of the separated colors were collected, mostly blue and green, thanks in part to Ishmael and Hannah being first on the scene. All but a tiny bit of violet was lost, as well as most of the red and yellow, and about half of the orange.

THE STONES

The stones in the wall shifted, puffing bits of stone dust out of the crevices between them. A deep-down pressure made its way up, shifting stones closer, ever closer, tighter and tighter still, until the stones burst wide open and a new posticum freed itself from the web of stones. The tightness was almost unbearable, and there would be no relief until the posticum closed once again. But the boy asked for it, and so it must be. The relationship with the boy's brother would be mended. Penance for the death of the boy's father would be served. And then they would have peace.

Peace and a long nap.

CHAPTER
28

Even though all the apprentices from the Hall of Hue scoured the buildings and cloister that night, they still found bits of color swirling around the next day, low to the ground. As Ishmael bent down to nudge a stubborn streak of yellow into a vial, Phoebe walked through the arch into the workroom and disappeared into Color Master's office.

"You cannot be serious!" Color Master's voice rang through the door. There was a bit of mumbling, and Phoebe exited, wearing the smock of the Hall of Hue. Her face was pale, and her unnatural silence made Ishmael wonder if the sound waves that stitched her together had unraveled. He also noticed that the pitch pipe encircling her wrist was gone.

Moments after Phoebe left the workroom, Color Master came out of her office, her hand on the doorjamb.

"May I have your attention, please?" Her eyes were deeply shadowed and creased with worry. Her red robes were wrinkled and smudged with color.

Color Master waited until all prisms were set down, all hands paused, all eyes on her. "The Sound novice, Phoebe, is to join us temporarily. Though she opened our jars innocently enough, the fact remains that we've lost the better part of our supplies and the majority of a year's work of distilling. There will be further investigation as to why this happened. In the meantime, Sound Master has released her from her duties there temporarily."

"But what will she do since she can't even see the colors? She's not going to sing, is she?" Jacob asked. He shifted his weight from one foot to the other.

"*Whose bread I eat, his song I sing,*" Thomas muttered.

"She will scrub the hall, do the dusting and cleaning, and take over novices' chores. That will free you to begin higher tasks, for everyone is desperately needed." Her gaze searched the room. "Is Luc here?"

Luc raised his hand from a corner of the room.

"Despite present circumstances, Luc, I'm glad you're still with us. We must attempt to replace our stores as best we can in time for our role in the Jubilee."

Ishmael looked closer at Luc. Something—Color Master's confidence or the sense of renewed purpose—seemed to breathe new life into him. His eyes had brightened, and he no longer looked hollow. Perhaps he would talk to Ishmael now, or at the very least, let Ishmael apologize.

Color Master turned to the novices. "The color we use for creation is taken from a yearly gift of light given to us from the astronomae at the House of Light. I have applied to them for an increase in our supply, but it will take some time before we receive a replacement."

"And the light here isn't strong enough to use?" Lilith asked.

"Not for posticum work. We can only use this light for making processed color."

"So what are we going to do?" The words flew from Rebekah's mouth with a hint of panic.

"We'll separate and distill color from the supply of light that we saved. That will guarantee the least amount of waste. The color we saved will also need to be distilled again, just to be on the safe side. This color is what we will use for the Jubilee posticum."

"We won't be using the prism-direct method of coloring?" an older apprentice said.

Color Master shook her head. "We can't. We simply don't have enough light, and we won't be able to get the quantity we need in time."

"You mean . . .?"

"Yes, we'll have to use the older methods."

The apprentice's jaw dropped. "But that will take too long!"

"What choice do we have? The increase of light from the astronomae won't come in time for the Jubilee posticum."

"Can't we get more light from somewhere else?" Lilith asked.

"Yes, we have received permission to seek out additional light from the posticums with an open portal to the Commons, but the strength of light from any source other than the astronomae could be questionable.

"The light that is released at the opening of a posticum is like a seed. It grows into its own fully developed source of brightness. The light in the posticums is newer and stronger than the light we have here, and the astronomae tell me that small quantities of this light can be siphoned off with little effect to the inhabitants of the posticums. The problem is that most of the posticums with an open portal to the Commons are very old as well."

Their faces turned glum.

"You see the seriousness of the situation. The majority of us will undergo light-gathering expeditions in these posticums with the hope of getting a large enough quantity of usable light to supply us until the astronomae can get us more."

"How long will that take?" Luc asked.

Color Master shook her head. "I can't answer that. It might take some time. There is some urgency for this expedition, because we have no control over the opening or the closing of the Jubilee posticum, and thus, we need as much light as we can get as soon as possible. We will begin our preparations and leave tomorrow. Are there any other questions?"

Lilith raised her hand. "What happens to the color we didn't capture?"

"The colors will break down in time. Distilled color is only permanent when it is used in the design phase of creation. If it is used on something else, it eventually decays. That's one of the reasons we need Phoebe here now. The workroom will be a very dirty place for the next couple of weeks until all the color has broken down."

That must be why the color on his boot crumbled off, Ishmael thought. A second later, he realized the colors inside the barn at home would have decayed by now, too. It would look much the same as it always had—only dirtier, if that was possible. He could never have color at home, because any color he produced would only be temporary.

Color Master's face hung heavy, aging her. She surveyed the room. The novices were gathered at the door to the supply room. The under-apprentices stood in the light storage area, still holding stone jars and stoppers in their hands. The older apprentices were at their workbenches with vials of half-collected colors and nearly empty jars of light. "There is much to be done." She nodded toward the workroom again. "As you were."

Ishmael worked listlessly all that morning. His eyes were gritty, his fingers ached from being clamped around his prism, and his arms were tired, even though it was still early in the day. But he couldn't stop. He had to show Luc that he was on his side.

Ishmael had almost finished with one vial when the enormous bell in the tower bonged. The bell bonged again. Then once more. The summons to Wright Hall for the announcement of the contest winners. One by one, the apprentices in the workroom turned to stare at Luc. He capped the jar of light he had been using. When he saw their stares, Luc glanced at Ishmael, but before Ishmael could open his mouth to speak, Luc quickly turned to leave the workroom.

Ishmael set his prism down on his worktable. Luc's coldness troubled him. He stoppered the vials of light and color, then set them in their holders with a small clink. The sound was echoed at the other worktables as the rest of the novices and apprentices did the same.

Rebekah waited for Ishmael to finish. "I never thought I'd be glad not to be in the running for this contest. I almost pity Luc."

"He didn't look worried," Ishmael said.

Thomas overheard their words as he followed them out of the workroom. "*The hidden heart still bleeds.*"

Together, the three walked through the courtyard to Wright Hall and took their seats by the other Hall of Hue novices.

Head Master appeared unsettled, his large eyes shifting from person to person, then door to bench, then ceiling to floor. While apprentices all over Wright Hall fidgeted, anxious to hear the winners of the contest, Luc sat still, painfully still, with an unnatural smile etched on his face.

When everyone was seated, Head Master rose. "I wanted to postpone announcing the winners of the Jubilee contest," he said, his voice carrying to the edges of the great room, "because of the unfortunate accident in the Hall of Hue, but I cannot." His expression was solemn. "The posticum has opened."

Several people gasped.

"We had hoped for a longer season of preparation, but work must begin immediately. Each Hall master received an abundance of fine entries, which were judged blindly so as to prohibit a show of favoritism. We have full faith in those who have been chosen."

The benches creaked as apprentices shifted their weight. Feet shuffled. Someone coughed.

"Without further ado, let me announce the winners. Representing the Hall of Shape: Dora, daughter of Joseph and Camilla."

A girl sitting in the Shape section looked shocked as people around her patted her shoulder in congratulations. Ishmael recognized her from the order and chaos challenge. She had drawn the simple shape that Michael had then complicated.

"From the Hall of Manufactory: Ethan, son of Jude and Elizabeth."

Cheers from the Manufactory section of Wright Hall rang out. Ethan's broad grin was visible from across the room.

"From the Hall of Motion: Thaddeus, son of Stephen and Orpah." The Motion apprentices threw their arms up in the air, as if their shouts emerged from their fingertips.

The names washed over Ishmael until Head Master announced, "Hall of Hue."

An eternity passed before Head Master spoke again.

"Ishmael, son of James and Talia."

SCENT

When the Scent apprentice had first arrived, Wright Hall was awash with the smell of anticipation, of hope, of excitement. It was a warm smell, one Keturah was familiar with from many occasions. But as soon as Head Master announced the name of the Hue artisan, the scent of fear diffused through the hall. Bubbling along the edges of that was the sour scent of disbelief and the rank smell of ill will.

She had no time to ponder that before Head Master announced, "From the Hall of Scent: Keturah, daughter of Aaron and Mehitabel."

Hearing her own name was a surprise. Keturah wanted to be happy. She wanted to be excited, but she couldn't get past an overwhelming sense of uneasiness. Though the ceilings were high in Wright Hall, the air seemed stuffy now. The noses on the carved faces above her seemed pinched, as if they sensed it, too. She turned her head away, wanting to recapture the scent of hope and excitement, but there was not a trace of it anywhere. Keturah sat stiffly, wishing she could escape, while the Scent apprentices surrounding her tried to cheer, but they, too, were caught in the unpleasant scent of fear.

Head Master continued, "From the Hall of Sound: Aaron, son of Mark and Abish. And finally, the Hall of Gustation: Gabriel, son of Jonas and Basha." The Sound and Gustation apprentices cheered loudly, completely unaware that anything was wrong.

When the announcements were over, Keturah stood up and rushed to the doors.

CHAPTER
29

On the opposite side of the room, Ishmael also stood up. He wasn't sure *how* he stood up. He couldn't feel his legs or feet or even his arms. He couldn't actually feel any part of his body. An enormous boulder had fallen on him, and he could scarcely breathe from the weight of it. Somehow his body took over and moved him out of his seat, down the aisle, and through the throngs of apprentices.

Rebekah offered an uncertain smile. Thomas slapped him on the back, saying, "You'll be great, Ishmael," but Ishmael dodged their well wishes. How could he be congratulated? This wasn't a means for celebration.

Luc was supposed to win.

Luc brushed past him, without smile or congratulations. Ishmael called out, but he realized his voice was caught under that same boulder weighing him down, and only a croak emerged, not even enough to catch Luc's attention.

Ishmael pushed against the flow of apprentices until he reached the end of the aisle. Color Master stood with the other Hall masters at the front of Wright Hall, but Ishmael couldn't get through the crowd to reach her. "Color Master!" he called.

Color Master looked up from her conversation with Manufactory Master, her long face looking almost guilty. Ishmael shoved through the crowd of staring apprentices.

"Color Master," he said, "you made a mistake." The words came tumbling out, a cascade of disjointed colors raining down like small pebbles.

Color Master shook her head. "Come," she said. "Walk with me."

In silence, they followed the crowd through the doors, then headed toward the courtyard at the entrance of the Commons.

"You are, no doubt, apprehensive," Color Master said.

Ishmael wanted to laugh. "Luc needed to win. *I* wanted Luc to win. *Everyone* wanted Luc to win."

His words seemed to fluster Color Master. "It's true that Luc *is* a very fine color keeper—one of the best."

"Then why didn't you pick his entry?"

Color Master hesitated, and in that brief moment, Ishmael thought he understood everything.

"It was because of our supply, wasn't it?" Ishmael asked. "Because we only have green and blue left."

Color Master sighed. "It's complicated, Ishmael."

"If Phoebe hadn't freed the light and spilled the color, you would have picked a different plan." Ishmael's words sounded petulant, even whiny. He didn't want to sound whiny.

Color Master smoothed her hair. "Phoebe *did* spill the colors, and our supply of light and color *is* limited. Circumstances being what they are, I chose your plan. It is simple, it uses the colors we have available, and it can be executed with the rudimentary coloring methods. It was the best of all the possibilities."

They ducked through the archway to the small courtyard by the gates of the Commons. Ishmael's legs moved jerky and stiff, like the hinged legs of a wooden doll trudging over the gravel pathways.

They reached the edge of the front courtyard, opposite where Luc's posticum used to be. A new archway had opened up in the wall. "I thought you might like to see the posticum."

Ishmael looked inside. There was nothing there—just a vague murkiness. He took a step forward to see better, but Color Master held up an arm to block him.

"Don't go any farther. There is nothing upon which to stand. You'd fall and continue to fall, for there is nothing to stop you."

Ishmael stepped back and eyed the distance from where they stood to the front gate. He turned to look at the wall opposite them, then turned again, and shook his head. "How is this here? My village should be on the other side of this wall, not this posticum."

Color Master smiled. "Your village *is* on the other side of the wall. All places are on the other side of the wall."

Ishmael shook his head again. "There are flowers growing on the hill just outside. There's no place for this posticum to be."

"It is simply a dislocation in space. It's probably best if you accept that this is where you'll be working now. Don't worry about the physics of it yet. It's just another place."

Ishmael looked back into the abyss.

"What do I do now?" His voice made the merest pinprick in that vast expanse.

"Fill the space," she said simply. "That is what we do here. Where there is emptiness, we fill it. Where there is blankness, we color it. We create in spite of any obstacles."

Ishmael looked into the posticum, overwhelmed at what he was chosen to do.

CHAPTER
30

Luc had been in a bubble of certainty. Color Master had promised him another posticum. It was inevitable that his name should have been spoken, that his name should have been trumpeted throughout Wright Hall as the chosen artisan for the Jubilee posticum.

But when the words from Head Master's announcement rose to meet him, the points and angles of Ishmael's name burst through the surface of Luc's bubble. In the sudden rupture, Luc plummeted. He hit hard reality, and the letters of *what should have been* dropped off one by one, until all that was left rearranged themselves into *Hue love bad*. A surge of heated anger flamed around him.

He pushed past all those apprentices making spectacles of themselves as they flapped their hands and hugged and cried

out their congratulations in giddy voices. The Hall of Manufactory even heaved their artisan up to their shoulders and carried him around. That should have been Luc on the shoulders
of the Hall of Hue apprentices. *What should have been. Hue
beloved.* He saw his younger brother, and he shouldered past
Ishmael before he could say anything.

Disgusted, Luc threw the doors of Wright Hall open with
too much force, not caring if they hit anyone on the way. He
ran across the Great Courtyard back to the Hall of Hue, but
instead of going to his tiny cell-like room—the sole privilege of
an artisan—he veered to the right, toward a small opening near
the Hall of Manufactory. *What should have been. Hue haven.*

Within minutes, he found himself in the stark landscape
of the Cairns. He picked up a rock. He knew the tradition.
He knew he should set the rock on top of a pile, and then wait
for the epiphany, but he was too full of rage for an epiphany.

What should have been. Hue weaves.

All of the events from the previous week that had been roil-
ing around inside him converged into something primeval and
violent. *What should have been. Hue vandals.* He took the stone
in his hand and threw it with all his might at a tower of rocks.
The rock struck the tower, and it tumbled down under the
force.

Luc picked up another rock and threw it, and then another.
Towers of rocks cascaded to the ground with each throw. He
hurtled stone after stone until his arms burned from the effort.
When that wasn't enough, he launched himself at a tower,

knocking it over with the full force of his weight. The stones fell, crashing into other stones, thumping the ground, and sending up puffs of dust.

Luc leveled cairn after cairn, numb to the sting of his scraped flesh. Out of the corner of his eye, he saw one majestic tower rising tall and immovable, as if mocking him. This tower was said to have been built by Godfrey Wright himself. Luc hesitated, staring at it. Did he dare?

What should have been. Hue, have boldness.

Did Luc dare? Indeed, he did.

Luc threw all of his weight at this final cairn, grunting with the effort, but the stones wouldn't budge. He tried once more, then collapsed at the foot of the cairn, wishing he could weep. His bubble of certainty was threadbare and tattered, leaving Luc floating free, unanchored, lost in the vast expanse of ruined cairns. *What should have been. Hue howl.*

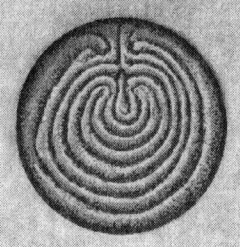

GUSTATION

When Gabriel heard Head Master announce his name as the artisan for the Hall of Gustation, he felt it first—ironically—in his gut, the center of blandness. The sensation spread upward to his chest (salty) and down to his abdomen (meaty). From there, his legs (richness) went weak, turning gelatinous and wobbly, and his neck (sour) seemed incapable of holding up his head. His whole body had turned numb, and he wasn't sure if he was weighted to the seat or floating in the air.

In his mind, his plan had been simple: to pair the tastes, sweet with bitter, rich with sour, salty with meaty, leaving bland on its own as a contrast because it had nothing of value to add. Head and feet, neck and legs, chest and abdomen. A good flavor with a bad. Simple elements joining to make something complex. Everything was partnered up (except for bland, as the contrast). The juxtaposition intrigued him, but he had never thought it would interest anyone else. He certainly never dreamed it would be chosen for the Jubilee posticum.

But it was.

And now, he had to hope that his very center—bland—would be strong enough to hold him together or his entire body might float off in discrete parts and he might never be solid again.

MANUFACTORY

When Ethan came into the Hall of Manufactory on the shoulders of some of the apprentices, cheers erupted, and the whirligigs and flying tops they had made for the celebration after the announcement flew through the air. Some of the structures had wings that flapped up and down, some spun as they fell, and some floated gently to the ground.

Only one apprentice stood apart from the celebration. Michael. The bandage wrapped around his arm made it too difficult to operate the devices. Even if his arm hadn't been bandaged, disappointment had lodged into his limbs, and he felt like a pulley that had gotten stuck.

Michael's plan for the posticum had been a good one. In fact, it had been more than good; it had been great. It had been conceived in the Cairns, after all. And the possibilities! He had designed a machine that folded all of the Halls' work into itself. Well, he hadn't worked out all the details yet, but it was a good plan, he knew it. It was an innovative plan. It was a plan that would have required all the chosen artisans to work together.

Even as he was getting excited again at the thought of

collaboration, the fresh fire was doused. His plan hadn't been chosen.

The possibilities were now impossibilities.

Ethan was the new artisan and his plan full of pliant covered gears and flexible hidden pulleys had been chosen instead.

And Michael would have to accept that.

He left the Manufactory workroom and headed for the Cairns. Maybe he needed another stone. Another epiphany.

At the entry to the path, he bumped into the Hue artisan who had gotten shut out of his posticum. Luc pushed past him without a word.

CHAPTER
31

Lost. Ishmael was completely lost, which was odd, considering he had won. Winning, losing. Finding, losing. One, but not the other. Won, but not the other.

His thoughts were all confused. The boulder that had rolled on him during the announcement squeezed the reason from him and left him squashed. Flattened.

But somehow, his feet must have still worked because after he left Color Master and the new posticum, he found himself on the path to the Cairns. Perhaps the boulder squashing him rolled him down the path of its own accord. Ishmael needed all the direction he could get, and if the only direction came from an invisible boulder leading him to a bunch of stones in an old quarry, well, that was better than simply being lost.

When he visited last, he had been overwhelmed with relief

at finding a place where he could wander with his thoughts. Now he needed to pin them down so they wouldn't float up and away. Then, he had gratitude. Now he had sheer and utter dread. But he hoped that going to the Cairns would help him sort it all out.

At the entrance, he stopped, stunned.

The vista opened before him, a great landscape of hewn rock and round stones, large and small. But where the tall and stately cairns had once stood, now they were leveled. Their stones littered the ground, helter-skelter, clogging pathways, settling into ditches, having exploded in all directions until there was no rhyme or reason left anywhere.

"No," he said, his voice barely making a sound in the forest of stone. "No!"

A head popped out from behind a large stone. Once again, it was the Manufactory apprentice, Michael. "I thought I heard someone."

"What happened?"

"I don't know. I found it like this." Michael shook his head and sat down. Ishmael joined him, feeling complete disbelief at the sight of wreck and ruin surrounding them.

The two sat, glum as overripe fruit.

"What should we do?" Ishmael asked.

"I think Head Master should see this."

Ishmael was itching to pick up a stone. He needed help. He needed direction, but he knew Michael was right. Head Master should see this. As he looked out over the ruins of the cairns, evidence of past apprentices' need for reflection, a tuft of green showed. Then another. Then he realized he saw tufts of all the colors peeking out from under fallen stones. A full spectrum's worth of dappled color.

He sat up, scanning the land.

"What is it?" Michael asked.

"I see more color here now. I only saw green when I came before."

"You must have more color to see now."

"I suppose so."

They sat, quiet for a moment, then Ishmael said, "You're here again. That must mean you're looking for more direction?"

"Not exactly." Michael tossed a stone from one hand to the other. "I wanted my plan to be chosen. I wanted the Halls to create together."

"Don't they do that already?"

"No—they work next to each other. They work side by side. I wanted the Halls to work *with* each other, to help each other in all things." He dropped the stone. "But Manufactory Master keeps telling me to stick to manufactory and stop worrying about the other Halls."

Ishmael wasn't sure how the Halls could work with each other. "It sounds interesting, but none of the other Halls can even see color, so how could anyone help the Hall of Hue?"

"I hadn't worked out all the details yet, but couldn't Motion move the color? Couldn't Shape design something to disperse color? Couldn't Manufactory build it? I'm not sure about Scent, Sound, or Gustation, but it doesn't matter now, because my plan wasn't chosen." Glumness settled on Michael once more as he gazed out at the broken landscape. Ruined towers everywhere. Ruined plans.

Ishmael tapped Michael. "Your plan wasn't chosen, but my plan was."

Michael sat up. "And?"

"I need all the help I can get."

Michael's face lit up. "Tell me more. What's your plan?"

"It's simple—that's the reason Color Master chose it. It's mostly just two colors with a few others sprinkled about." Ishmael would have been embarrassed, but Michael's enthusiasm erased any shame he felt about his plan.

"That sounds straightforward enough. Can we build a machine to deliver the color? I have some ideas that might work—compression and expulsion—"

"Well, actually, we've already got some methods of coloring."

"Oh," Michael checked himself. "Of course you do."

"But the methods are old and very slow. It's easier if we deliver the color directly from pure light."

"So why don't you do that?"

"Our light supply is mostly gone."

"Hmm." Michael crossed his arms and thought for a minute. "So you need a faster method of delivery, or better yet, a new supply of light. Wait a second, why can't you just use the light we already have?"

"It's not pure enough."

"So if we could purify the light we already have . . ."

Ishmael's eyes widened. "That might work."

"I'll go talk to Ethan immediately to see what he thinks, then I'll start working on some plans. I'll let you know when I've got something usable." He took off through the scattered stones, hopping over and around them as he ran toward the path.

Underneath the ruins, tufts of color danced in Ishmael's sight, struggling to free themselves from the stones covering them. They flickered and flared, rising and popping, one after the other, like bubbles of joy. He watched. This pageant of color was like an exhibition of the deepest desires of his heart, and although he had come here lost, he didn't feel so lost anymore.

SHAPE

Dora struck out from her Hall late that afternoon. Head Master's announcement had caught her by surprise. When her name had been called, her mouth had formed an O, and ever since then, she felt like she was moving in a circle, around and around, covering the same ground and never getting anywhere. This, on top of that dreadful challenge where her hexagon was turned into a crowd of lines going every which way, gave her a feeling she hadn't been able to shake.

It was a feeling she couldn't easily identify. She couldn't wrap a line around it, nor enclose it with a series of dots. She prodded it and poked it, but it was a strange feeling, and she needed to examine it in the light of day outside the Hall of Shape. She wanted to pick it apart in a place where she wouldn't be influenced by the lines and circles that usually surrounded her.

She needed to go to the Cairns.

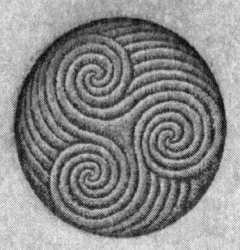

MOTION

Far above the courtyard in an upper room of Wright Hall sat Thaddeus. It was the same place he had sat just yesterday, but this time he didn't come at the request of Motion Master. This time, he came of his own free will. He found himself needing repose, needing to witness the sight of a natural stillness—not the engineered stillness of home—before the end of the day, before he turned his thoughts entirely to the work of the Jubilee posticum.

His plan had been based on the challenge he had participated in: order and chaos. He wanted both order and chaos in this posticum, because there was beauty in order and there was also beauty in chaos. There was order in motion, but there was order in stillness, too. There was chaos in motion, but Thaddeus wasn't sure if there could be chaos in stillness.

Tomorrow, he would begin his duties for the Jubilee posticum—most likely gathering energy for the wind—and he wouldn't have the opportunity to look for chaos in the stillness for some time. So he snuck away from all his well-wishers after the announcements, up to the quiet room in Wright Hall.

He sat by the window savoring the stillness until it was

broken by a figure moving from the Hall of Shape. As the light dissipated into dusk, he saw that the figure was a girl—a girl who moved with a rolling grace.

He watched her walk across the square, as if she were the only one in the Commons, as if she owned the entire courtyard. As he watched her, he realized she did own the courtyard, because he couldn't take his eyes off her as she moved through the space. This was far better than stillness. This was far better than chaos. If given the opportunity, he would follow that girl wherever she went as long as he could watch her rolling grace.

The girl, of course, was Dora, the Shape artisan.

She headed toward the Hall of Manufactory, and Thaddeus felt a stab of jealousy. Why would she go there? But then she passed Manufactory and headed toward the Cairns. She stopped when another figure emerged from the alleyway.

It was that Manufactory apprentice who had competed with them in the first challenge. Thaddeus could see her stiffen at his approach. He watched Michael talk with a great deal of animation. He gestured back toward the Cairns, then toward the Hall of Hue.

The whole while, Dora stood there, unmoving, arms crossed. Thaddeus couldn't see her expression, but the longer she stood there, her rolling grace suspended, the more he believed that the concept of chaos in stillness was entirely possible.

She was living proof of it.

CHAPTER
32

Y ou wanted to see me?" Luc popped his head into Color Master's office that evening. His face was puffy and bruised.

"Come in, please. Sit down."

Luc lowered himself into the chair across from Color Master.

"Luc," Color Master said slowly. "I know that you expected to win this contest."

Luc fingered his prism and met Color Master's eyes. "You said that I would get another posticum."

"I said we could make arrangements for you to be a part of another posticum. That's not the same thing. To be honest, I'm not certain that the wall will open another posticum for you alone." Color Master swiveled in her chair, turning her gaze to the view out her window. "It's impossible to predict what the wall will do."

Luc knew only too well how unpredictable the wall was. "Then why didn't you pick my plan?"

"Ishmael's plan was the only viable one."

"Not the only viable one, surely. My plan would have worked."

She shook her head. "Not with the colors we salvaged. My responsibility is first to the colors and the posticum, and second, to the apprentices." She swiveled around to look at him. "I had to choose his plan, but choosing his plan puts me—and by extension, you—in a difficult position. What if the wall won't open another posticum for you?"

"Why wouldn't it? The wall always opens posticums."

"Yes, the wall always has in the past, but no one has ever missed the closing of their posticum before." She leaned forward. "If the wall won't open a posticum for you, what does that mean for the apprentices in all the other Halls who are waiting for their posticums? What if your presence here brings the work of the Commons to a complete standstill?"

The realization of what Color Master was saying began to sink in.

"You mean the wall might not open *any* other posticums until I'm gone?"

"That's exactly what I mean."

Luc hung his head in his hands.

Color Master continued. "I see two options here. You can go home, leave the Commons, and relinquish your role as a color keeper."

"And the other option?"

"I fear the second option will be just as distasteful to you."

"What is it?" Luc asked, though deep down he already knew the answer.

"You know that no apprentice may lay claim to a posticum unless he or she has put their mark upon it?"

"If I want to have a posticum at all, then I must make my mark in this posticum?"

"Yes, but therein lies the difficulty." She swiveled back and forth in her chair and tapped her fingers together. "This is Ishmael's posticum. He would be in charge. If you want the opportunity to lay claim to this posticum, it would be conditional on mentoring Ishmael through the creation process. But you must remember, it is his posticum. You can leave your mark, but you cannot change his plan in any way."

Hue, have boldness.

"And if I refuse?"

"You can always go home."

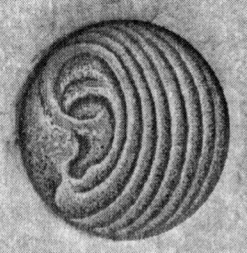

SOUND

As Aaron put one foot in front of the other, his long legs feeling longer than usual, he was overcome with emotion. This was the last time he would be treading this path, this path that the soles of his shoes had grown accustomed to over the years. Another apprentice followed behind him—a girl. The great bell would answer to her now.

Aaron wound his way up the curving steps, but he didn't count them this time. He didn't wonder about who had built them or who had come before, and he pushed away the thought of who would come after him. That was hard to do, since the new bell ringer was right behind him, and her labored breathing up each step was a constant reminder that the silence of the morning and the hush of the evening were no longer his.

When they reached the top of the stairs, the girl looked around her in wonder. With shining eyes, she said, "This will be mine, every day?"

"Yes," Aaron said curtly. "Every morning and every evening and before each meal and all gatherings."

The girl turned to look out the window. Aaron remembered doing the same thing his first time with the bell.

He wadded up the wool and put it in his ears. "Here," he said, handing a bit of wool to the girl. "For your ears. It gets pretty loud."

Aaron grasped the rope, sliding his fingers over the surface worn smooth over time. He heaved himself up, his arms strong from the daily practice, and let the weight of the bell carry him. The sound rang out, over and over and over, and Aaron wasn't sure if he could let go.

CHAPTER

33

Ishmael was the first apprentice back to the Hall of Hue after breakfast. He wished he could talk to Luc. He wished he could tell him that he was on Luc's side, that Luc should have won, that he didn't want to be the artisan for this posticum. But Luc skipped breakfast, so Ishmael went looking for him.

He found him at the entrance to the tower. Seeing Ishmael, he pivoted, but before he had a chance to walk away, Ishmael said, "Luc, wait."

Luc stopped walking, but didn't turn around.

"I wanted you to have this posticum. You know I did. Your plan should have been picked, not mine. What you did in the tower room was really amazing." Ishmael stopped, as Luc slowly turned around to face him.

"What I did in the tower room? You think that's what my plan was?"

"Wasn't it?"

Luc barked out a laugh. "No. My plan was the same one I used for my posticum."

"But—"

"My posticum was perfect," Luc said. "And then you came and ruined everything." He glared at Ishmael, his face hot.

The words burned through skin, then flesh, then bone, seeping deep into Ishmael's body until they settled into his core. It filled the sliver of space left and poisoned him.

He couldn't believe he had been so stupid about everything: stupid enough to wander away from Papa, to leave Mam to search for Luc, to think Luc would ever return. He had been stupid to not go home when he had the chance, stupid to think he could help Luc at his posticum, stupid for entering the contest with such a stupid idea. Stupid to believe he was strong enough to leave the Commons.

Luc folded his arms and leaned against the wall. "If I want the opportunity to claim the Jubilee posticum, Color Master told me that I have to mentor you through the process."

"I don't even want to color the posticum," Ishmael said.

"Too bad." Luc pushed away from the wall. "You've been chosen," he said over his shoulder as he strode away.

Ishmael listened to Luc's retreating footsteps, and his words echoed in Ishmael's mind. *You've been chosen.*

No, Luc was wrong. He hadn't been chosen; his plan had

been chosen—only because of how little color and light they had—a plan that was just as simple and stupid as he was. When Ishmael thought of showing his plan to Luc, of Luc mentoring him to bring its simple stupidity into reality—he cringed. It wouldn't be so bad if he had created a vision that he could be proud of, that he was excited about. Then working with Luc might not be so awful.

He wished he could regain that sense of peace he had when they worked together in the tower room, when they dappled the wall with specks of color and all differences blended together into a sight so fine that it had made his heart soar. When Luc actually felt like a mentor. But far too much had happened since then to return to that. He was not the same, Luc was not the same, and Ishmael feared they could never regain the easiness they once had with each other.

When the sound of Luc's footsteps faded, another sound sidestepped into his consciousness—the swishing of a scrub brush and something else. Something repetitive. Something quiet. Something irritating. He heard no colors in this sound.

It was a voice intoning words.

Phoebe sat scrubbing the floor at the entrance to the workroom. He watched her dip the scrub brush into the water, tap it against the side of the pail three times, then scrub around and around. Her voice swooped up and down, the words sometimes quick, and other times sustained. She was in a world of her own, scrubbing away. Singing.

Anger rose in him once more. If she hadn't emptied their

stores, he wouldn't be in this position. They would still have color, and Luc would have been chosen for this task instead of him.

He walked toward her, and kicked over her bucket of water.

The water sloshed out, spreading in a pool around her so that she knelt in a half inch of scrub water. The dirty water darkened her dress, crawling up and over each fiber. She looked up at him, bewildered, pale, and wet.

But the satisfaction he had anticipated didn't come. He backed away, staring at the puddle of murky water. When he bumped into the workroom doorway, he turned and hurried inside, ducking behind a row of empty jars feeling just like that dirty water.

CHAPTER
34

Within minutes, all the Hue apprentices had assembled in the workroom ready to begin their tasks of the day. Color Master walked in and threw a spectrum into the air, and the apprentices quieted. Ishmael peeked out from behind the jars.

"It goes without saying that we must pull together to help Ishmael and his spectrum. His plan relies mainly upon green and blue, of which we have an adequate supply. Consequently, we will delay our expedition departure until after the opening ceremony when Ishmael illuminates the posticum. In the meantime, we shall continue distilling color. Now, back to work."

The apprentices scattered, and Ishmael returned to his worktable. Jacob sat perched on a stool next to it. "Head of the posticum, head of the spectrum."

Ishmael detected the slightest bit of resentment in Jacob's

voice, as if Ishmael wanted this in the first place. "Just because my plan was chosen doesn't make me the head of the spectrum. In case you've forgotten, green is still in the middle." His words seemed to mollify Jacob.

"I suppose so. Are you going to share the details of your plan since we're all in this together?"

Ishmael retrieved the rolled-up parchment from the corner of the table. He hated the thought of showing it to the rest of the apprentices as much as he hated the thought of showing it to Luc. Artless and simple. Not grand at all. Not like what he had done with Luc in the tower room.

Lilith, Rebekah, and Hannah pulled up stools to join Jacob at Ishmael's table. Matthew and Thomas followed. Matthew wore a swathe of fabric tied around his waist like a belt.

"What's with the belt?" Hannah asked.

"Remedy for hiccups. Thomas said it helps."

"Hallelujah," Rebekah said. "That'll make Color Master happy."

"I think it's going to take more than a belt to make Color Master happy right now," Matthew said.

Ishmael unrolled the parchment and slid empty glass vials over the curling corners. One of the vials rolled off and shattered on the floor.

Ishmael jumped up, but Rebekah said, "Sit down. I've got it."

Rebekah came back seconds later with Phoebe carrying a dustpan and broom. Phoebe looked at Ishmael hesitantly, afraid he might throw something at her.

"I'm sorry," he said, "about the water."

Phoebe nodded, then swept the broken glass together. "Go ahead with whatever you were doing. I'll try not to bother you."

Hannah smoothed the parchment. There before them lay the simple and artless rendering. Ishmael had distributed green along the bottom two-thirds of the parchment and blue at the top. Reds and yellows and purples and bright orange intertwined along the edges of the page.

"Like Color Master said, I picked green for the main color, blue for the heavens, and bits of the other colors to accent it."

Phoebe had finished sweeping the shards into the dustpan and leaned on the broom, staring at the parchment, squinting, tilting her head to see. From the disappointed look on her face, Ishmael could tell that she saw nothing. He caught her eye. She shrugged and turned away to empty the dustpan of its shards.

"Matches up perfectly with our remaining stores of color," Jacob said, rolling a glass vial around in his hand.

"It is lovely, though," Hannah added.

The novices turned to stare at her in disbelief.

"Lovely wouldn't be the first word that came to my mind to describe this," Jacob said.

"I just mean that I like its simplicity," Hannah said.

"Yes. It has great simplicity," Lilith agreed. "But I like that it has all the colors in it."

"It's so different from Luc's posticum," Rebekah said.

"And we were so sure Luc was going to win," Thomas said.

"I wonder what Luc's entry was," Rebekah said. "Anyone know?"

"It was the same as his other posticum. He wanted to re-create it," Ishmael said.

"How do you know?" Rebekah asked.

"He told me."

Ishmael stopped. He had assumed Luc would have used dappling in his entry, which is why Ishmael hadn't. Perhaps he still could. And if he did, perhaps it might remind Luc of their work in the tower room. Perhaps it might lessen Luc's anger at him. Perhaps it would swallow the sting. Cover it over with a glorious variety of color.

Ishmael studied the parchment and thought of Michael. It might be done. "We need to know how much color we have. I thought you could count how many vials there are of each of your colors right now, as well as how many are currently being collected."

Color Master appeared behind Lilith. "That's a good beginning. After inventory, I would suggest making swabs. You'll need them for the color transfers. Bolts of linen and baskets of sticks are in the storage room. It's laborious work, but you've done it before. I have complete confidence that your spectrum is up to the task."

They each grabbed a slate and chalk to tally their numbers, leaving Ishmael and Color Master at the worktable.

The wheels were turning in Ishmael's head. If Michael could indeed build a machine to purify the light, then he could dapple the posticum to his heart's content. But first, he needed to know how much light he would need. "Color Master, how big is the posticum?"

She hesitated, then said, "Forty square miles."

Ishmael's right hand slid off the worktable. Forty square miles?

"It's quite a bit larger than our usual posticums, but . . ." Color Master sighed. "It was supposed to be a celebration."

He tried to write forty square miles on his slate in his best script, but his hand didn't seem to be able to control the chalk and the numbers came out ill formed. He would never be able to get enough light to dapple that much. For that matter— "Will we have enough color?"

"Ah, that is the question, isn't it?" Color Master smiled grimly. "You must take care in your calculations so that you allot just enough light for the ceremony without giving too much."

"Ceremony?"

Color Master frowned. "I figured Luc would have spoken to you directly after breakfast about the ceremony. No? Every posticum opens with a ceremony where the Hue apprentice releases light to illuminate the posticum. Once there is light within, then the work begins."

"Yes, but—" Ishmael still held out hope that he might be able to dapple.

"But what?"

"We need the light for color."

"Light for the opening ceremony must take priority. When

you release the light, you release a spark, which will become a fully developed light source. A sun, if you will."

"So if I don't release light, the apprentices from the other Halls wouldn't be able to do their work?"

"Correct. Releasing the light is only part of it, though. You must color the dawn at the same time. Come."

Ishmael followed her to the rack of full vials.

"What colors draw you to them right now?" she asked. "Don't think—just reach out. Close your eyes if it helps."

He did as she suggested, and let his fingers be pulled forward by some inner sense until he touched the glass vials in front of him.

"Ah! Indigo, orange, and violet. Excellent!" She grabbed the three vials, handed them to Ishmael, and headed to her office. "The colors are intense, so you won't need very much."

Color Master walked into her office and patted a stone jar on her desk. "I will bring the light for you tomorrow. You'll need swabs," she said, holding out three small twigs with their tips covered in linen.

"You must have your color ready before you release the light, for the light moves quickly—in the blink of an eye—and once it's gone, there's no coloring it. The powdered color is very fine and will disperse with the light as it escapes from the jar.

"There are two tricky parts, however. First, you must ease the lid off slowly, otherwise the light flashes out in a blinding glare. It's more effective to do it gradually. Second, you must blow the color into the light continuously. It mixes itself into the light as you blow, and if you blow in a great huff, it gets patchy."

Images of violet and orange smears of color crossing the sky danced through his head. Ishmael's hand holding the swabs sank down. "I'm not sure I can do this."

Color Master looked at him with concern in her eyes. "Well," she said, taking a deep breath, "let's practice blowing. We'll use this string so you can see how gently you'll need to blow." Color Master held one end of the string up. "Watch me." She took a deep breath, then exhaled so slowly and gently that the string hardly moved. "You try it," she said as she handed the string to him.

Ishmael took a deep breath and let it out, sending the string dancing.

"I didn't get it on my first try, either," Color Master said. "Gentle this time."

Ishmael took a deep breath again, held it for a minute, then released it. The string shimmied again.

"Remember," Color Master said, pointing to the string, "you'll be blowing color—not a string. Try thinking about the color instead. Maybe that will help you."

Ishmael held the string tightly in his right hand and imagined that it was a group of color swabs. He pictured layers of violet and orange and indigo, producing delicate gradations of color. Ishmael breathed deeply one more time and let it go with barely an exhale. The string hardly moved.

"Excellent!" Color Master said. "Again."

Ishmael pictured the colors again, took a breath, and released it. It was as if Color Master had done it herself.

"One more time, for good measure."

Ishmael did it once again. *Inhale, hold, release.*

"Do that tomorrow morning, and the Jubilee ceremony will be off to an auspicious start." Color Master clapped him on the back.

"And if I don't?"

"Let's not consider the alternatives." She winked at him.

CHAPTER

35

H ead Master called the first meeting of the artisans that afternoon in an upper room in Wright Hall. Ishmael studied the faces of the others as they arrived: friendly, serious, round, angular. He considered the set of their eyes, the planes of their foreheads, the curves of their eyebrows. He regarded the tilt of their heads, their manner of moving, their facial expressions, even the way they listened. Up to now, they had just been apprentices in the other Halls. But the conversation he had with Michael at the Cairns about working *with* the others sprouted in Ishmael's mind, and now he saw possibility in each of them.

As soon as the last artisan arrived and took his seat, Head Master began. "This is a grand gathering. I am absolutely delighted with your plans. The result is bound to be impressive."

He looked through his thick spectacles at each of them. "However, there is much work to be done. Because the posticum has already opened, work must begin immediately. At the opening ceremony, Aaron and the Hall of Sound will present their anthem."

Aaron, the former bell ringer, nodded.

"Ethan and the Hall of Manufactory suggested that they lay a stone threshold across the posticum entry to discourage the wall from closing. Though we've never done this before, I think it is a wise precautionary measure."

Ethan gave a quick nod, and Head Master continued.

"Following that, Ishmael from the Hall of Hue will release the necessary light into the posticum, and work will begin in earnest. Following the opening, the work will pass from the Hall of Shape to Manufactory. Once Manufactory has finished their work, the schedule must become more flexible. You must do your tasks in a timely manner and keep the work moving along, while being sensitive to the fact that the Hall of Hue is working under imperfect conditions." Head Master clasped his hands together. "Any questions?"

When no one responded, he continued. "While you won't necessarily understand the specifics of each other's work, it would be good to have a general idea of all the plans."

He turned toward the opposite end of the table. "Dora, let's start with you. Do you have your initial drafts ready?"

Ishmael watched as Dora's long slender fingers unrolled a

large scroll. "I have a detailed drawing of the landscape. I've based most of my structures on the curved shape of the dot." The posticum entrance was centered at the bottom. The upper right area was water. The rest of the land was divided into eighteen overlapping circular sections. The shoreline curved from corner to corner, separating land from water.

"Considering the troubles with the Hall of Hue—" her silvery voice paused as she glanced up at Ishmael, "we thought it might be easier if two-thirds of the area was water, leaving only one-third as land. That way there would be less detail for all concerned."

Ishmael was touched by her kindness. "Thank you," he said.

"I would also like to adjust things a bit here," Dora said, pointing to the top left corner. "It has too much line in it, but we should be ready to turn the plans of the coastline over to Ethan soon." She looked at the Manufactory artisan.

He nodded. "We'll start immediately on the scaffolding, then. I expect it'll take us a week to build the coastline and fill the area with water."

"Wait," Ishmael blurted out, looking around at the others. They sat there, as if Ethan hadn't just said the most extraordinary thing ever. The Motion artisan rolled a pencil on the surface of the table, back and forth and back and forth. Aaron, the Sound artisan, tipped his head, as if listening to the echoes of Ishmael's voice in the chamber. Keturah touched her nose delicately with one finger. No one looked dismayed by what had been said.

"A week?" Why was no one else dumbfounded by this? "Color Master told me this posticum is supposed to be forty square miles. How can you possibly build scaffolding for forty square miles in a week? And where will you get all that water to fill it?"

Head Master smiled at him. "Ishmael, though this is new to you, it is not to us. The walls of the Commons are riddled with posticums. Each Hall has taken part in countless creative challenges and posticums. What the Shape and Manufactory apprentices propose has been done in similar ways before. A posticum opens, the House of Æther provides materials, and we create."

Ishmael bit his lip.

Head Master continued, "The other part of the speed is simply practice. The apprentices have had years of experience here—experience that you haven't had yet."

Ishmael nodded, one stiff nod. He was certain he would never be able to do his part in such a short amount of time, even if he had years of experience.

"Dora, the rest of your plans are underway, then?"

"Yes, Head Master."

"Do you foresee any difficulties?"

Dora shook her head.

"Excellent." He turned back to Ethan. "And Manufactory?"

Ethan glanced over at Dora. "Aside from the challenge of

bearing the weight of so much water, we should be fine. My plan is based on flexibility and stability using covered gears and pulleys."

"Do you have enough supplies?"

"Manufactory Master has one of the apprentices organizing our storage room so we know exactly what we have."

Head Master's mouth twitched in a smile. "Good. Once you've got the foundation and water set, we'll schedule a tour for the artisans so you'll know what to expect. Thaddeus, how about you?"

"The plan for motion is based on chaos and order."

"And how will you execute that plan?"

"Waves."

"Excellent." Head Master looked expectantly at Ishmael, and Ishmael realized it was his turn. He looked down at his parchment and cleared his throat. "Our plan is simple. That's probably its only redeeming quality."

"Ah, simplicity. There is beauty in simplicity," Head Master said gently. "Do you have enough color?"

"I hope so. The salvaged color is mostly green and blue."

"Are you comfortable using the older techniques to transfer the color?"

"I've practiced a few of them. That was one of our first lessons."

"Undoubtedly, you will become more comfortable as you work." Head Master moved on to the Hall of Sound.

"Aaron?

The tall boy in the corner tipped his head in a way that reminded Ishmael of Phoebe.

"Connections," he said, his voice pleasant and smooth.

"Can you elaborate?" Head Master asked.

"Sound touches everything; it connects to everything. Past to future. Tangible to intangible. Emotion to logic. My plan is to forge as many connections as I can between sound and the other elements of this posticum."

Ishmael blinked. He understood very little of what Aaron said, but it seemed like something Michael would appreciate.

Head Master turned to the petite Scent artisan. "Keturah?"

"The focus of my work will be the scent of possibility."

"And Gabriel?"

Gabriel sat across the table from Ishmael. His face was open, and Ishmael tried to figure out what color he would represent in the spectrum if he were a member of the Hall of Hue, but Gabriel was not red, or orange, or any of the other colors. Gabriel was not Hue; he was Gustation. He probably had a taste assigned to him, something far from Ishmael's ability to comprehend.

"My plan involves opposition and contrast with flavors," Gabriel said.

Possibility, connections, wave, opposition. Ishmael had no idea how waves would manifest chaos and order or what the scent of possibility smelled like, or how sound could be connected to everything. He had no idea how taste could have opposition and what any of this had to do with a palette of green and blue. He missed the rest of what Gabriel said as his thoughts struggled with these ideas. He didn't belong here. Their plans had so much sophistication to them. His plan was nothing but the scribbling of a simpleton.

MANUFACTORY

Michael gazed at the mess before him. The storeroom was filled with bolts of fabric spread onto the tables and unrolled halfway across the floor. Rolls of heavy paper stood up in the corner, though one roll had fallen and leaned on a table. Drawers holding thin sheets of metal lay open, the sheets half in and half out. Blocks of wood and stone were haphazardly stacked, with a lone pencil shoved into a crack. Barrels of filler—sand, gravel, fluff—had disgorged their contents, which lay scattered on the floor. Buckets of nails and tacks spilled into each other, and dozens of bottles had glue slopped over their sides. There were even a few whirligigs and flying tops from the celebration scattered over the rubble.

Ugh.

Until his arm healed, Manufactory Master said he should clean and sort, so the mess was left to him. Him and his bum arm.

However, Michael was certain no one would notice how quickly or how slowly the storeroom was cleaned and organized. He was certain no one would notice if some of the materials mysteriously wound up elsewhere, like in an innocuous little machine that helped concentrate the diffused light of the Commons. Though Dora hadn't understood what Michael wanted to do and sent him on his way, he was sure he could figure out how to make a machine on his own to help Ishmael. He just needed some time to tinker.

—PART IV—

COLLABORATION

All things counter, original, spare, strange;
Whatever is fickle, freckled (who knows how?)
With swift, slow; sweet, sour; adazzle, dim.

Gerard Manley Hopkins, "Pied Beauty"

SCENT

On the morning of the opening ceremony for the Jubilee posticum, Keturah stood with the other members of her Hall at the edge of the archway. She was close enough to smell the posticum. Or rather, she would have smelled the posticum if there had been anything to smell. Curiously, she smelled nothing.

It shook her to the core. She knew that the posticum was a void. It had to be a void until the artisans filled it, until *she* filled it. But even the sight of the nothingness troubled her, and she wished she didn't have to witness this. It seemed not dangerous exactly, but not safe, either. It was like seeing someone naked when, more than anything, she wanted everyone to be fully clothed.

Her thoughts turned to the apprentices from the other Halls— the apprentices who would work on the posticum with her. *Please let them* . . . please let them what? She couldn't finish her thought, because she didn't know how to finish it.

Today was the day for Ishmael to release the light. Keturah turned away from the empty posticum to look for him in the crowds of apprentices, but she couldn't see him. She couldn't do her work in this vast nothingness until the others began theirs.

Yearning overcame her again, yearning for the other Halls' apprentices to fill this vast space. Please let them *do?* Please let them *complete?* Ah, here it was. *Please let them create.* And quickly. Then she could layer this Jubilee posticum with possibility, with fragrances both sweet and pungent.

Until that time, the posticum was empty, and the utter nothingness of it frightened her.

CHAPTER

36

A faint rumble of voices met Ishmael as he walked toward the courtyard. The chill in the air worked its way through his tunic and trousers, and he found himself in a cold sweat. His mind was blank, but his lungs recalled their task: *inhale, hold, release.* He practiced the breathing pattern all the way through the square into the smaller courtyard.

The darkness made it difficult to see anyone, but Ishmael could spot his brother standing where his posticum used to be, his hand resting lightly on the wall. The look on his face was difficult to read. Maybe insecurity. Maybe jealousy. Maybe fear.

Ishmael wished he could run to his brother, he wished Luc would encourage him, he wished they could do this together, but there was little chance of that. Ishmael scanned the crowd to find Color Master, but instead caught a glimpse of Phoebe, who stood alone, apart from both the Hall of Sound and the Hall of Hue apprentices.

He made his way toward the newly opened posticum. His spectrum of friends stood in a cluster near the front.

"Good luck," Hannah whispered.

Matthew tightened the belt he wore around his waist. "No hiccups today. I don't want to distract you."

"You can do this, Ishmael," said Lilith.

"Thanks," Ishmael said.

Then it was time.

Head Master stood by the entrance to the posticum. He held a lantern in his hand, which he lifted to get everyone's attention. "We undertake this posticum in celebration of this Jubilee Year to honor our founder who built the foundations of this great community."

He nodded at Sound Master, who lifted his arms in some sort of cue to the apprentices gathered before him. A single voice hit a high, lilting note and held it. Deeper voices wove through the high note, singing words of praise and honor. They were joined by other voices, and the sound swelled until the stones rang.

Ishmael, who was by now used to the sound of singing thanks to Phoebe, tried to appreciate the intricacy of their voices, but his nerves prevented anything other than the repetition of *inhale, hold, release.* So he simply let the music wash over him, pulse through him, wrap around him until he felt like a very small piece in a very great work.

When the singing ceased and Sound Master finally lowered his arms, Head Master signaled to Ethan. At his feet was a setup involving a rectangular stone, a wedge, and dozens of smaller round stones. Ethan took a mallet and knocked the wedge out, allowing the stone to be rolled into the entry. He forced it into place, making sure both sides lined up with the wall. Satisfied, he turned to Ishmael.

Inhale, hold, release, Ishmael thought one last time as he made his way toward the jar of light Color Master had left at the entry. With shaking hands, Ishmael pulled the swabs and a container of violet from his satchel. He handed the swabs to Thomas, and carefully opened the vial of color. When he looked up to take a swab, he finally saw Color Master standing behind the Hue apprentices. Though he could barely make out Color Master's face, he saw her smile.

Ishmael dipped the swab into the vial, tapping the twig against the side of the glass. He could feel the heaviness of the violet clinging to the linen. He shook some of it back down into the vial, and when he sensed what he thought might be the right weight, he handed the twig to Thomas. Ishmael corked the vial of violet and exchanged it for the orange.

He repeated the process, gathering a greater amount of orange, and then added a tiny bit of indigo for balance. He handed the swabs to Thomas and returned the vials to his satchel.

When all was ready, Ishmael wiped his sweating hands on his smock so the swabs wouldn't slip when he blew the color. He tried to work up some saliva so he could sense the air flowing out as he blew the color, but his mouth was dry as dust. *Inhale, hold, release.* Ishmael knelt down by the jar and reached for the swabs that Thomas held.

Clasping the lid of the stone jar in his left hand and the swabs of color in his right, Ishmael took a deep breath. The crowd stirred and someone coughed. He knew most of the people there would only see the light, not the color, but that didn't make this any easier. He didn't want to fail.

The lid squealed as Ishmael turned it round and round until he met no more resistance. How different this was from the dappling he had done with Luc. How much weightier it was than what he had done in the barn. He took a deep breath again, moved the swabs close to the jar, and bent over them. Color Master's voice spoke clearly in his mind, telling him to think of the colors. Ishmael lost himself in the vision of the grand, sweeping dawn he hoped for—swirling violet, layered with a glowing orange and a hint of indigo that would illuminate the sky in a way he could only have dreamed about until this moment—and eased open the jar, releasing his breath across the color-tipped swabs.

He exhaled until his lungs were empty, until every possible bit of color had been breathed into the light, until there was nothing left in him, and he gasped for air.

Ishmael looked into the posticum, certain of his triumph.

But there was nothing. The posticum appeared as dreary as it had before, full of gray murkiness.

Ishmael didn't see light. He didn't see color. He wondered if

Color Master had brought an empty stone jar, instead of the reserved one full of light. He heard a hiccup from Matthew's direction and a snicker from someone else. Someone shushed them. Ishmael hung his head, not daring to look up, the swabs and jar swimming in his vision.

He dropped the twigs on the ground and screwed the top back on the stone jar, wondering how he would get through the rest of the Jubilee if he couldn't do something so simple as releasing light the right way.

It was then that he heard a gasp.

"Ishmael!" It was Hannah.

Ishmael looked up. Astonished, he watched as the night rolled away to reveal all the colors he had envisioned. Swirling and mingling together, the colors danced in a beauty that he scarcely believed possible. It was as glorious as he had hoped . . . No, it was *more* than he had ever dared to hope.

In the growing light, he saw Color Master with her face raised toward the dawn. He saw Luc staring at the horizon, his attention caught by the sight. He saw the other artisans and apprentices shuffling around, uncomfortable in the presence of something they couldn't understand. But the color keepers were united in speechless wonder. Never had any of them seen such a sight.

When the light had fully encompassed the sky, Head Master turned to Ishmael with a kind look on his face. "Well done, Ishmael, well done." In a louder voice, he said to the others, "Let the work commence!"

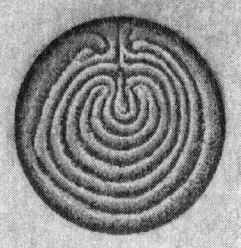

GUSTATION

Gabriel turned toward the refectory shivering in the cool air. Instead of hunkering over the stove watching the toast darken, Gabriel had stood with the other chosen artisans directly in front of the posticum entrance watching the darkness in the sky fade.

It was a glorious thing. There was darkness, and then there was a brightening, a lightening, a rising up, and the darkness gave way to full light. He couldn't quite put his finger on how it was different from any of the other dawns he had seen, but there was a power in this dawn. This was not just an ending or a beginning, but both at the same time. A contrast. An opposition.

Gabriel felt lifted up and weighted down—his head rising, extending upward, reaching for the heavens; his feet planted firmly, sinking down, as if embedded into the foundation. It was a curious sensation, like being stretched or mixed or kneaded. The kind that results in something sweet. Something bitter. Or both at the same time. Bittersweet.

How utterly perfect.

CHAPTER
37

T he Hue apprentices swarmed Ishmael, jostling the Gustation apprentice in their rush. When Head Master had announced the chosen artisans two days ago, no one had known what to say to him. Now, congratulations flowed from all sides.

"Not bad," Jacob said, slapping him on the back.

Rebekah jumped up and down beside him. "How *did* you do that?"

"If that's what's possible with just a smidgen of color, I can't wait to see the finished posticum," Hannah said, giddy. They walked across the courtyard to the refectory, pushed along by the crowd of apprentices.

When they reached their table inside the refectory and all the apprentices were seated, Head Master stood. "Our thanks to the Hall of Gustation for the imminent feast."

Celebration was in the air, and cheers rang out. It took some time before they quieted down. Head Master looked out at their exuberant faces with soberness. "Unfortunately," he continued, "before we can turn our attention to such an excellent repast, I must request information relating to an unfortunate incident at the Cairns."

Ishmael caught Michael's eye across the refectory.

Head Master continued. "An act of vandalism occurred sometime in the past week. If you visited the Cairns recently or saw anything that would assist us, please inform either me or your Hall master. Now, let your exuberance return, and let us give thanks for this food!"

The Gustation apprentices had engineered a celebratory breakfast of spiced bread, thick slabs of bacon, tart citrus juice, porridge, sautéed mushrooms, and a heavenly hot drink made with milk and cinnamon and cloves and mounds of whipped cream. No one but the other Gustation apprentices recognized the significance of this breakfast—it contained six of the seven flavor profiles they studied, but everyone recognized that it was special as they feasted.

Ishmael finished eating early, overcome by the reverberation of the dawn colors that appeared in his head as he ate, and he headed back to the workroom. As he crossed the threshold, a familiar tread of footsteps sounded behind him, a tread he knew as well as his own.

Ishmael stopped walking, and Luc burst around the corner to face him. It had been twenty-four hours since he had talked to him, but Luc appeared no less angry.

"Head Master warned me that I must help while Color Master is gone, so I might as well start now." Luc held up his arms. The brilliance with which all the apprentices glowed had dimmed on Luc. He seemed like a candle that had just been snuffed out, but smoke still leaked from the wick—a wick still burning on the inside.

Out of mercy, Ishmael was sorely tempted to tell Luc that he didn't want his help, but there was just so much he didn't know, and Color Master would be leaving soon with the rest of the apprentices. Ishmael reached for a scroll of parchment on his worktable, not knowing what to say. He rolled the parchment tightly. "You don't have to help me. I know you're angry. You've got every right to be."

Luc watched the parchment wind tighter and tighter in Ishmael's hands and said, "Oh, that's wonderful. You know I'm angry."

Lilith and Matthew walked in just then, but stopped when they saw Luc. It was the first time he had returned to the workroom since the announcement, and they felt the tension that his presence brought.

"Luc." Lilith flicked her long straight hair over her shoulder nervously. "That was some feast, wasn't it?"

Ishmael tied the parchment and settled it into a drawer at his worktable. If Lilith was flustered by Luc's presence, there was no hope for the rest of them.

Luc pushed away from the bench as Jacob, Rebekah, Hannah, and Thomas followed behind Lilith. Matthew moved over to the far side of the table, hiccupping.

"Luc. Hi," Jacob said. The others murmured hellos, and then an awkward silence descended on them.

"So what now?" Luc said as if to mock their discomfort. "Is this your plan?" Luc pointed to the unrolled parchment on the table, still secured by the stone lids.

When no one replied, he walked over and examined the plan. "This? Really?" he said, eyebrows raised.

Ishmael felt the shame all over again, and it made him defensive even though he knew the plan was rubbish, even though he had scrapped this plan in favor of dappling. That is, if Michael came through.

Thankfully, Hannah came to his rescue. "It's not so different from your posticum," she said. "The only difference is that green is dominant instead of yellow."

Luc glared at her.

As if to cut the tension, Matthew said, "You never had a chance to tell us what Head Master said at your meeting yesterday."

Ishmael glanced at Luc. "He said as soon as Manufactory has the basics ready, we'll have a chance to visit the posticum. Then it'll be our turn. We begin with coloring the heavens and the water."

"But didn't you color the heavens just now?" Rebekah asked.

Luc turned away from them, speaking to the empty workroom. "That was just the dawn. That amount of color is not enough for an eternity of dawns."

"So what do we have to do?" Lilith asked.

"One of the best ways of coloring water," Luc said, turning back around, "is to dump the vials of color into the water."

"You can't be serious," Lilith said.

"I'm entirely serious. Color disperses easily in water."

"What about the heavens? How will we color that?"

Luc pulled out one of the linen-wrapped twigs that Ishmael had used for the ceremony that morning. "Swab."

Before he could elaborate, dozens of apprentices crowded into the workroom, their bags littering the floor. Hopeful talk filled the air as everyone prepared to leave in search of more light. Ishmael couldn't help but feel glum, for Color Master's presence was like a safety net to him—and now his safety net was being whisked away, leaving yet another big void, and the only things left to fill it were Luc's anger and the misery that accompanied it.

Color Master threw a spectrum into the air, and the talk quieted.

"This is a most vital expedition—and, I might add, a most difficult one. Please stay focused on the work at hand. Do not, I repeat, do not wander in body or in thought. Your safety and the future of the Hall of Hue depend on it." Color Master turned toward Ishmael and the novices. "We shall return as soon as we possibly can. Luc, will you assist us to the gate?"

He nodded and picked up a bag.

Color Master looked at the novices one last time, nodded, and then said, "Onward!"

With that, the apprentices gathered bags, tools, and containers, and left.

"Before Luc returns, I want to show you all something," Ishmael said. "Follow me."

"Where to?" Thomas said.

"The tower room." Ishmael knew this was a bit of a gamble because he wouldn't see Michael until this afternoon, but Ishmael couldn't wait to show the other novices the dappling in the tower room.

When they reached the top of the tower stairs, the novices fanned out into the room, wide-eyed and surprised.

"Wow," Hannah said.

Lilith studied the dappled walls before her. "Who did this?"

Ishmael had almost forgotten just how stunning the mural was. "Luc and I."

"But how? When?" She touched a spot of indigo.

"With a spectrum." Ishmael demonstrated, catching a ray of light and flicking a speck of green at the wall. "Luc taught me this before his posticum closed. I thought we could do this in the Jubilee posticum."

Jacob frowned. "You think *we* can do *that*?"

Thomas murmured, "*You need a sharp ax for a tough bough.* None of us is that sharp yet."

"It's really beautiful, but . . . Do you think we have enough color to do this in the posticum?" Hannah said. "There's an awful lot of color on these walls."

"Hannah's right," Lilith said. "As intriguing as it is, I don't think we have enough of all the other colors to get the same effect."

"And how are we supposed to transfer the color since it's already been removed from its spectrum?" Jacob said.

"That's just it," Ishmael said, nearly jumping in excitement. "One of the Manufactory apprentices is working on a way to purify light. It won't matter if we have enough distilled color, because we'll be able to work straight from the light!"

Silence. Thomas looked at Hannah. Lilith pursed her lips. Rebekah crinkled her nose, and Jacob just shook his head.

Surprised by their lack of enthusiasm, Ishmael said, "Why don't you want to do this?" He looked at Jacob. "You yourself clearly didn't like my plan."

"So?"

"So I would think you'd want to do something better."

"This," he indicated the dappled wall in front of him, "is beyond our capabilities. None of us can do this, except you."

"I can teach you. Luc taught me in twenty minutes."

Matthew looked doubtful. "Even if we learn how, don't you think Color Master would want to approve the change in plans? There are rules we're supposed to follow."

"I don't think the other Halls are supposed to be involved," Lilith said. "Especially with the light. That's just too risky."

"He's using light that we already have. What's risky about that?" Ishmael said. "Besides, what I'm suggesting is not all that different from my original plan. The large blocks of color would just be broken up with some dappling of the other colors."

"Not that different? *He who closes his eyes cannot see what is before him,*" Thomas said. "This is not what we're supposed to do."

"What do you mean? We're supposed to color. This is color." Ishmael felt his voice rising.

"But this is not something we know. We have to stick with what we know."

Ishmael looked around at the others. "Do the rest of you feel the same?"

Hannah broke the silence. "I'm not sure this is the best time for experimenting. Why don't we just do the first step—the heavens and the waters—in the regular way? Then we can go from there. We can see how it goes, and then maybe we can replicate this."

Ishmael agreed, but he wasn't happy about it.

MANUFACTORY

The Manufactory apprentices hauled cart after cart of materials from the storerooms at the Hall of Manufactory to the posticum. There were vats of cryogenic liquid, miles of heavy cable and fine cable, an uncountable number of metal tubes, and yards and yards of waterproofed canvas, all formed of stardust from the House of Æther. The apprentices built scaffolding outward from the entrance using the metal tubes and the cable to form a reinforced path. From there they built a fibrous network that would become the coastline with the finer cable. They stretched miles of waterproofed canvas until it hung suspended from the scaffolding and the network, one edge to the next. Once it stopped bobbing from their movement, they poured a freezing agent on it, turning it solid.

Back in the Hall of Manufactory, Michael had missed the beginning stage of the posticum. While the others built scaffolding, he pushed all of the detritus in the room to the center of the floor, and there it sat, a big soup of pencils and shavings and nails and papers all jumbled up in piles of stardust. It was a ploy to make it look like he was making progress sorting and organizing when really, he spent his time tinkering with an object hidden in the corner beneath a linen cloth—an apparatus he had designed of glass lenses, mirrors, a bit of rope, and some glue that would concentrate diffused light.

Michael knew the other Manufactory apprentices would be finished with the foundation soon, so his time for tinkering was quickly drawing to a close. He had made plans to meet Ishmael at the Cairns to see if the condensed light was strong enough, so Michael snuck out of the Hall carrying the wrapped apparatus tucked under his arm and hurried through the alleyway leading to his usual place behind the largest cairn. He set his device down and unwrapped it, but before he could go any further, he heard footsteps. He poked his head out, relieved to see it was only Ishmael.

"I couldn't wait any longer," Ishmael said, sliding to a stop by Michael. "I really want to know if this will work."

"Of course it will work!" Michael opened a small hatch at the top, revealing a mirror.

He explained the process to Ishmael—the light collection, the condensing tube, the filtration—pointing out the different parts, and finished with, "And this is where the condensed light collects."

"And that's all?" Ishmael looked doubtful.

"That's all." Michael's confidence in his little machine was surprising, yet encouraging.

"How long will it take?"

"That's the one thing I can't be certain about because

I don't know how intense you'll need the light. Let's give it a try." Michael opened the hatch for a few minutes, allowing some light in, and then closed it and began turning the crank. A grinding noise came from the apparatus.

"Is it supposed to sound like that?"

"Have faith in me, will you?" Michael said with a smile, continuing to turn the crank.

"Can we check now?"

"No faith and no patience, either, eh?"

Ishmael laughed. "Nope."

Michael stopped turning the crank. A slight glow emanated from the box.

Ishmael pulled out his prism to form a spectrum with the escaping light. The spectrum was weak, but it was definitely there. "I think it's working!" He flicked a few spots of color onto one of the stones. The color was faint.

"You just need to have some faith."

But an hour later, they had only condensed a small portion of light.

"Maybe I need to make this opening larger," Michael mused. "And let the light collect for a longer period of time before I begin cranking."

"Maybe it needs to be up higher to get more of the light," Ishmael suggested.

Michael looked at Ishmael with surprise. "Of course! And if I feed the light into more hatches . . ." Michael picked up the apparatus, shifted a few of the knotted ropes, circled one spot, then flipped it over and circled another spot. He picked up the linen covering and began walking toward the entrance.

"Where are you going?" Ishmael called out.

"I need to make some adjustments so it'll be more efficient." He waved without turning, hurrying back to the Hall of Manufactory.

Ishmael touched the few specks of color on the stone surface and couldn't help but feel excited.

CHAPTER

38

W hen the Halls of Shape and Manufactory were finished
with their initial work, Head Master granted permission for the
chosen artisans and their assistants to view the posticum.

A small crowd gathered in front of the entrance after breakfast.
Ethan, the chosen Manufactory artisan, stood blocking the way.

"The introduction to the posticum is only for chosen artisans and their assistants." His words were met with groans from
several of the gathered apprentices who had hoped to sneak in
unnoticed. "The rest of you will get to see the posticum once it's
finished. Now, we'll take the artisans and assistants in by Hall,
beginning with the Hall of Hue. Sound, Scent, Gustation, and
Motion will follow in that order. When you enter, don't go beyond
the stone barrier."

Rebekah leaped up from where she had been sitting on the

gravel path of the courtyard to join Jacob right behind Ishmael. The other Hue novices crowded around her. "I can't believe we get to see it first! This is so much better than wrapping swabs!" In the week since Ishmael released the light, he had dropped the discussion of collaborating with Manufactory, and instead, set the Hue novices to producing a large number of swabs, quills, and sifters in preparation for their work.

"I'm so excited that I can't even think of a fitting proverb," Thomas said.

Their enthusiasm was contagious, and Ishmael, too, felt a zip of excitement, a delight in the possibility of what might be. This was going to be his posticum, his place to fill with color. He couldn't wait to see the improvements Michael made to his light machine and be able to send specks of color dancing over everything once again. He looked at the faces of his friends, feeding his optimism with theirs, then he saw Luc, and his smile faded.

When Ethan stood aside, they filed into the posticum, Luc bringing up the rear. Ishmael stopped long before he reached the stone barrier, astounded. When Color Master had brought him to the posticum just after it opened, there was only a dim empty vastness. Now the vastness was outlined with a foundation below and air above, with an expanse of water at a shoreline.

From the entryway, a stretch of land led outward, soft underfoot. To the right, the terrain gave way to an area covered with small round pebbles. Beyond it lay a shallow sandy beach and water as far as the eye could see. At their left was a barren foundation.

It was overwhelming.

Ethan stood by the stone barrier. "What do you think?" he asked with a smile.

Ishmael was speechless. In a weak voice, Hannah said, "It's bigger than I thought it would be."

Rebekah had become very, very still, and Jacob looked off into the distance.

Thomas said, "My Gram used to say, *Worry gives small things a big shadow.* She never said anything about big things, though." His long limbs slumped down, as if the weight of the entire expanse had settled on him.

Lilith elbowed him and pointed toward Ishmael. "Don't you have anything more positive to say than that?"

Thomas shook himself. "Oh. Um. How about, *A little ax can cut down a big tree?*"

Luc laughed out loud.

Ethan didn't seem to catch the dread that flowed from one Hue novice to another.

"One last look," the Manufactory artisan said. "Then I need to bring in the Sound apprentices."

Ishmael looked up at the limitless heavens above him. The immensity of what lay before him imprinted itself on Ishmael's soul. Yes, this was going to be his posticum, but he no longer felt any delight in the possibilities, only a growing dread.

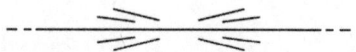

By lunchtime, all of the chosen artisans and their assistants had viewed the Jubilee posticum. Manufactory was ready to begin their next phase of construction, and the Hall of Hue was given authorization to add color.

After lunch, Ishmael walked with Hannah to the posticum, each carrying a basket of vials and swabs. Jacob and Lilith followed, so as to provide moral support, while the others stayed behind to continue working.

Ethan, the Manufactory artisan, met them at the entry again. "We're moving on to the foundation over there," he said, pointing to the left. "Thaddeus from the Hall of Motion is coming, too, but his work shouldn't disturb you."

Ishmael and the other novices nodded their thanks and turned toward the water. When they reached the edge, Hannah set down her basket.

"So much water," Lilith said. "I wish I could send some of it back home. It's too much for us and not enough for them."

"We can't possibly have enough color for this," Jacob said. "Do you think we should do green instead? We have more green than blue."

The sight of the water spread out before them made Ishmael numb. "I suppose now wouldn't be the time to remind you that Michael can help us concentrate the diffused light? That we could try using our prisms to generate the color?"

"We said we'd do blue in the traditional way," Hannah said. "Let's stick to the plan."

He didn't know what else to say, so Ishmael took off his sandals and waded in, letting the water slip over his feet, soft and cool. He walked onward until the water lapped at his knees.

Bending over to look into its depths, all he saw was a reflection of himself, slightly distorted.

The dull, pale heavens and flat, colorless water seemed so somber. "I wonder what this will look like colored."

"Remember the opening ceremony," Hannah said. "You used the tiniest bit of color for that, and it was amazing. It will be great." Under her breath, she added, "I hope."

They were interrupted as Thaddeus, the Motion artisan, hailed them from the entrance. His hair stood up in wild swirls, and he carried a bulging skin bag tightly cinched at the neck.

Ishmael walked back to the shore where the others stood.

"How's the water?" Thaddeus asked.

"It's large."

Thaddeus laughed. "It is, isn't it? Let me know if I'm bothering you." He headed for the edge of the water at the other end of the shore.

Hannah reached for her basket. "Are you ready?"

Ishmael grabbed one vial of blue and tucked it into his pocket. "I guess so."

"Security vial?"

He nodded. "Not that one vial is good for much of anything."

"You never know," Lilith said. "It's probably good to have it, just in case."

Ishmael split the remainder into two piles: one for sea and one for sky. Hannah and Lilith took the vials for the sea and walked over to the water's edge. They dumped vial after vial into the water, dropping the empty ones back into the basket. When they drained all of their vials, they joined Ishmael and Jacob, dipping swabs, scooping out the color, and blowing it into the heavens.

After two vials' worth of blowing, Hannah stopped to stretch her jaw. "My cheeks are sore," she said. A wind suddenly appeared that ruffled the twist of fabric holding back her hair. Hannah looked in the direction of the gust.

Ishmael raised his swab into the wind and watched as the breeze carried the color away.

"Brilliant," Jacob said.

Hannah's eyes brightened when she realized what Ishmael had done. "Thaddeus. Of course. He was carrying the wind when he came in."

"Collaboration does have its benefits," Ishmael said. They smiled at each other, and Ishmael called to Thaddeus.

Thaddeus, standing farther down on the shoreline, paused. Ishmael grabbed the basket of vials and hurried toward him. Hannah and the others followed.

Thaddeus's thumb and forefinger pinched the neck of the skin bag. "Is the wind too strong for you? I had hoped it would have a rolling grace."

Ishmael put down the basket of vials. "Actually, the wind can help us."

"Help?"

"It moved the color."

"Really?" The skin bag bobbed in Thaddeus's hand as the breeze played with it.

"Do you mind if we work near you? So we can use the wind?" Hannah said.

Thaddeus shrugged. "Sure. I don't mind."

Ishmael handed out vials. They each held swabs up in the air while the wind nudged the color off. Specks of blue swirled, lifting up into the expanse until they could no longer see them.

Thaddeus watched what they were doing with interest. "So that's what Color Master meant."

Hannah paused. "What?"

"She told me once that color is a wave and that it responds to other waves."

"You see the color?"

"Not exactly. But I see the waves in the air—the currents—and they seem more solid somehow." He grinned. "And they definitely have a rolling grace."

When the last vial was emptied, they laid it to rest, nestled among the other vials.

"I guess that's it," Ishmael said. After all that worry, this seemed strangely disappointing. It was done, for good or for bad, and he could do nothing to change the outcome. "Thank you."

"My pleasure." Thaddeus cinched up the skin bag and turned to leave, the bag flapping empty at his side.

Lilith gathered up the basket of empty vials and the bag of swabs. Ishmael looked out into the water, searching for a sign of blue, but saw nothing. "The color we had wasn't enough to make even the smallest change," he said. This was nothing like dappling the tower room, or even like releasing the light. There was nothing here.

"Give it some time," Jacob said.

Ishmael shook his head. "I don't even see where it was dumped in."

The four began walking back toward the hall.

"What's done is done, and now we need to think about what comes next," Hannah said.

Ishmael didn't respond. The morning had drained his spirit. His head and heart were as empty as Thaddeus's flapping bag, as empty as the vials clinking in their baskets. If he had to think about what came next, he could no longer be empty. He'd have to fill himself with thoughts and with emotion and with worry.

"So . . ." Lilith nudged him with her elbow. "What is next?"

Ishmael sighed. "We tell the Hall of Sound we're done."

"And after that?" Jacob said.

"We color the foundation."

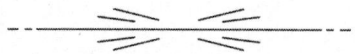

At supper that night, Michael sought out Ishmael. "I made all the adjustments. It's ready now. You want to try it in the posticum?"

"I don't think we can use it," Ishmael said.

Michael looked crestfallen. "Why not?"

"The posticum is just so huge. It's going to take a massive amount of light to color it. Besides, none of the other novices want to. They think we'll get in trouble for breaking the rules of creation."

The disappointed look on Michael's face made Ishmael say, "But we can at least try it when Ethan tells me the foundation is ready. No one can object to that."

"Ethan told me he's almost done. Do you want to meet me in the posticum tomorrow morning before breakfast?"

Ishmael looked around to see if anyone had overheard their conversation. "I'll be there."

Michael grinned and hurried to the Manufactory table where he piled his plate high, well satisfied.

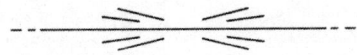

That evening, Ishmael flopped on his cot with a heavy sigh.

Thomas lifted his head from his pillow. "I heard things didn't go so well this afternoon."

"That's an understatement." Ishmael drew a deep breath.

Jacob rolled over to face Thomas. "It didn't look like we added *any* color. It looked as blank when we finished as when we began."

Hearing the words hurt, but they were the truth. Ishmael couldn't deny it.

Matthew hiccupped from the far side of the room.

"*The best of the thirty-six plans is to run away.* You're not going back home yet, are you?"

Ishmael glared at Thomas.

"So what are we going to do?" Matthew asked.

"I'll figure something out," Ishmael said. "In the meantime, we have to carry on as best we can." He would just have to hope that Color Master returned quickly with a large supply of light or that Michael's machine actually worked.

"Well," Matthew said, "maybe tomorrow will be better."

"Maybe." What Ishmael didn't say was that he was worried that tomorrow might actually be worse.

CHAPTER

39

Ishmael snuck out of the dormitory before dawn and hurried to the posticum, where he met Michael holding the contraption in his arms. It now featured a few more openings, as well as a rather tall tripod. Michael fairly bounced with excitement.

When they walked through the entry into the Jubilee posticum, Michael looked around in amazement. "Ethan's done nice work. Look at how level the land is." He bent down to run his fingers through the gravel at their feet, then studied where water met ground. "And that shoreline. Nicely done, indeed."

Ishmael felt a pang of jealousy. "I wish I could appreciate Ethan's work like you do."

"I could teach you the fundamentals of Manufactory when this is all done if you want."

"I'd like that."

"Let's set up over there." Michael pointed to an innocuous place at the edge of the wall.

Ishmael helped Michael attach the machine to the tripod, then pulled out his prism, ready to catch the flash of light that was sure to come.

Michael slid open the door.

The light burst out in a clean flash, and Ishmael caught a spectrum. He held it there, stunned by the beauty of the colors in this still-stark place. "If this works—"

"*If* this works? You saw the light from it just now. Of course it works! But I can't say it won't look somewhat different from color spread by hand, since I can't see that."

Ishmael began flicking specks of green onto the foundation. He had forgotten how much patience the process took. He fell into a meditative rhythm dappling, covering the land in the lightest flecks of green. It seemed miraculous—Ishmael wondered why he could see the specks of green now when he couldn't see even the slightest bit of blue before when they colored the water and the heavens. Perhaps it was the machine. Or perhaps it was the ground itself.

The spectrum began to fade, and he realized he needed more light. "Can we try some more?"

"Sure. We can work until breakfast if you want to—no one knows I'm here." Michael slid the panel open, allowing another flash of light to escape. Ishmael caught it with his prism and the spectrum blazed. Ishmael's thoughts turned to Luc, and without realizing it, he began flicking specks of yellow. He almost wished

Luc were here so he could see what they were doing. He dotted the ground, overlaying the green with yellow. Ishmael wondered briefly if the colors would mix and turn yellow-green, but he quickly dismissed the thought. They hadn't mixed in the tower room.

Ishmael relished the thought of surprising all of the novices. What would they say when they saw this? What would Color Master say? He laughed just thinking of it. When the spectrum began to fade again, Ishmael tried a third color, indigo. The indigo was delightful, though not quite the perfect complement to the yellow, nor the perfect analogous color to green. It was complex, though, and Ishmael was pleased with the effect.

Michael walked along the shoreline, restless.

As the morning broke, the indigo, orange, and violet of dawn covered the sky. Ishmael looked out to the water and was surprised by the faintest touch of blue. He stared at the water, and the blue grew stronger as the light brightened. He looked at the sky. The dawn colors had faded to blue. Blue everywhere. His heart lifted at the sight.

Everything would work out. The test section had turned out far better than Ishmael had dreamed of, and he saw no reason to stop. In that instant, Ishmael made a snap decision that he should finish the foundation immediately.

"Why don't you get some breakfast?" Ishmael called to Michael. "I think I have the hang of this . . ."

"And you weren't sure this would work!" Michael laughed as he headed out with a wave.

Ishmael knew the work ahead of him was substantial, but it gave him a thrill to imagine the entire foundation dappled. His simple plan had morphed into something much more complex, much more beautiful, much more satisfying, and he couldn't wait to see it finished.

CHAPTER

40

That evening, a ravenous but triumphant Ishmael made his way to the refectory for dinner. He met the novices at the door.

"Where were you all day?" Thomas asked. "Ethan was looking for you. And we made swabs until we ran out of twigs and were forced to whittle feathers down into quills. I've got blisters to prove it." Thomas held out his left hand, fat blisters on knuckle and thumb.

Ishmael stifled a yawn. "I was working in the posticum."

"Without us?" Hannah said, a trace of hurt in her voice.

Ishmael didn't realize Hannah would be upset. "I have a surprise for you. You know how you thought dappling would be too hard?"

"*Thomas* and *Jacob* thought dappling would be too hard.

The rest of us thought dappling would be against the rules," Lilith corrected.

"What did you do, Ishmael?" Rebekah asked, a note of alarm in her voice.

Ishmael began to have a feeling that they might not like his surprise until they actually saw it, so he said no more. "I'll show you later. Right now, I'm so hungry I could eat the entire Hall of Gustation."

The warmth of the refectory welcomed them, and the novices took their seats. Conversation was sparse during dinner. Ishmael spent the time shoveling food in because the faster he ate, the faster he could show them his work. Not everyone was so enthusiastic, though. Thomas and Jacob had seconds.

When they were finally done, Ishmael hopped up. "Come see." He led the way out of the refectory to the posticum entrance, imagining their surprise and admiration.

It was true they were surprised as soon as they stepped foot in the posticum—but the biggest surprise was reserved for Ishmael. The group stopped short just inside the entrance, confused at the sight that met them. There were no dapples, no speckles of color anywhere. There were no individual colors, except for the blue in the sky and the water.

The foundation, once speckled with each of the colors, was now a solid dark shade. All the colors had merged together. It was a shade that Ishmael—and the rest of the other novices—had never seen before. Michael's contraption sat a little to the side, seeming very out of place.

"*The gift of nuts to toothless people is no gift at all,*" Thomas muttered.

"What did you do?" Hannah said, her voice sounding very small in the vast expanse.

Instead of answering her, Ishmael knelt down and ran his hand over the ground. "I don't understand." He picked up a handful of the dirt as if expecting to see the individual colors speckling each grain. But there was only the single shade of dark, and he let the dirt slip through his fingers. "That's not how it looked when I left it." He looked up at the other novices. "It was just like what I showed you in the tower room."

Jacob raised his eyebrows. "It's not like that now."

"How could you have done this without telling us?" Lilith said.

Ishmael shook his head. "It was supposed to be different."

"Yes, we were supposed to work on it together."

"No, I mean it was supposed to be all the colors."

"That's not the point. The point is that you did this without us. We're a spectrum," Lilith said. "Or we're supposed to be."

With that, she pivoted and walked off, trailing a cloud of disappointment and hurt feelings. The others followed her, except for Hannah. Hannah picked at the hem of her tunic. "I know you meant well."

"It was different before, I swear!"

Hannah looked out at the landscape. "The color isn't the problem. Lilith is upset because you did this without her—without any of us."

Ishmael knelt down again and scooped up some of the dirt. "Everything should have been different." He turned back to Hannah. "I don't understand what happened."

"Maybe Luc could tell you."

Ishmael's heart sank, knowing she was right.

Hannah made a small movement with her head, took a deep breath. "I did some research earlier about the astronomae."

"Why?" Something in the tone of her voice alarmed Ishmael.

"We need more light, and the need will be constant for some time to come."

"But Michael knows how to filter and condense the light here!"

Hannah looked down at the foundation. "I'm not so sure. Even the light the apprentices gather might not be enough to help with the Jubilee posticum, and it definitely won't be enough to build up the stores of color. Think about it, Ishmael. It will take years to gather enough color for another posticum."

"What are you saying?"

"I'm going to ask to train with them and harvest light instead of color."

Ishmael thought he might fall through the foundation of the posticum. "But what about our spectrum? Who will be the steward of blue?" He pointed to the sleeve of her uniform. A splotch of blue remained from when they colored the waters yesterday.

"There won't be any blue to be steward of if I don't go. I *have* to do this." Hannah appeared unmovable. "I can't stay here, knowing I could do something about the lack of light if only I were willing. Not when I *am* willing."

"You sound like Lilith," he said. "Please don't leave yet. Wait at least until the posticum is finished."

She tapped a finger on the stone next to her. "I can't."

"You can't?" Ishmael repeated. "You just want to go off to be some hero." Ishmael's voice spiraled up.

Hannah stood, her chin lifted to an angry angle. "Is that what you think?"

Ishmael slumped. "No." He picked up a small stone and tossed it back and forth between his hands. Part of him wanted to throw it as far as he could.

Hannah curled her arms around her waist. "I'm not doing this for glory."

He could tell she had been hurt by his response. Ishmael wished he could take back his words, but all he could do was replace them. "I need your help with this posticum."

"You didn't seem to think you needed our help today."

"I thought this plan would be the solution to our problems. I wanted to prove that I can do this . . . I'm sorry, I really am."

She nodded and they stood there without speaking, just staring out at the blue sea.

Ishmael didn't know what else to say. Hannah didn't, either. She uncurled her arms, rubbed her hands together, and left.

Ishmael turned to watch her as she walked to the posticum exit. Her shoulders drooped, and the bounce she usually had in her step was gone. He wished she would turn around. If she turned around, he would know that everything would be fine. If she turned around, he could say something more, something important. He could apologize again, and maybe she wouldn't go.

But Hannah kept walking. She reached the entrance and passed through, and then she was out of Ishmael's sight.

Ishmael stood up, each part of his body aching. How could this have gone so wrong? He needed an ally right now, someone on his side. He needed a brother.

CHAPTER

41

It was late, but Ishmael tracked Luc down in the nearly empty workroom, staring into a spectrum.

Luc looked up when Ishmael walked in. "Brother of mine," he said without a trace of emotion.

Ishmael licked his lips, suddenly nervous. "Luc," he said.

Luc raised an eyebrow and waited silently for Ishmael to speak.

"I think, that is, we all think . . . Without Color Master here . . . I need . . ." Ishmael slumped against a workbench, and his words faded into silence.

"You need my help?"

Luc's tone was so understanding that Ishmael almost believed he had been forgiven, that Luc had returned to being the older brother Ishmael had known and loved all these years.

"Please. I don't know what to do."

"About what?"

"Come see the posticum."

Ishmael explained what he and Michael had done while they walked to the posticum. When they arrived, Luc studied the foundation.

"It was supposed to be like what you and I did in the tower room. And it was—at least it was when I left before dinner. But something must have happened."

"Your colors mixed," Luc said, kneeling down to study the foundation. "You made a new color."

"But how? This didn't happen in the tower room."

"The walls—the surface of stone—already has color so the dappled colors can't permeate it. This," Luc pointed to the foundation, "was colorless, so the colors soaked in and mixed together. While the color is nice—deep and rich—I'm afraid you're going to have to contend with Color Master. I don't think she'll take kindly to you associating with apprentices from other Halls." Luc touched Michael's contraption. "Especially when she finds out he was doing your work."

"But he wasn't doing my work! He just gave me the light—"

"It's not the way things are done here," Luc interrupted.

Ishmael was desperate. "Is there anything I can do? Can I pull the colors back out—like with the second law of color? Make a spectrum and let them separate?"

Luc shook his head. "It's kind of hard to fix something that covers the whole foundation."

"I'm doomed." Ishmael slumped down.

Luc walked a few paces, then said slowly, "Not necessarily."

"No?" Ishmael clung to a shred of hope.

"What if you covered the foundation with trees and bushes and plants? That way you could hide the new color, and Color Master will never have to know."

"But I'd need hundreds and hundreds of plants and trees to cover the foundation," Ishmael said with dismay.

"It's up to you, little brother. But I know what I'd do." Luc walked off, his hands in his pockets.

The problem was that Ishmael *didn't* know what he should do. He liked the new color. It was warm. It was comforting. It held most of the colors, except blue. Seen against the blue of the sky, Ishmael felt like the spectrum was complete. But would Color Master be angry about the way he colored the foundation? Luc thought so, and if Luc thought so, he must be right. Ishmael didn't want to face her anger. Luc's anger had been bad enough; he couldn't possibly face anyone else's.

CHAPTER

42

T he next morning, he found plans from the Shape artisan lying on his worktable.

"These were delivered yesterday," Matthew said. "From Shape."

Ishmael fingered through page after page showing diagrams of trees and plants, some tall and spiky, some squat and fat, some round and bulbous, but all with the same pattern of roots, stem, and leaves.

Several of them looked familiar. Ishmael could see influences from the trees and plants at home. One tree had cascades of branches flowing down to the ground. Others showed flowers and fruit hanging from stems and branches and vines.

"So now what? Or do you need to consult with your assistant from the Hall of Manufactory first?" Jacob asked.

Ishmael tried to ignore the sarcasm in Jacob's voice. He knew

Jacob felt like Ishmael had betrayed their spectrum when he dappled the foundation with Michael, but there wasn't much he could do about it now. He could only add it to the list of good intentions gone awry. Ishmael studied the forms of the plants and trees. Maybe Luc was right.

"Luc suggested that we cover the foundation entirely with trees and plants. If we have enough, and if we cover all those trees and plants with green, you won't see much, if any, of the mixed color underneath," Ishmael said.

"You're going to hide the color?" Lilith asked.

"I don't want to get in trouble with Color Master."

"It's a little late for that, isn't it?" Jacob said.

"And we won't have enough green," said Matthew. "That is, if you're using the green that's already distilled."

"You're right, I don't think we have enough green right *now*, but if all the light that Color Master brings back is distilled into green—that should be enough. And don't worry, I'm not going to chance using anything but distilled color." Ishmael grabbed his slate and chalk, and began scribbling numbers on it. He tapped the chalk on the slate. "You know, I think we might just be able to do it. We'll need about ten to fifteen more vials, though."

"That might be possible." Lilith looked around at the others. "How should we apply the color?"

"Quills would take too long, and swabs just wouldn't work. See?" Ishmael held out the plans from the Hall of Shape.

Jacob nodded. "Too much detail."

"Maybe dusters?" Lilith said.

They looked at her blankly.

"They're like sifters, but on a much bigger scale."

"How do you know this?" Ishmael asked.

"I read up on other methods of coloration after we saw Luc's posticum."

Ishmael decided to ask Ethan for more flora to cover the foundation.

And then? Well, they'd just have to work quickly to color it all.

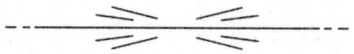

Ishmael walked through the entryway into the workroom of the Hall of Manufactory and looked around, appalled. Stuff was everywhere: most of it was piled up in the middle of the floor, some spilled off workbenches, and some crowded the shelves. But the sight confirmed his plan for the posticum: he could barely see the floor for all the stuff that was on top of it. If there were enough trees and plants, the ground of the posticum would be covered.

Ethan sat at his drafting table, surrounded by parchment. Below him were wadded-up balls of paper. "Ishmael!" Ethan said, sitting up so quickly that he nearly tipped over his stool. "How goes your work on the posticum?"

Ishmael grimaced. "I wonder if you could adjust the plan a bit?"

Ethan set his pencil down and swung his legs around to face Ishmael. "Do you need fewer plants?"

"Actually, I wanted to see if you could cover the foundation with more flora than are in the plans."

Ethan crinkled his eyebrows. "More? I figured we'd build only two of each kind of vegetation because of the color shortage. We were going to send over most of the flora this afternoon."

Ishmael shook his head. "I'd rather have the foundation covered. Can you do that?"

"Yes, but are you sure?"

"I'm sure."

"If you think that's best." Ethan picked up his pencil again. "I'll let you know when we're done."

"Thanks." As Ishmael left, he heard Ethan directing the other Manufactory apprentices to make more leaves and stems.

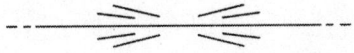

Dozens of carts rolled over the courtyard stones pushed by the Manufactory apprentices. If Thaddeus, the Motion apprentice, had been watching from the tower above, it would have looked like a mass exodus, a caravan of epic proportions. He would have thrilled to see the movement, but he wasn't watching. He was in the Hall workroom, thinking about Dora, the girl from the Hall of Shape, who walked with a rolling grace that captivated him.

Down in the courtyard, there were few people to witness the carts delivering the flora to the posticum. The carts bumped over the uneven surface, jostling the flora inside, setting the leaves quivering. Burlap-wrapped trees and bushes and plants, shovels and spades, were all bound for the posticum. This was going to take some time, but soon the foundation would be covered.

SHAPE

Several days later, Dora walked across the courtyard with a spring in her step. She carried nothing. Empty hands, empty fingers. No pencil, no paper, no round-handled basket. The emptiness was a new feeling, a curious feeling since she had been tied to the plans for the Jubilee posticum for days now. She had been working on a long-necked land animal whose neck was much too long for its legs. It would never balance. The geometry of it was not right. Too much line, not enough circle. Dora needed a break.

Also, she needed to confirm that the Hall of Manufactory had followed her designs with the flora, that there were large areas of merriefield, a tiny, low-growing plant with three circular leaves, as well as smaller plots of the less-detailed, spiky tallgrass in the posticum.

If she were honest, though, she had an even more profound reason for checking the posticum. It was a reason that had been blossoming in her mind over the past week, ever since that Manufactory apprentice talked to her. He had told her about his hope to collaborate, to help the Hall of Hue, but at the time, she had been miffed because of what he had done to her hexagon at the challenge, and she sent him off, saying she didn't understand what he meant. His words had stayed with her, though, and she began thinking about how all the pieces of creation fit together.

Dora loved the principles of Shape, and she knew she could design shapes well, but without the efforts of the other Halls, the shapes she made would be pretty hollow. Where would the Hall of Shape be without Manufactory? The output from the Hall of Shape would only be drawings on a page without the skills of Manufactory. Likewise, where would Manufactory and Shape be without the Hall of Motion? Their shapes would be stiff and stagnant. And the other Halls? Undoubtedly, their work had to be part of one great whole.

As she walked along, she realized that just as Shape was dependent upon Manufactory and Motion, the work of the other Halls was dependent upon the Hall of Shape. She had a responsibility to Scent, Sound, and Gustation in the structures Shape created for them.

Hue was different, though. Hue didn't need separate structures for their work; they overlaid it upon what already existed. There were no specks or splinters Shape needed to design for Hue. Nor did they need Hue to add to their designs.

The Shape apprentice stopped walking.

If Shape wasn't dependent on Hue and Hue wasn't dependent on Shape, then they could help or hinder each other at will. They could be allies for no reason other than sheer goodness.

That was a beautiful thought.

It excited her, and she began walking toward the posticum again. Dora thought of the Hue artisan. Over the past few days, she had watched his shape change as his shoulders sagged more and more under the burden of responsibility he carried. She herself could do something more to help him, couldn't she? She had already made the water cover the majority of the land to help, but Michael must have thought there was something she could do since he had approached her. She didn't know the first thing about color—she only knew shape, but she would find some way.

By that time, she reached the wall surrounding the posticum. It was all she could do to keep from charging in, but she placed her fingertip on the stones, tracing their shapes and the lines between them in order to calm herself. She stretched out the moment of anticipation until she couldn't bear it anymore, then ducked through the archway.

Though she had worked on the merriefield drawings for days, she wasn't prepared for the reality of the sight. She found herself utterly entranced by the curving pathway through trees leading down to the water. It was neither line nor circle, but somehow both. She paused to look for the low-growing plants, and there they were, clumped in masses underneath the trees. Farther on, she saw fields of the grasses ruffled by the wind. Yes, it was exactly as she wanted.

Ethan, the Manufactory artisan, stood by the water. He held a small tool in his hands, which he twisted and turned while he waited.

She called out to him, and he spun around, a friendly smile on his face.

"Is the flora acceptable?" he asked, walking to her.

"It's lovely."

"I'm pleased with it myself. If it passes your inspection, I'll notify the Hue artisan to let him know it's his turn."

The Shape apprentice lifted her head. "I'll take the message, if you'd like. You must have other things to do?" Maybe this was the opportunity she needed to discover how she could help Ishmael.

He laughed. "You wouldn't mind? I have a list of things to do about a mile long. Adding this extra flora set my schedule back."

"I won't be missed," she said. Not for the short amount of time it would take to walk to the Hall of Hue and deliver a message. She could look at the Hue artisan's face, study its shapes and its planes, and see if the answer to her question of how to help lay in its lines and its curves.

They left the posticum together, heading toward the corner where the Hall of Hue and the Hall of Manufactory met.

"Ishmael really asked for more flora?"

"He did indeed. It's funny—no one from the other Halls has ever requested a change in the plans. But then again, I suppose no one from the other Halls has ever been in a situation like the Hall of Hue. Thanks again." He stuffed the device into his pocket, and they separated at the entrance to the Hall of Hue.

She linked her fingers together and walked to the workroom, nervous excitement shooting through her. She peeked through the door, taking stock of all the shapes in the room. The long, rounded glass vials; the squat stone jars; the wide, flat worktables. It pleased her.

She spotted Ishmael in the midst. The Shape apprentice was more determined than ever to be an ally to the Hall of Hue. "Excuse me?" She knocked on the door.

Ishmael looked up. He recognized Dora and smiled. It seemed like a million years ago that she competed in the order and chaos challenge.

"Ethan asked me to deliver a message."

He rose from his bent-over position into a straight line, and it made Dora want to encase Ishmael in a protective circle. "Ethan said to tell you he was done with the trees."

The roundness of relief and then lines of apprehension played over his face, one after the other, and he said, "Already?"

"Was that sooner than you had expected?" she asked, taking a step closer.

"Yes."

"But why did you ask for so many more trees? I thought you were running out of color."

Worry lined his face. "I am. You wouldn't understand. You're not from Hue. It's complicated, and I don't have time to explain."

Her jaw dropped open into a small oval—a circle that had been squashed—when she realized what he had done with those four small sentences. He had started with a conclusion—a dot—that he drew out into a line and then another line, line after line until he had boxed her up and labeled her as a member of the Hall of Shape, incapable of being or thinking or doing anything else.

She looked away, only to notice that the other Hue novices had stopped their work and were staring at her. This was not going the way she had hoped. "Just because I'm not from Hue doesn't mean that I don't understand complicated things or that I can't help."

The Shape apprentice turned and left. So much for goodwill. So much for being allies.

As Dora walked away, she wondered if that's what she had done with Michael when he had asked for her help: boxed him up and labeled him a Manufactory apprentice, incapable of anything except following directions and building things. Overcome by shame, she realized that's exactly what she had done.

When she reached the Great Courtyard from the Hall of Hue, a gust of wind swirled around her, blowing away all of the dots and lines and shapes confining her. It made her catch her breath as it pushed her onto the stones surrounding the fountain. She sat down hard. When she pulled her hair away from her face, an unusual sight caught her eye. In front of her, a spiral of dust twisted in the air, going around and around. She stared at it, mesmerized.

"What are you looking at?" a voice asked her.

Without turning her head, she pointed toward the spiral of dust. "The shape . . . it's so fluid. It's neither circle nor line."

The breeze died, and the dust fell to the ground. She finally turned toward the voice.

It was the Motion artisan, Thaddeus. He had kind eyes and hair that stood up in every direction. The shapes she could find just in his hair! It made her smile.

"Did you want to see it again?" he asked, the waves embroidered on his uniform pocket rippling merrily.

"Yes, but . . . the wind dropped."

Even as she spoke, the wind swirled around her again. She looked at the Motion apprentice. He had a sly look on his face.

"You did that?"

He smiled. "Beginner's stuff in the Hall of Motion." He lifted his hand and the dust began to swirl.

CHAPTER
43

O nce Dora informed Ishmael that the trees were done, he called a halt to the novices' work and led everyone to the posticum to see the trees and plants they would be coloring the next day. The sight was astounding. Trees covered the mixed color of the foundation, so that in some places it hardly showed. Every place they turned was lush with vegetation.

Lilith stood, jaw slack, helpless at the sight.

"*Where there are many hens, the people eat eggs,*" Thomas said. "And where there are many trees, the Hall of Hue covers them in green."

"We'll never be able to color all of these using swabs and sifters!" Rebekah put her head onto Jacob's shoulder and he put his arm around her awkwardly.

What *had* he done? Ishmael looked out over the landscape.

There were so many trees. So many, many trees. No wonder Dora had asked him why he had asked for more trees. This was insanity.

The next morning, Ishmael and the novices made their way to the posticum. They brought a cart containing all the vials of color, and each carried a basket of swabs and sifters. Luc came, too, his first time working with the novices in the posticum. How grateful Ishmael was for Luc's support now. Luc looked eager, almost excited. Ishmael figured it was because he looked forward to working in a posticum again.

The more Ishmael looked at Luc, the more unsettled he became. Luc's demeanor was odd, almost as if he expected something. As if he *knew* something. Apprehension made Ishmael move faster toward the posticum. He burst through the archway, catching himself on the stones for balance.

The trees were still there. The trees were everywhere, as far as the eye could see. Trees blocked the view to the blue water. Trees blocked the blue sky.

And those trees were slowly turning the dark color of the foundation. From the bottom up, the dark color was soaking into the trunks, making its way upward toward the leaves.

The novices hurried in behind him.

"This," Matthew said, "is not good."

Thomas muttered, "*The end is the crown of any work.*"

"Oh, be quiet, Thomas," Lilith said. "That's not useful right now."

The basket of sifters swung from Rebekah's wrist. "What should we do?" she asked, the shock registering on her face.

Ishmael looked at Luc.

"It's too late for you to do anything," Luc said, smiling. "The color is easing its way through the tree trunks and will reach the leaves by this time next week. Your posticum—or should I say, *my* posticum—is going to have a single color, just like I wanted."

Ishmael turned to his brother, agape. "You told me to do this because you wanted it this way?"

Luc patted the trunk of the tree nearest to him. "If I couldn't have a replica of my own posticum, I wanted something close. Though the heavens and the waters are blue, the rest of the posticum will be this one shade."

"This posticum is supposed to have all the colors."

"It does," Luc said with glee. "They're just mixed together." Ishmael felt sick.

"The color is already moving along. But you haven't learned that function of color yet, have you? Not even the fastest color keeper could color the tops of the trees in time." Luc laughed. "My work is done," he said as he turned and walked out of the posticum.

Shock paralyzed Ishmael for only a moment. He turned to Lilith, eyes wide. "He tricked me."

"What are we going to do?" Jacob asked.

Ishmael grabbed a vial of green out of his basket. "I've got to talk to Michael. Start with the sifters on the low parts. All of you! I'll be back as soon as I can."

"Michael?" Ishmael stood at the entrance to the Hall of Manufactory, his hands shaking and his breath coming in gasps.

Ethan saw him first. "What's wrong?"

"I need help."

To Ethan's credit, he said nothing, but guided Ishmael to a back corner, grabbing Michael on the way. Ishmael hadn't had the heart to tell Michael the colors mixed right after it happened, so he filled them in, then finished with, "I don't know if it was the light, or the fact that I used all the colors in one sitting, but I've got to stop this. The posticum *must* have all the colors represented."

Ethan thought for a moment. "What if we built a machine that could speed the color work?"

Ishmael's eyes were still wild, panic-stricken. "You'd never finish it in time. Luc said we have by next week until the color permeates everything, and we've got miles of land to cover."

Michael looked at Ethan, and said, "Nozzle, compression chamber, pump?"

"Exactly." Ethan turned to Ishmael. "Look, leave that to us. Do what you can manually and we'll meet you at the posticum as soon as possible with some mechanical help."

Though Ishmael knew they had good intentions, he had

little hope that they could do anything. There had to be some other way. Ishmael loved color—all color—and he couldn't allow Luc to make another world that had no diversity of color. Though it might kill him, Ishmael vowed to get those treetops green so this posticum would have the full spectrum of colors.

Instead of returning to the posticum immediately, he ran to the library in the Hall of Hue, hoping to find a faster way of spreading the color. He realized he still clutched a vial of green in his hands, so he carefully slid it into a long, thin pocket in his tunic.

When he arrived at the library, he found Phoebe standing at the top of a rolling ladder, wiping dust from the shelves of books on the upper tier. "I thought you'd be at the posticum today," she said.

"Quick! Do you know where books on coloration methods are?"

"I think I saw books about coloration over there." She pointed below, one shelf over. "Can't help but read the titles as I'm dusting, you know?"

"Thanks." Ishmael went to the shelf and grabbed a pile of books. He paged through, seeing direct transfer, indirect transfer, multiple layering. He didn't understand half of what he read, but nothing looked applicable. Nothing looked fast.

Phoebe's voice spiraled up and around and around while she dusted, background noise to Ishmael's rising anxiety.

He closed the book, and pulled the vial of green from his pocket. There must be a better way. He lifted the stopper from the vial and peered inside, hoping to get some inspiration.

He didn't. Ishmael picked up the stopper, ready to cap the vial, but paused. The color in the vial quivered.

"Phoebe, come here," he asked her.

She stopped singing, descended the ladder, and walked toward him.

"Never mind," he said. "It stopped."

She shrugged, then picked up the dust cloth again, immediately launching back into her vocal exercises as she ascended the ladder.

It happened again. Ishmael stared. The color in the vial seemed to move to Phoebe's song.

He watched as she kept singing. The green rose. When it reached the rim, it danced up and over, hitting his fingers before he stoppered the vial.

"Phoebe!"

She jumped. "What? Are you never going to let me finish dusting?"

"You—you made the color move!"

"That's ridiculous. I can't even *see* the color."

"Not you, your song. Sing again."

She sang a pattern of notes as Ishmael unstopped the vial.

He nodded. "See? Argh. No, you can't see. Trust me, the color is moving when you sing!"

She stopped singing again, and the color sank back into the vial.

Could it be possible?

"Give me your dust cloth," Ishmael said, setting it on the

table in front of him. "I want to try something. Will you sing again?"

"I guess so." She began making funny noises deep in her throat. "Warm-up exercises," she said and made a few more of the noises.

Then she opened her mouth slightly and sound came out, quietly at first, then louder and louder until reverberations from the sound shook him. The sensation was curious—so different from the singing she usually did while she cleaned.

Color lifted out of the vial and hung in the air, a thin vapor of green. It danced through the air and touched the rag, staining it.

"How can this be?" Ishmael whispered. Color was subject to direct manipulation—you had to move it by hand, by swab, by quill, by wrap, by brush, by any number of means that Ishmael didn't even know about. It couldn't move on its own unless directed. And yet, here was green on Phoebe's cleaning rag, and he hadn't moved it.

Phoebe wasn't even a member of their Hall. She couldn't *see* the color, let alone have the skills to move color. Could it be that color was subject to will? To song? To something else entirely?

She stopped singing when Ishmael picked up the rag, not trusting what he had seen. He opened the rag, stretched it out, and turned it over and over in his hands. The green had transferred. He laughed.

"What's funny?"

"Not funny, just . . . unbelievable!" he said. "The rag is colored, through and through." Ishmael pinched the corners of the cloth, holding it up for her to see. "You colored this." He handed it to her, and she balled it up, ready to dust again.

"No—you can't dust yet. This is amazing! Are there others from your Hall who could do this?" he asked.

She looked at him like he was a dunce. "That was just a vocal exercise on dynamics—it's one of the first lessons that we learn."

"Dynamics?" Ishmael asked.

"How loud or soft the sound is."

Ishmael nodded his head. He didn't understand what dynamics were, but the rag had been colorless, and now it was green. "And the other Sound novices could do this?" he asked.

She nodded. Ishmael was so happy that he surprised them both by hugging her. Just as quickly, he released her. "Sorry!"

Phoebe backed away from him and crossed her arms. "What is going on?"

"I think you may have solved one of my problems. Come with me."

"But what about the cleaning?"

"Oh, hang the cleaning! This is more important."

He grabbed the vial of green and raced out of the library toward the posticum, Phoebe trailing behind him.

CHAPTER

44

An uncharacteristic smudge of green snaked across Lilith's cheek. A cloud of green hung in the air over her, and puffs of green came from farther afield where Jacob, Matthew, Thomas, and Rebekah worked.

"Where have you been, Ishmael?" She looked annoyed with him. Before Ishmael could answer, Lilith turned to Phoebe. "And what are you doing here?"

"I've come to help," Phoebe said.

Lilith put her hands on her hips. "You can't even see color. How are you going to help?"

"I found a new way to color the leaves," Ishmael said. "I want to show everyone together."

Lilith pushed her hair off her face, leaving behind yet another streak of green on her forehead. "Another experiment? Really, Ishmael? We don't have time for this."

"I know, but this will make the work go faster." Ishmael called for the others.

They weren't far, and Ishmael heard irritation in their voices as they approached.

"I had just gotten to the top of that tree when you called," Jacob said. "What do you want?"

"Phoebe has something to show you. She's come to help." He nodded at Phoebe.

"Right now?" she asked.

Ishmael pulled the vial of green from his pocket. "Anybody have a swab?"

Jacob handed him a swab from his pocket.

"Wait. Where's Hannah?"

"I think she went to the far side of the posticum," Jacob said. "She probably couldn't hear you call."

Disappointed by Hannah's absence, Ishmael dipped the swab into the green and held it up. "Go ahead," he said to Phoebe. "Sing."

She opened her mouth and began to sing. The sound eased the green off Ishmael's swab. The color swirled through the air, twirling and jumping, until it landed on a low leaf of the nearest tree.

Ishmael couldn't help but be thrilled at the sight. Lilith's jaw dropped. Phoebe sang until Lilith walked over to the leaf and touched the spot of green, rubbing her thumb gently over the ridges of the leaf. The green stayed. Phoebe's voice trailed off as Lilith looked at her in amazement.

Just then, Michael burst through the trees, holding a contraption that looked just as strange as the last one. "I've got it!" he declared.

No one noticed.

"Did I just see that?" Rebekah asked. Ishmael nodded.

"See what?" Michael asked.

"Phoebe, did you—? The color—?" Lilith said.

Phoebe nodded also, and Lilith let out a whoop of joy. Jacob picked up Phoebe and swung her around.

"*The song of the heart brings joy to the hearer,*" Thomas said.

Matthew twisted his fingers through a narrower belt he wore around his waist, tightening it, and Jacob broke out into the widest grin Ishmael had ever seen.

"Wait! What did she do?" Michael said, looking from one to the other.

"Do it again!" Lilith said.

"Do *what* again?" Poor Michael had no idea what had happened. "Ishmael, tell me what's going on."

Ishmael held out a vial of green. "Her song moves color."

Michael's eyes lit up, and he beamed at Phoebe.

Lilith held the vial, and Phoebe began to sing again. The green rose in a cloud, swirling around them and growing denser as Phoebe's song grew louder. It kept coming, pouring forth, and as Ishmael watched the cloud strengthen, he realized he had no idea just how powerful this could be.

The green hovered.

Ishmael squeezed Phoebe's arm, watching the green sway and shift. There was a terrifying beauty in the power of her song as it led each particle of green up, floating, into the sky—a beauty that he could never have anticipated.

Phoebe straightened her shoulders and dug down into the ground with her heels, as if she could harness power from the foundation, filter it through her feet and legs and torso, and give voice to that power. Ishmael could see the effort it cost her, straining her voice. The sound dipped, then jumped, and her voice soared.

The green rose again, blotting out the copse of trees nearest them. Phoebe kept singing, and the wave of green draped itself upon the crowns of both the small, young trees as well as the larger trees from the topmost leaves all the way down to the roots sticking up out of the foundation. In a moment, about twenty of the closest trees in the copse were covered in green, trunks and leaves.

Lilith touched Phoebe lightly on her shoulder and nodded. Phoebe stopped singing and gasped for air, breathless from the exertion. She put her hand out and leaned on one of the trees. After a minute, she sank to the ground.

Thomas, Lilith, and Ishmael followed. Matthew walked over to a leaf and touched it.

Michael, still beaming and blind to the near-disaster, said, "Did she do it again?"

"What just happened, Ishmael?" Phoebe turned to him. "Did it work? You all looked strange, and I wondered if I did something wrong."

"When you colored the rag in the library, you colored a spot about this big." Ishmael held his hand out, making a circle with his thumb and forefinger. "Just now you colored about twenty trees."

She turned to look at the tree she rested against. "The whole thing?" Her eyes traveled up the trunk to the topmost branches.

"Yes, the whole thing."

"Twenty of them?"

"Leaves to roots."

"Oh." She looked at the trees. "No wonder you looked strange."

"I've never seen that much color loose—except the time you emptied all the jars in the workroom," Ishmael said. He looked at her, and she looked at him, and they burst into laughter.

"That's not funny!" Lilith protested, but then she giggled, too.

"We would have had a much easier time collecting the color if we had known you could do this," Jacob said.

"*I* would have had a much easier time cleaning up the workroom if I had known I could do this."

That sent them into peals of laughter again.

"But how does the color get there?" Michael asked.

"I directed my song outward and let the sound carry it."

"Maybe with less color, the placement will be more exact?" Ishmael said.

Michael thought about that for a second. "Possibly."

"Wait, why are you here?" Rebekah said.

"Yeah, why *are* you here?" Jacob said.

Michael held up the device in his hands. "Ishmael asked for help, so I come bearing help."

"What is that thing?" Thomas asked.

"If you have some color, I'll show you."

Lilith held out the vial to Michael. He dumped what was left of it into a funnel and began turning a crank. Simultaneously, he lifted a nozzle on the other side and pointed it toward a tree behind him.

A fine green mist emerged and drifted onto the foliage.

"Can you aim it any higher?" Jacob suggested.

Thomas stepped forward, dropped his bundle of vials and said, "Give it to me." He took the nozzle and lifted it as high as he could reach. The color sifted down through the leaves, staining them green. When he ran out of color, he put the nozzle down.

"It's not fancy, but it's faster than what we can do with sifters and swabs," Thomas said. He surveyed the trees left to color in that section. "We might just be able to do this in time. But as Gram said, *Do not praise yourself while going into battle; praise yourself coming out of battle.*"

"We could ask Sound Master for more help, too," Phoebe said. "There's a full Hall of apprentices that can do what I just did."

"Do you think he'll agree?" Lilith twisted a lock of her hair. "What's he like, anyway?"

"Sound Master is brilliant with sound. Listen. Can you hear the music in the wind? It's a marvel. He composed that music." Phoebe looked up toward the sky. She closed her eyes and cocked her head.

Thomas lifted an ear. "But I thought Aaron had to do all the sound in here."

"Oh, he did. It's just a variation on the work Sound Master did years ago."

Ishmael listened. He heard a branch rubbing against another and in the distance, the sound of the waves churning in the sea. It sounded sort of . . . *blue*. He looked at Lilith. She shrugged her shoulders. Thomas shook his head. Jacob frowned, while Matthew wore a look of intense concentration, trying hard to hear music in the wind. Michael was still perplexed by what had just happened and tapped one of the tree trunks, as if hoping to figure out what exactly Phoebe had done.

Phoebe opened her eyes and hummed a few notes. "I don't know if he'll allow the others to come or not. He's a bit . . . temperamental."

"How could he not?" Ishmael picked up a stone and tossed it in the air, catching it.

"Yeah," Michael said. "How could he not?"

CHAPTER

45

"Absolutely not," Sound Master boomed.

Ishmael and Phoebe had come right over and explained the situation to him.

"I can't see how this would benefit the Hall of Sound," Sound Master continued. Everything about him dwarfed Ishmael—his voice, his girth, his whiskers. "We sing, your color moves? It appears to me that it benefits the Hall of Hue, as it allows the Hall of Sound to do your work, correct?"

This was not going well.

"It's not just moving one thing to another place," Ishmael said.

Phoebe took over. "This could benefit everyone at the Commons, and it would just be for the next two days."

"My answer is still no."

"But, Sound Master—"

He sliced through the air with his hand. "No arguments, Phoebe. You have been released from your duties here because of a debt you owe to the Hall of Hue. The other novices have their own work to do. As it is, you are far behind your fellow novices, and I don't know how you are going to catch up. I will not jeopardize the progress of the others to solve problems," he said with a sideways glance at Ishmael, "for this color novice."

"But—" she said.

"Are you a novice in the Hall of Sound or the Hall of Hue?" the Sound Master thundered.

Phoebe seemed to shrink. "The Hall of Sound, sir," she whispered.

"Remember that," he said. He nodded, then dismissed them, motioning toward the door.

They shuffled out, and the latch clicked with a sound of finality as the door shut. From the other side came the echo of Sound Master's footsteps as he walked in the opposite direction.

The ensuing silence dropped on them like a wet blanket, heavy and cold.

"I'll never be able to color all the trees in time now." Ishmael dreaded the thought of the thousands of trees awaiting attention.

"Is that so bad?"

"Yes! Color keepers are supposed to honor each color. All posticums are supposed to have a minimum of the three primary colors. If Luc has his way, only one of those colors will be represented, and there won't be balance. This is the worst thing a color keeper could do. There won't be diversity. There will just be monotony everywhere."

The two apprentices left the Hall of Sound and walked through the courtyard.

"Thank you for trying, Phoebe." Ishmael hung his head. "Do you think . . ." Ishmael paused. "No, never mind. It's too ridiculous."

"What? Tell me."

"I wondered if you thought maybe . . . *I* could do those vocal exercises? You could teach me, and maybe I could move the color?"

She looked uncertain. "Ishmael, I can't even see color. If I am blind to the most basic element of your art, what makes you think you'd be open to the most basic elements of mine?"

He didn't want to tell her about how he saw colors when he ate, and how none of the other Hue apprentices did. "It was just an idea."

She clucked her tongue. "Fine. Open your mouth, like this." She relaxed her face, letting her jaw open slightly.

It felt ridiculous, but he did as she said.

"Now, take a deep breath, here in your gut, and let it out." A lovely high tone burst forth from her core.

Ishmael took a deep breath and let it out with a croak. "So much for that idea." He started walking back toward the posticum. "I'd better go. I have about a million trees to color."

"Oh, never mind that." Phoebe grabbed his arm. "I'm coming, too. I'll try to get just the leaves this time."

"What? You heard Sound Master. You can't help."

"He never said *I* couldn't help. He only said he wouldn't release *other* novices from their duties to help."

Ishmael thought back over what he had said. She was right. "Are you sure you want to do this?"

"Positive."

Ishmael smiled. "Let's go, then."

They hurried back to the posticum. After a few trials, Phoebe figured it out: aim high and let the color drape over the jagged edges and soft curves of the leaves.

Ishmael let Lilith hold the vials while Phoebe sang. Thomas and Michael had gone off to a different section and the others had returned to their areas, so Ishmael gathered several vials of green and a couple of swabs and headed toward a section of trees that hadn't been colored yet, all the while listening to Phoebe sing.

Phoebe's exhibition opened up so many questions. How did the sound of her voice carry the color? How did it have the power to do so? Ishmael could imagine the wind in the heavens and the waves of the water carrying color, the currents of water and air pushing it along by the force of their strength. But song? He didn't understand even the most rudimentary parts of it. How could it move the particles of color?

The breeze brushed against him, and he closed his eyes, trying to understand. With his sight darkened, he no longer saw color through his eyes. It was still there in his head, but the colors were dimmed, and he found that by dimming the colors, he could sense other things around him. The breeze. The ground underneath him, heavy, dependable. The light falling softly down. The stones of the wall. The far-off roll of the waves. The silence. There was much about the world that Ishmael did not understand, but he felt the beauty of it all.

By the end of the day, he and the other novices had each colored almost two dozen trees, scaling the trunks, blowing the color off the swabs, and descending. Thomas and Michael had colored double that with Michael's device. But Phoebe and Lilith had colored acres of leaves as far as her sound could travel.

But still, the dark color moved up the tree trunks, threatening to bring Luc's plan to fruition. Time was running out.

CHAPTER

46

In utter exhaustion, Ishmael went to the workroom that night to gather more vials of green for the next day. Before he had taken three steps into the room, Color Master's door opened, revealing Color Master herself.

She looked older, more tired, and the red of her tunic had dimmed and darkened. Even her sharply arched eyebrows seemed subdued.

Color Master motioned toward her office. "Come, sit."

Though his legs didn't want to move, Ishmael found his way to the office and sat across from her.

"I looked for you at the posticum as soon as I arrived so I could tell you the outcome of our expedition." Color Master folded her hands in her lap. "I must admit, I was somewhat surprised by what I saw there. Would you like to tell me what happened in my absence?"

Ishmael's throat was so dry, dry as the dark dust that covered the foundation, but he needed to lay down the shame and the fear and the worry he had carried for far too long. "I wanted to do something better at the posticum, something that Luc could be happy with, since it's meant to be his."

"Something better than your plan?"

"Yes." He told her about dappling the tower room wall with Luc, and Michael's wish to work together, and Thaddeus's wind moving the blue. He told her about the novices' hesitation about dappling, and Michael's machine, and the glory of the dappling on the foundation. "I covered the foundation, speckling it with all the colors. The variety made the foundation look alive, almost. It was so beautiful. But when I went to the posticum later that night, the colors mixed somehow."

Color Master nodded her head. "Yes, yes. Adding more than one color at a time on a newly created structure in a posticum can be done, but it must be done slowly to give the colors a chance to set. That is why your colors mixed. Did Luc not tell you that would happen?"

"No."

Color Master pursed her lips. "And what about the trees?"

"When we found the colors mixed, Luc told me that I should cover the foundation in trees and plants so you wouldn't know. I was afraid of getting in trouble, so that's what I did. Manufactory made even more plants, but as soon as they were delivered and installed, I realized what a mistake I had made." Ishmael looked down at his shirt.

Color Master gave him a look of compassion. "Ishmael, there is no right or wrong way in creation. Each Hall in the Commons relies on the ingenuity of its apprentices for progress. We make what might be considered *mistakes*, but we learn from them, and we move on."

"I doubt anyone has ever made as big a mistake as this," Ishmael continued.

"I doubt anyone has ever had as big a posticum as this," she replied with a chuckle.

"When we went back the next morning to add color, we saw that the dark color had begun seeping up into the trees. And when Luc saw it, he said that's how he wanted it all along."

"Did I hear my name?" Luc had silently approached and now leaned against the doorjamb, his arms crossed over his chest.

Ishmael wheeled around so quickly that his seat shifted.

Color Master made a small sound. "You have much to account for."

Luc pushed himself off the doorjamb and stood up straight. "I've done nothing wrong."

Color Master rose, her large frame matching Luc inch for inch. "You've also done little right. Your presence is requested at a tribunal council tomorrow."

"For what? For making helpful suggestions?"

"For sabotaging the work of the Jubilee posticum. For deceit. For vandalism."

Luc raised his eyebrows. "Judged and found wanting, no doubt." He shrugged, then pivoted and walked away.

Color Master turned around to face the wall. Several seconds passed before she said, "Your presence is requested at the tribunal as well." Color Master spoke quietly, but Ishmael could tell what effort it took to control her voice. She faced Ishmael again.

"Am I to be sent home?"

Color Master's voice loosened. "No. The posticum must be finished."

"But why? Won't the color from the foundation just continue to spread?"

Above Color Master hung a mobile of color circles the Halls of Shape, Manufactory, and Motion had given to Color Master when she became Hall master. She gently tapped the mobile, sending it spinning.

"The light you used, though condensed, is not strong enough to maintain its color, let alone cover all the trees in the posticum adequately. It will fade, and those structures that do not receive more color would cease to exist."

"I don't understand."

"Each of the seven Halls brings some vital thing to creation. Without Shape and Manufactory, the structures would not be formed. Without Motion, they would not move. Together with Sound and Scent and Gustation, we bring these structures the four elements of beauty. If one element is missing—for example, color—the components of these posticums become unbalanced. They need the presence of all four elements to push against each other, to bear each other up. If all four aren't present, the struc-tures will fall. Although the color from the foundation is soaking up into the trees, it's not a large enough quantity to completely cover the flora. The color will eventually stop and what isn't covered will be left in ruins."

Ishmael wove his fingers together, a small and powerless web made of inept fibers, speckled with flecks of green. "Can one of the older apprentices finish the posticum? Someone with more experience?"

The colors in the mobile dipped and bobbed as they slowed. Color Master reached her finger for the circle of red. "A posti-cum must be finished by the artisan who began it."

"Me," Ishmael said glumly. He unraveled his fingers.

"The road we travel down is not always an easy one." Though Color Master spoke to Ishmael, it seemed as if she needed to hear the words, too. "Tomorrow is a new day."

Ishmael slid forward on his chair. "I'm sorry about the color."

"Don't be sorry about the color." Color Master waved away his apology. "To be honest, it intrigues me. No, what worries me is how you are going to finish all of those trees."

"Were you able to gather more light?"

"Yes, some. The other apprentices are bringing it by the end of the week. But it will take time to distill it—I'm not sure it will be done when you need it."

"May I use some of it straight? To color directly?"

Color Master's eyebrows arched in surprise. "Sometimes I forget you're a novice. Other times, I am surprised by your aptitude. Of course you may use some of it straight, if you think that's best."

The mobile above Color Master's head rocked in the breeze from her hand. "Ah. There's one more thing I should tell you. Hannah left earlier today for the House of Light. Head Master told me." The circle of blue turned sideways so Ishmael couldn't see it anymore. Red and orange and yellow and green, then nothing, then indigo and violet. The hole gaped in the spectrum. Ishmael turned away to shut out the sight. "May I go now?"

Color Master nodded. Ishmael left the office and headed to the dormitory.

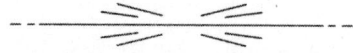

The room was already dark when Ishmael reached it, but no one was asleep.

"Color Master is back."

Thomas groaned. "*The pain of the little finger is felt by the entire body.* Are we all in trouble? Or just you?"

"I don't know." He fell into his bed, exhausted. "There's a tribunal tomorrow morning for Luc. I have to go. Can you three take over the work at the posticum while I'm gone?"

"Of course," Matthew said. "Thomas can keep working with Michael, Lilith with Phoebe, and the rest of us can climb trees."

"I never thought my height would be an advantage," Thomas said into the dark room. "But, then again, *When you have what someone needs in your haversack, everybody seeks your friendship.* Are the other apprentices back, too? Maybe they can help."

"Not yet. We're on our own for now."

"Not true," Jacob said. "We've got Michael and Phoebe along with our spectrum, and they count double for each one of us."

Ishmael knew he should tell the others about Hannah, but if he said the words that might mean that they were true—that she really had left—and their spectrum was no longer complete.

CHAPTER
47

The next morning before breakfast, Ishmael was summoned to see Head Master. With dread in the pit of his belly, he walked across the Great Courtyard to Head Master's rooms and tapped at a plain wooden door.

"Come in," Head Master said.

The room was simply furnished but for a curious thing on a side table: a miniature circular track mounted on a base, with pulleys, ramps, and a pendulum swinging from a column. Ishmael's gaze followed the track around as it rose and dipped. At one point, the track stopped. Several thin slabs of stone stood upright, followed by a reservoir of gravel hanging over a small cup. A short distance from that, the track continued again, leading to a wheel mounted on a column. A small, polished ball waited in a dimple at the top of the track. Each part of the machine was colored in the most brilliant, beautiful colors, one flowing into the next in such a skillful way that Ishmael couldn't tell where one color stopped and another began.

"I see you are interested in my machine." Head Master smiled.

"What does it do?"

Head Master rose from his seat and nudged the ball out of its resting place. It swooped and dipped along the track, gaining momentum as it sped on its way. It hit the stone slabs and knocked them over, which triggered a mechanism that drained the gravel from its reservoir. The gravel filled the cup, the weight of which tipped the ball back onto the track. The ball rose up the wheel and landed exactly where it started.

"Fascinating, eh?"

Ishmael marveled at it. "Yes."

"Although the ball ends up back where it began, the circumstances around it have changed." He pointed to the slabs of stone knocked over, and the gravel in the cup. "It makes one think, doesn't it? But I didn't ask you to come here to talk about my little machine. Please sit."

Ishmael took a seat opposite Head Master.

"Do you know why you're here?"

"Because I ruined the posticum?"

Head Master chuckled. "No, my dear boy. You have not ruined the posticum by any means. You are here because I want you to consider a question." He leaned forward, putting the tips of his fingers together. "It's an important question, one which we sometimes neglect in our daily duties."

Ishmael waited, hands folded.

"What is it that you want?"

Ishmael hadn't expected that. After a minute, he said, "I want to do the right things. I want to change all the wrong things I've done."

"All? Even the ones that have led to good?"

Ishmael couldn't see any good that had come of his actions. He came to bring Luc home with him, but that hadn't happened. He tried to help Luc with his posticum, but it shut without him. He worked so Luc would win the Jubilee posticum, but instead, he himself ended up winning. As for the posticum itself, well, nothing had gone as he would have liked. "Has anything led to good?"

"Oh, yes. You have done much, much good. But I'm not going to tell you what it is. I'm going to let you discover that for yourself."

"I don't think I'll ever be able to. I've failed at everything I've tried to do since I've come here."

Head Master considered this; then he turned to the machine on his table. "I made this machine while I was an apprentice here. Do you know how many times I had to rework it?"

Ishmael couldn't imagine Head Master as an apprentice.

"Two-hundred sixty-three times." Head Master smiled at the memory. "Each time I failed, I learned another bit of information that helped me on my next try. What some call a mistake or a failure is merely a stepping stone to what comes next."

"But—"

Head Master held up his index finger. "You cannot change the past. You can only move forward. So move forward with the knowledge you have gained. See what comes next."

His words disappointed Ishmael. "I don't think I can. I'm stuck—there are so many trees, and now the mixed color is soaking into the trees. I'm afraid that's all there will be."

Head Master nodded slowly. "And you wanted all of the colors in the posticum." Head Master smiled. "The mixture is only one manifestation of the colors. Where else are all the colors found?"

Ishmael paused. "In light." The first law of color: *All color is contained in pure light.* If a beam of light is cast through a prism, the colors, which had been hidden, reveal themselves. "But how does that change anything?" Ishmael asked.

"You'll figure that out," he said. "Do your work without worry."

Ishmael paused at the door. "Head Master, how do you know about color?"

His eyes twinkled. "I studied color once upon a time, too."

"But you said you made that machine. I thought you were in Manufactory."

"Apprentices who have multiple abilities are rare, but there are a few of us, and those few usually end up doing uncommon things." Head Master winked at Ishmael, then dismissed him.

"Luc, son of James and Talia, you stand before the tribunal to be judged." Head Master sat at the front of Wright Hall on the raised platform, a small table in front of him. The seven Hall masters flanked Head Master, with four seated on his right side and three on his left. Luc stood below, alone, in the center of the floor. Ishmael was surprised to find Phoebe in the front section when he arrived. He sat with her, both of their faces somber. Michael was also there.

"What are you doing here?" Ishmael whispered to Phoebe.

"Witness."

Before Ishmael could say more, Head Master read from a parchment in his hand. "Your charges are as follows: You have sabotaged the work of the Hall of Hue in this Jubilee posticum. You have broken the oath and duty of a color keeper. You are accused of influencing novices in the Hall of Hue to do likewise."

Head Master continued, "You are accused of deceit, for having led Phoebe, a novice in the Hall of Sound, in a path that would prove disastrous for the Hall of Hue."

Ishmael faced Phoebe, his eyes widened in silent surprise.

She nodded.

"In addition to the charges relating directly to the Hall of Hue, you stand accused of having vandalized the Cairns."

Head Master looked over the parchment to Luc, perhaps hoping to see some remorse for his actions. There was none. "What say you to these charges?"

Luc smiled. "What would you like me to say?"

"What is your plea? Are you guilty or not?"

"Yes, I've done all these things. But I feel no guilt for what I've done."

Head Master's eyebrows puckered. "Is your breach of faith so deep that you have no shame for your actions?"

Luc stood straight and tall. "Why should I feel shame? You told me I needed to put my mark on this posticum."

"You were meant to put your mark on this posticum within the boundaries that have been set by the Hall of Hue. You stepped outside of those boundaries. You daily spoke the oath and duty of a color keeper, in which you promised to honor each individual color and its place in the spectrum. You committed to uphold the laws of the Commons and seek harmony in the use of your skills. Your actions have not been in accordance with your commitment. There are consequences to such acts." Head Master's voice lowered even more, pleading with Luc. "I give you one more chance. Do you have any remorse for your actions?"

Luc hesitated, but only for a split second. "No."

"Then you are no longer welcome here. I hereby banish you from the Commons and its immediate environs. I strip you of your title of color keeper, and forbid the usage of a prism. You are to leave immediately, returning from whence you came." Head Master rapped a gavel on the table in front of him. "Color Master, please escort him out."

Before Color Master could descend, Luc was gone.

THE STONES

The stones knew things when no one else did. They sensed the cycle of creativity and work and rest. They felt the apprentices from the Halls pass through their portals. They noted the shape and the size of the apprentices, the way they walked, the things they carried, the things they said, the things they left unsaid. They could tell a lot about an apprentice by the way he or she stepped through the posticum. Some never lost their sense of wonder. Others, like this one, walked through with a sense of entitlement.

They recognized him immediately. He was meant to go home with his brother. Why was he still here?

Luc put his hand on the stone wall, patting it like an old friend. The stones read the lines and whorls written upon his hand and recoiled. His history was mixed, but the lines were dark now, so very dark. As they read, they saw that he had never intended to go home. What's worse, he had betrayed his brother. The stones shivered.

They would have closed up the posticum right then without

a second thought in order to protect the betrayed one, if it hadn't been for the threshold stone, that pesky outsider. This apprentice—the one who shouldn't be there—walked through, and the stones could do nothing to stop him.

CHAPTER
48

As Ishmael walked with Michael and Phoebe out of Wright Hall, he swam in loss. When Papa had gone, the loss had seemed like a hole, an empty well. But with Luc, the loss felt large, like it overflowed from his very center and threatened to flood the whole Hall of Hue, the entire Commons, every single last posticum. Luc was gone, and though Ishmael had wanted Luc to return home, he never wanted it to be like this. He could only hope that some good could come of this. Perhaps Luc might provide some help to Mam. Perhaps he would see some remnant of Ishmael's color left in the barn. Perhaps he would make color again with the glass pane. Perhaps Luc could find contentment, if not happiness.

"I'm sorry about your brother," Phoebe said. "I don't understand why he used me to sabotage your light, though."

"Maybe his anger made him want to destroy something," Michael said. "I saw firsthand what he did to the Cairns. Maybe that just wasn't enough."

"I don't think any of us can understand what Luc thought at the time," Ishmael said. "I don't think we'll ever find out now, either."

"I suppose you're right," Phoebe said. After a few moments, she said, "When someone from the Hall of Sound leaves, we sing a special melody—an elegy—for that person. I will sing one as I work today. Maybe it'll help."

Ishmael nodded, grateful for her kindness. "I can't go back yet. Will you tell the others?"

Phoebe touched Ishmael's arm, then followed Michael to the posticum.

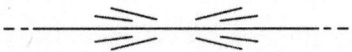

Ishmael needed the solitude of the Cairns. He still wasn't used to the sight of it, defaced and messy. The elegant towers of rock were mostly gone, and the land was littered with the remains of dozens of them. He walked through the hillside picking his way around the demolished cairns. Luc really had ruined everything—their color, the posticum, the cairns. Worst of all, though, was the ruin of Ishmael's trust.

Ishmael pushed thoughts of Luc away, and turned around to see how far he had come. The hillside rose up before him, and the alley to the Hall of Manufactory lay far in the distance.

This would do.

He found the largest stone he could move, and rolled it end over end to an even bigger stone. Using another stone as a wedge, he lifted it up onto the base stone. He sat down nearby to catch his breath, trying to think what else he could do to save the color in the posticum. He was afraid it was hopeless. He had done all that he could.

His mind wandered to Head Master's words. What good had he done? As he thought about his actions of the past weeks, he realized that his only fault was that he cared too much. He cared too much about his family, which led him to seek out Luc. He cared too much about Luc, which led him to choose the wrong bag. He cared too much about the Jubilee posticum, which led him to want to make it better. He cared too much for color. He cared too much about everything. The thoughts moved through his mind, one metamorphosing into another. Caring too much had turned into too much care. Too many cares and a whole lot of uncertainty about what he should do.

Had he really done all he could?

He thought of Michael's plan for the posticum and how he had wanted to collaborate.

Then he thought of how Thaddeus used the wind to move the color, and how Michael built the device to condense light, then built another device to move the color. He thought of how Phoebe sang color onto so many trees. How they all had helped. That was what Michael had wanted to do, wasn't it? He wanted all of the artisans to work together. Was that possible?

Could the other Hall artisans help—in ways that Ishmael couldn't even begin to understand? Shape? Scent? Gustation?

The thought of asking Dora for help made him wince. He hadn't meant to be unkind when he said she wouldn't understand—he had merely been frustrated by the situation he found himself in—but it was clear she had left their workroom on the verge of tears. Now the tables were turned, and he was the one who didn't understand. He wasn't sure how Dora could help, but perhaps she would have something to add to the process.

He wasn't sure how any of the other artisans could help, but this—all of this—was bigger than him, far bigger than his capacity to think or do or understand. He needed to ask them all for help.

As he looked out over the hillside, a ray of light streamed down on a single tuft of green.

Feeling more at peace than he had in a long time, he left the Cairns with only the merest suggestion of a plan in his mind. Ask for help, and expect help to come.

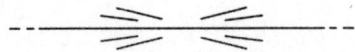

Since Thaddeus had already helped once, Ishmael went to see him first.

"Most of my work is finished or on hold," Thaddeus said. "I'd be glad to help."

Together, they went to the Hall of Shape.

Dora stood at the entrance, blocking the door. "Yes?" she

said. Her mouth formed a straight line. Line after line after line, she could sense her face breaking into linear shapes: straight eyebrows, flat eyes, a perpendicular nose, a mouth like a trench. She still felt slighted from being boxed up the day before yesterday by Ishmael. Then she saw Thaddeus, and the lines of her face softened.

"I thought that you might be able to help us," Ishmael said.

"Me?" Dora nearly squeaked in surprise. Her eyebrows rose into a lovely curve, as if they were desperate to pull away from the unnatural line in which they had been stretched.

"Yes, you," Ishmael said.

"Oh," Dora said, her mouth in a circle, the shape she liked best. She looked at him, at his young neck and his young face and remembered how she had thought they could be allies, just out of sheer goodness. She realized they still could.

If she let them.

Sheer goodness.

The lines she carried on her face curved, bending upward and around. "Of course," she said, and with those two words she became allied to the Hall of Hue.

Ishmael explained the situation to her: the trees, the time, the contraption that Michael had made, the phenomenon of Phoebe's song, the past help and the hope of future help from Motion. "I thought that since some of the other Halls have been involved, that you, too, might have something to contribute," he finished.

A bubble of joy rose in Dora, a complete circle. It grew until it enclosed all three of them. She was asked to *help*. She was asked to help the *Hall of Hue*.

"I find that the answer to most problems is that you need more circles and fewer lines," she said.

"More circles?"

Dora laughed, a high, round sound. "Yes. And though I could say that it's complicated and you wouldn't understand, I won't."

Ishmael flushed.

Dora linked arms with Ishmael and Thaddeus, and Ishmael led them toward the Hall of Gustation. "Another stop."

Thaddeus blew a wind that preceded them, sneaking through the cracks in search of Gabriel. It found him in the garden, bent over a row of fledgling plants, and swirled around him, head to toe.

Gabriel had never been called quite this way, but the flush of heat that the wind ignited in the sweetness at the top of his head to the shiver it left behind at the bitter soles of his feet told him he was needed. He met the others as they came. "You wished to see me?"

Ishmael smiled, a deluge of gratitude and friendship and hope washing over him. "We need your help."

Gabriel nodded.

"Now for Aaron," Ishmael said.

When Ishmael found Aaron and explained the situation to him, the Sound artisan said, "Phoebe did what?" and then he gladly came along to lend his voice to hers, forging more connections between the Hall of Sound and the Hall of Hue.

Keturah rounded the corner of the Hall of Scent and smiled when she saw the artisans gathered. "I expect you'll want me, too?"

As they walked the short distance to the posticum, Ishmael told them about the help from Michael and Phoebe.

When he finished, Dora nodded. "Too much line and not enough circle."

Bemused, Thaddeus turned to her. "But you haven't even seen the process."

"It doesn't matter. Like I said, when there's a problem, the solution is usually in the balance between line and circle. It's easy to think that the line is the answer to all questions. It's direct. It's uncomplicated. It's distinct. But the line is flat. The line is simple. The line is at its best when it works as a foundation, not as a single entity. Most things need a circle to be complete."

"But what can we do? I don't see how this will help us color the trees," Ishmael said.

"I would guess that the color is being spread in a line when it should be spread in a circle."

Thaddeus's eyes lit up. Even her mind had a rolling grace. "I think I understand. If the color were spread in a circle, it would have a farther reach and the work would go faster."

Gabriel knew that color was not flavor, but what if it acted the same way? What if it overlapped his elevation map? "Maybe you need to aim the color higher to find the sweetness."

"The higher the projection, the greater the dispersion," Thaddeus said, almost to himself.

Aaron's brow furrowed. "What does that mean?"

"It means if we can send the color up higher, it will come down on a larger area."

Aaron pictured waves of sound stretching out, connecting. If he connected his voice to Phoebe's, how much farther could the color go? "I need to find Phoebe," he said.

Keturah, for her part, wasn't sure how she could help, but she carried with her a vial of the scent she had created for this posticum: the scent of possibility. She uncorked it, and let it waft over the group.

Ishmael was the first to smell it, and it bolstered his confidence. "Let's find the others." He paused, observing each of them. He had never felt so loved, so much a part of something. The large blueness of the sky beckoned, and he wished Hannah were there to feel a part of this, too. "Thank you—all of you."

Thaddeus and the other artisans nodded and waved off his gratitude. A spray of green was clearly visible in the distance. "They must be this way," Ishmael pointed. The artisans moved through the trees toward Michael and Thomas, discussing the shape of the nozzle, the boost from the wind, the connection of the patterns, and the height of the launch.

When they reached Michael, he listened to their plans and his eyes lit up at the joy of cooperating with all the Halls. He got to work immediately adjusting his machine.

Phoebe went off to sing with Aaron, and as Ishmael watched them, he knew she sensed the glory of the colors around her. He could see how Aaron felt the motion cradling his sound.

Ishmael watched Gabriel as he melded flavor with color next to Keturah, and he saw recognition on Gabriel's face—the recognition that taste and scent were part of one great whole.

Beyond them, Thaddeus released a gentle breeze that swirled Dora's straight lines into curves, and she laughed chasing after them.

There was joy in this place, even if Ishmael couldn't quite reach it from the chasm of loss he was in. He knew he would eventually. For now, there were trees. Many, many trees—each one an opportunity to proclaim the glory of color. He grabbed the condensed light from Michael and headed out of the reach of Phoebe's song and far from the range of Michael's second machine. Though he hadn't intended on using the condensed light again, the need for color surpassed the need for pure light. The trees might not be as intensely colored, but at least they would be colored.

When he found himself in the midst of a grove of pallid trees, he set down the machine, ready to fill the chasm of loss with work.

CHAPTER

49

At the end of the day, Ishmael was pleased with what he had done. It wasn't as far-reaching as Phoebe's song, but it was nearly as good as Thomas's work with Michael's second machine, and they were making progress. He estimated that they had covered almost two-thirds of the trees. He would have kept going, but he had used up the last of the condensed light so he decided to head back to gather some vials of green and see if any of the others were around.

The first sign that something was wrong was the missing cart of distilled color. They had left the cart at a crossroads, where everyone could return and restock as needed. But when Ishmael arrived, the cart was gone.

It was, at first, simply an irritation. Grooves from the wheels showed in the soft, dark foundation, so at least he could follow it, but tracking it down wasted time, and time was something they just didn't have.

He pursued the wheel ruts for a short distance before they took an odd turn. Instead of going toward the unfinished trees, they turned toward a section Ishmael knew had already been finished. What's more, everyone else knew it had been finished, too.

It was then that he heard the voices, and one of them knocked him sideways.

Luc.

"Give it to me," he said.

"No!" Thomas said.

Then came Matthew's voice, soothing and calm. "Let's talk about this before we do anything rash."

Luc would never allow them to finish the work of coloring here—not if it meant a full spectrum of color. Ishmael berated himself for not realizing this sooner. He took off running, suddenly fearful for his friends and for the posticum.

Ishmael burst through the trees into a clearing. Luc stood by the cart, with one hand outstretched. Thomas held Michael's machine behind his back. Matthew stood to the side, his feet planted in a firm stance. Gabriel, arms crossed, stood next to Thomas.

In the split second after Ishmael registered what was happening, Luc opened a vial of orange and threw it at Thomas. He recoiled, but not fast enough. The color caught Thomas full in the face. Orange covered every speck of his skin. He tried to wipe it out of his eyes, but there was too much and the orange just transferred to his hands.

Ishmael ran to Thomas's side, using his tunic to wipe the orange from Thomas's face, but the color had already soaked into his hair, his skin, his mouth, and nose.

Gabriel stood, his bitter feet rooted at Thomas's side. "Thomas wouldn't give Luc the machine."

"No, and I'm still waiting for it," Luc said. "So glad you could join us, little brother."

Ishmael studied Luc, trying to find any evidence of the older brother he had once been. The brother who had helped Jerusha untangle her yarn, patiently weaving the end over and under and through the mess. The brother who had seized Mam's hand as she stumbled on a stone. The brother who had crept out of bed to show Ishmael the night sky and tell him stories about the stars. The brother who had taught him color. He saw no evidence of that person, and the loss overcame his anger.

"Why are you here?" Ishmael finally asked. "Why didn't you go home?"

"My posticum was supposed to be my home. Now this is my home. If you are not happy with how things have turned out, you have only yourself to blame, little brother."

"Stop calling me that."

"Why? Don't you want to be associated with me?" He laughed. "Have I fallen in your estimation? No longer the hero?"

Truer words were never spoken. "No hero of mine would do something like this."

"You ruined my posticum, so I wanted revenge. But then that Sound novice missed the stores of green almost entirely and botched everything else. The little disaster forced Color Master to choose your entry for the posticum instead." Luc practically spit the words out.

Ishmael met Luc's eyes. They were hard as glass, and again he was struck by how different Luc was now from the person he had known back home.

"You didn't used to be like this," Ishmael whispered.

Luc reached into his pocket and pulled out his prism. He held it to his face and studied its flat surfaces. "No? Perhaps not. But you didn't used to be like this, either."

Ishmael touched the prism in his pocket, unsure of Luc's next move. "Like what?"

Luc turned away, facing the trees behind him. "So self-righteous."

"There's a difference between being self-righteous and being right."

Luc whipped around, pointing his prism at Ishmael's face. He flinched. "You don't know what you are talking about."

"Perhaps not," Ishmael said, "but I do know the spectrum. I know the rules of color. I know how color works. I know the joy that color brings."

Luc laughed, then rubbed his hand over the tree trunk he leaned against. "You're very sincere, but you're wrong. What brings me joy is knowing that I am the best color keeper. That's why I made my posticum golden. Everywhere you looked, you would see me. My color, my world."

"*The mouth that eats pride at breakfast speaks tolerance at lunch.* I think you forgot about lunch," Thomas said.

Luc took two steps toward him.

Gabriel stood taller, blocking his way, even though Luc was much larger. "Leave him alone."

"Now might not be the best time for proverbs, Thomas," Matthew said.

"No, now would be the best time to hand over that machine of yours." Luc stretched out his hand again. "I had hoped this world would have only one color—even if it wasn't *my* color, at least it wouldn't be yours. I underestimated you, little brother. But enough is enough. Hand over the machine."

"No." Ishmael's thin shoulders shook under the full weight of responsibility for this posticum, for the color, for Thomas and all the other artisans who had helped him. He reached for the prism in his pocket.

"Ah, ah," Luc clucked. "If you fling your prism about in anger, you never know what might happen." He twirled his prism and caught a ray of light, which grew into a glorious spectrum.

Ishmael didn't know what to do. Clearly Thomas was in pain, and he needed to get him to the infirmary. But he couldn't leave Luc here. He couldn't leave the color here. He couldn't leave the posticum unfinished.

Luc laughed. "See? Even with something as simple as a

spectrum, I'm the better color keeper, and you? You'll always be the little brother." He laughed again.

Matthew cleared his throat. "I think Ishmael just wants to do his work. I think he wants to stop fighting."

"It's too late for that," Luc said, brandishing the spectrum. He spun it, twirling it so the colors flashed until yellow showed. It grew, forming a sphere, just like when Ishmael first saw Luc in his posticum, only this massive sphere of yellow dazzled in a way that the other never did.

Ishmael looked at Thomas, staring blindly, a look of pain on his face. Gabriel stood by him, his jaw locked, his hands clenched. For their sakes, he couldn't give up. For Color Master's sake, and Head Master's sake. For Hannah, who had sacrificed so much. For Phoebe, who was a victim of Luc's ambition. The ground underneath him, strong from Ethan's work, bolstered his courage. He thought of all the Halls, and the apprentices who had worked so hard to make this posticum beautiful—Michael, Thaddeus, Dora, Gabriel, Aaron, Keturah. For their sake, he couldn't give up. The edges of the prism cut into Ishmael's hand.

Luc laughed again, the yellow globe resting on his prism. "This is my world now."

Ishmael just noticed Michael, who stood off to the side. He was nearly twitching trying to signal something to Ishmael. He looked at him, then looked deliberately at the light condensing machine in Ishmael's right hand, then looked up in the air, and his eyebrows rose.

Ishmael's eyes widened. Of course! He wasn't sure if this

would work, but he was willing to try. He opened the hatch at the top of the machine to allow light in, and immediately began turning the crank.

"Oh, please," Luc said. "Don't tell me you're going to try to . . ." But he stopped, because he had no idea what Ishmael was going to do.

Ishmael wiped the prism on the edge of his tunic.

"If you make a spectrum, it will be no different from mine. Light is light."

"That's where you're wrong. Some light is stronger, especially when it's bolstered by the light from others." Ishmael nodded at Michael and Gabriel, then slid the compartment open, and a flash of blinding light flew out. He lifted his prism to the sky, remembering Gabriel's admonition to aim high. He caught the light, and he held still, allowing the light to burst forth into the most glorious spectrum of color imaginable, arcing into the sky. Streams of color shot upward, higher than the tops of the trees above them, with a brilliance that made his eyes ache. It dwarfed Luc's sphere of yellow, which slunk away to join Ishmael's spectrum.

Second law of color, of course. *In the presence of the complete spectrum, a color will always take its place among like kind.*

Ishmael held his arm steady. "It's over Luc. You need to return home."

Luc lowered his head and charged, knocking Ishmael to the ground. The prism flew from his hand, landing with a loud crack behind him, shattering into pieces.

Gabriel cried out just before Ishmael's head knocked against the root of a tree. He pointed up at the sky. "I see something!" he gasped. The spectrum arced gracefully over their heads.

Luc's clenched fist had pulled back to punch Ishmael, but at Gabriel's words, he turned around to see.

The spectrum *was* still there, glowing with luster over their heads, the colors distinct and beautiful.

Luc sat there, stupefied.

Ishmael himself was shocked. He had expected the spectrum to dissolve when his prism lost contact with the beam of light. But he hadn't counted on the strength of the light.

What's more, Gabriel and Michael saw it, too.

The spectrum remained high above their heads. The longer they watched it, the more impossible it seemed, and the more glorious it was as it blazed across the sky. Luc's hope for a one-color posticum would never be realized. Ishmael's hope for a reconciliation would never be realized, either.

The future seemed crystal clear at that moment. Ishmael pushed Luc away. "You're not the master here. And we are no longer brothers."

Luc looked hard at Ishmael, then shoved the cart of vials as he stalked past it through the trees deep into the heart of the posticum.

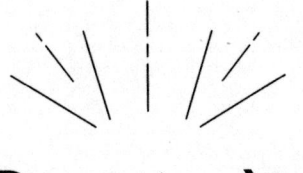

PART V

CLOSE

He fathers-forth whose beauty is past change:
Praise him.

Gerard Manley Hopkins, "Pied Beauty"

CHAPTER

50

Gabriel, Michael, Matthew, Lilith, Jacob, and Rebekah met Ishmael outside of the infirmary, looking battle-scarred and weary. Gabriel's face was streaked and mottled with orange. Even Lilith had lost her usual polish.

Phoebe dashed across the courtyard to join them, twisting the pitch pipe that she once more wore around her wrist. "If only I had been there! I could have kept the color away from you and Thomas."

Gabriel shook his head. "Don't blame yourself. You were in a completely different section."

"How is Thomas?" Phoebe asked.

Before Ishmael could answer, he saw another person hurrying toward them. "Is that—?"

The others turned around. Matthew squinted, then his eyes widened at the sight of the sleek figure dressed in white.

"Hannah!" Lilith cried out. They flew into a hug, joined by Ishmael and the other novices. Phoebe, Gabriel, and Michael hung back, not wanting to intrude, but Lilith pulled them into the circle.

"Color Master sent a message to the House of Light. I came as soon as I heard."

"Color Master thinks that the quantity of orange that got into his eyes overcame his color receptors, and they simply shut down," Ishmael said.

Tears sprang to Lilith's eyes, and her hand rose to her mouth. Hannah wrapped her arm around Lilith's slight frame.

Phoebe patted their shoulders, but it gave little comfort to any of them.

Ishmael continued, "She's hoping that, with enough time, all the color receptors in Thomas's eyes will revive, but she's uncertain about the orange receptors. They might have been permanently damaged."

With visible effort, Lilith swallowed her emotions and stood taller, ready for action. "What are we going to do now?"

Ishmael suspected that his plans would not be received well. "We will not be returning to the posticum."

"What?" The word flew out of Lilith's mouth.

"It's too dangerous," Ishmael said. "Thomas—"

"Thomas is the reason we should do something!"

"But Lilith," Jacob broke in, "Nothing we do in the posticum would help him. Besides, Luc could do the same thing to any of us. How can we be color keepers if we can't see the colors?"

"He's right, Lil," Hannah said. "If not for yourself, then for the sake of the Hall."

Lilith flung her hands down in frustration. "How can you just give up like this? We can fight him. We're ready now."

"No. This is supposed to be a Jubilee celebration, not a battle."

"How are we going to color the animals, then?"

"We'll color them at the entrance and release them there."

"But—"

"No." Ishmael's word was final.

Lilith turned away from them. Matthew put his arm around her. Rebekah joined them to offer what comfort she could.

Phoebe cleared her throat. "Can we at least be there at the entrance to help color the animals?"

"You can come if you want to, but I'm just going to make some rolls of color wrap. You don't have to be there to sing."

"I think if I sang even a single note, Sound Master would execute me." She smiled wryly, but Ishmael knew that she was in deep trouble.

"Sing?" Hannah said, looking from one to the other.

"Oh, Hannah, you've missed a lot," Ishmael said.

Her eyebrows crinkled, and she looked like she was about to cry. "I'm so sorry."

"Did you see the blue before you left?"

Hannah shook her head.

"Then you must come, too." Ishmael wished there was some way he could tell her that he was grateful for what she had done, and how he had missed her, and how sorry he was for what he said before she left, but he couldn't find the words. Nothing sounded quite right. No words captured the importance of what he wanted to express. "How long will you stay?"

Hannah tried to smile through a frown. "I think I made a mistake."

Lilith grabbed her arm. "Are you back for good?"

Hannah nodded, and Lilith and Rebekah squealed.

"So you'll all help?" Ishmael asked. He looked specifically at Jacob, grateful that he had understood why Ishmael didn't want to risk sending them into the posticum again.

They nodded.

"All right. I'll let you know as soon as I get word from the Hall of Motion that the animals are ready."

Lilith looked at him slyly. "Why don't you let us prepare the color? I'd like to do this to take my mind off Thomas."

"All right," Ishmael said.

Hannah, Rebekah, and Lilith walked off, arm in arm. Ishmael watched them, glad that their spectrum was a little bit more whole.

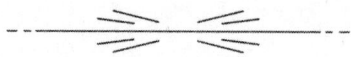

As soon as Ishmael heard they had two days before the Hall of Motion would finish the animals, he went to see Ethan. He asked for one last thing.

Ethan agreed to the plan. "It's a bit unusual," he said, "but I'll ask Michael to help."

Ishmael knew Michael would be willing.

"Would it be all right if we tinker with the original prototype a bit? If we can adjust the size and scale of each piece, it might make it easier since we're a bit rushed. In fact, maybe Dora wouldn't mind if each apprentice built his or her own design off the general shape. Each piece could be individually formed. That way, we wouldn't have to cast a true prototype, which would save us time."

Ishmael nodded his head, envisioning it in his mind. "I think that will be fine."

"The pieces won't be permanent, though. You did know this, right?"

"Yes, but once something is in the posticum, its shadow is there forever, right?"

"That's what I've been told." Ethan checked his clipboard. "I'll ask Thaddeus to release them late tonight."

"I don't know how to thank you, Ethan."

"Don't mention it. We're in this together, right?"

Ishmael smiled, the truest smile he had in days.

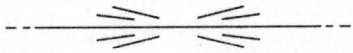

Next, he went to find Gabriel. Something had been bothering him. Ishmael found Gabriel in his Hall and without preamble said, "I want to know something. I guess the answer doesn't really matter, but it's something I've been wondering about. Did you really see the spectrum in the posticum sky?"

"I don't know what I saw, but I saw something—and it was so perfectly beautiful that I wanted to hold on to it forever."

"I wish you could," Ishmael said.

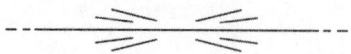

Ishmael turned toward the Cairns. Since he had no other pressing work to do, he spent the morning cleaning up the scattered stones, sorting them into piles according to size. When he could do no more, he placed one stone on top of another, beginning a pile.

Memories flooded his mind—memories of home and color and family and friends and texture and pattern and line and circle. The flash of brightness and darkness as he rolled down Commons Hill with Luc. The smell of the sheep in the barn. The sound of the wind whipping the laundry on the clothesline. The taste of Mam's porridge. The sight of the broken latch on the springhouse door. The shape of Simon's toy blocks. The motion of the sheep grazing in the field. His green-stained boot as he walked to the Commons. All these things came together here. Scent, sound, gustation, manufactory, shape, motion. He had lived in absolute ignorance before, all these gifts only wisps of smoke, just out of his grasp.

He let the memories drain out until his mind lingered on one particular memory. It was a memory of Mam sharpening the blade shears before shearing season. She was so careful, so exact, that Ishmael had marveled at her skill. "I didn't know you could sharpen the shears," he had said.

"There are many things I can do that you don't know about," Mam had replied.

Ishmael had been so worried about Mam when he came here, but with this memory came the feeling that she was stronger than he realized. In that moment, he knew Mam would be fine on her own, just as he would be fine here—but perhaps he could visit sometime soon, just to make sure.

When he felt emptied of memories, he knew it was time to see Color Master.

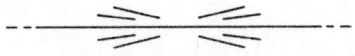

Ishmael sat in Color Master's office, his gaze moving from the swathes of color on one wall to the mobile spinning lazily above.

Color Master smiled and folded her hands over her knees. "I find it serendipitous that you were the apprentice. Regardless of our color supply, you were right for this posticum."

"I'm not so sure."

"You should be."

"But so much of the posticum is different from how I planned it."

"Most apprentices, if they had been in your shoes, would have given up long ago. You carried on. You found solutions to your problems. It might not be exactly as you envisioned, but someday, you may come to think of it as being better than you planned."

Ishmael doubted that. "You said once that it would take me a lifetime of study to understand color."

"Yes."

"I think I'm beginning to understand what you meant. Each color says something distinct to me. And when they're mixed together? They say something entirely different."

"Exactly." Color Master reached up and touched the mobile above her head and sent it spinning.

The sight reminded Ishmael of the first time he had met Color Master, and how he tried to fool her into thinking he couldn't see color, and how she fooled him instead with the packet of color for his food. He had no idea back then what would transpire in the coming days and just how bound he would become to the beauty in the colors.

When Ishmael left Color Master's office, the other apprentices in the workroom paused, sensing that something had changed.

Something *had* changed.

Ishmael.

CHAPTER
51

The morning dawned with a strange bleakness, as each dawn had in the days since Luc left. It had been Luc who had colored the dawn in the Commons each morning, and no one had replaced him since he left. The gray light gradually changed into day without art or artifice, with only the new bell ringer to broadcast the change from night into day.

By the time Ishmael arrived at the posticum, the apprentices from the Hall of Motion had already delivered the animals, and crates of all sizes awaited him.

Lilith, Rebekah, and Hannah stood near a cart.

"Did you see the posticum?" Ishmael asked Hannah.

"I was waiting for you to arrive before I peeked."

Ishmael went to the entrance and pulled Hannah next to him. It had been empty, but for the water, when she had left. She gasped at the sight and her eyes filled with tears: the green merriefield, sprinkled with the cheerful flowers bobbing in the breeze; bits of yellow and violet showing through the verdant tallgrass; the dark tree trunks in the distance, some leaves colored orange from the struggle with Luc; and farther still, a vast expanse of green.

"I should have been here to help," she said.

"You *did* help, more than I can say."

"It's beautiful," she said, wiping her eyes dry.

Uncomfortable with her tears, Ishmael cleared his throat. "Are you going to tell me what you're planning now?"

Hannah giggled, and Lilith said, "How about if we show you?"

He nodded, so Lilith pulled a jar of light from the cart. Then Rebekah pulled a duplicate right after her.

Ishmael couldn't have been more surprised. "Pure light?" He reached out to touch the jars. "How did you get this?"

"I brought it with me from the astronomae," Hannah said, shyly.

Lilith linked her arm through Hannah's. "We thought we could use it to dapple the animals."

"Because that's how you wanted it," Rebekah said.

Ishmael was stunned.

"We asked Color Master to teach us how to dapple. Did you know she was the one who discovered that method?"

Ishmael shook his head. "But the colors will mix together."

"Color Master said some of the color might remain on the

animals, because the surface quality of their skin or feathers or fur will allow the color to set before it comes in contact with the other colors. But yes, some of it will probably mix."

Jacob, Matthew, and Phoebe arrived then, and saw the jars of light. Matthew smiled at Lilith with unabashed pleasure. "You're ready?"

"We figured one person could hold the animal, while another holds the spectrum."

Ishmael hardly knew what to say. He didn't have to say anything. Though Thomas was still in the infirmary, their spectrum was complete and he was anchored right in the middle of it.

They set to work in teams. Once the color began to seep into the fur or feathers or skin, they released the beast into the posticum. They worked for hours until their arms ached, but the variety of patterns they each made kept them laughing: swirls and curlicues, spots and stripes, zigzags and uneven patches, all dappled with the full spectrum.

When they colored the last beast—a large hoofed animal with the merest bump rising from the center of its forehead—the supply of light had been depleted.

The work of the Jubilee posticum was finished.

Phoebe smiled. "I'd better go. Thanks for letting me help."

"No—wait." Ishmael said. "I want you to see something." He pulled a new prism and a small mirror out of his pocket, and then stepped into the interior of the posticum. "I just want you to know that I couldn't have done this without each of you, and Thomas. Thanks."

Lilith's eyes shone, and Hannah hugged him.

Ishmael wiped the mirror on his pants, and then held it against the prism. He did not wait to catch a ray of light or make a spectrum this time. He only wanted to reflect the light, the way Michael had when he condensed the light. He lifted his gaze, and aimed his prism and the mirror directly upward, toward the sky, hoping that Thaddeus had delivered the Hall of Manufactory's work. As the others stood there watching, an area of lightness grew over their heads. It burgeoned outward, billowing and puffy. The breeze that had been soft a minute before blew cold.

The mass above them grew dense as the grasses flattened and the petals of the flowers shivered. A small flake fell, landing on Lilith's nose. She brushed at it, but it melted at her touch.

More flakes fell from the sky, landing on the branches of the trees, the leaves of grass, the beasts still grazing in the field. As they watched in silence, the nearly transparent flakes blanketed the field, until nothing showed but the straight lines of the dark tree trunks in the distance.

Ishmael lowered his arm. He had come to the Commons looking for Luc, and it was here in this posticum that he would leave Luc.

SCENT

Keturah held a small basket with twelve sections, each containing a petite glass vial. While she had been helping the Hall of Manufactory add scent to the crystal flakes, there had been some mix-up about the delivery of the scent for the fauna. Even though both the flora and the fauna scents were ready for the posticum, the vials containing the scents of the fauna had accidentally been left behind. So Keturah carried the needed vials from the Hall of Scent, but she was afraid it might be too late to use them.

When she arrived at the posticum courtyard, the memory of the nothingness of the posticum from the opening ceremony assaulted her—the fear, the emptiness, the very blankness of the place. It made her shiver. How different it was now. How grateful she was for all the work the other artisans had done. How she rejoiced in it.

As she came close to the archway, a few of the stones surrounding it shifted, sending out grit and dust.

Keturah poked her head in. A fluffy brightness covered the ground and the trees, giving off a familiar scent. These were the crystals she had scented the day before, crisp yet sweet, perfect for this fluttering stuff. It had the smell of both beginnings and endings, of eternity and beyond—almost that smell she awoke with so many weeks ago, the smell of the newborn babe.

Hill and field were draped in a vast blanket of this strange substance, softening the view into the horizon. The trees and bushes nearby were covered in it, as were a few of the large animals she could see in the distance—the animals that should be scented with the vials she held in her basket. Overcome by this wonder, she found she couldn't be bothered by the unfinished work. That could come later.

More of the flakes fell from the heavens, dropping softly onto her head and arms and hands, her nose and eyelashes. She took a step inside, then another. Her foot sank through to the ground, making an impression.

It was cold in the posticum. She shivered, and the glass vials clinked in her basket, but she couldn't tear herself away from the beauty of what was before her. Keturah set her basket down, and lifted her face to the sky.

She stretched out her arms and laughed, twirling around, mouth open, her tongue catching the falling flakes.

GUSTATION

Gabriel also carried a basket—a bushel basket of seedpods from the gardens on the far side of the Commons. He chewed a nib from a pod as he walked through the courtyard, tasting its complex bitter flavor. It needed sweetness—a great deal of sweetness—but then it would be nearly perfect. He could taste it in a hot drink with mounds of whipped cream on top. Or baked in a cake. Or frozen and whipped. Or . . .

He realized he had stopped walking, thinking about the endless possibilities. It was, without a doubt, the best flavor he had ever created. Or at least it would be, once he added sweetness to it. It lifted him up and weighted him down, just as it had before, on that morning that Ishmael had opened the posticum. Bitter, strangely enough, *and* sweet.

On a whim, he decided to stop at the posticum to test the flavor of the nib there, to see if he needed to add anything else. Gabriel walked through the entry, and peeked inside. Keturah was there, twirling in the field. She didn't notice him as he watched her spin. She didn't see his smile or the way his eyes lit up when he, too, opened his mouth and caught one of the crystalline flakes on his tongue.

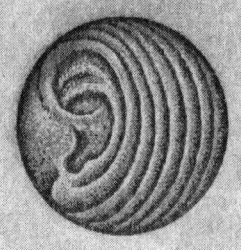

SOUND

Aaron, the former bell ringer, rushed up the steps. Panting before he even reached step number seventy-five, he realized how quickly he had lost his stamina for these steps, as if they weren't his anymore.

That's because they weren't.

But he had seen the wall buckling around the posticum, and he knew the threshold wouldn't be tolerated much longer. Though he didn't know what the wall would do with the large stone, he suspected it wouldn't be pretty.

The new bell ringer wouldn't know about the posticum until far too late, so Aaron had taken it upon himself to alert the Commons. Really, though, he just wanted to ring the bell one last time. He took the steps two by two, wishing he had Thaddeus's speed. When Aaron reached the top, he gave his legs and his lungs only a split second to recover before he flung himself at the ropes, never mind the wool for his ears.

He had made his decision and he didn't want to be the second artisan in the history of the Commons to be left out of a posticum.

Motion

The sound waves carried over the courtyard to Thaddeus, who stopped what he was doing, sensing the motion of the waves from the great bell all around him. He let the waves bump into him, wishing he could ride these sound waves, wishing that he could harness their motion.

But he couldn't. He hadn't yet figured out how to do that.

So he did the next best thing: he ran to the Jubilee posticum, all the while wondering if Dora could sense the motion from the sound waves, too.

SHAPE

There were times for dots, and there were times for lines, and this was definitely the time for a line. Dora ran in a straight line to the arch of the posticum.

MANUFACTORY

Michael had been overjoyed to help Ethan create more of the "order and chaos" flakes, but he was finished all too soon with these tasks and was requested to organize Manufactory Master's office since he had done such a good job with the storeroom. Although he was pleased with all the collaboration he had done with the other Halls, he still wished things had worked out better with his prototype. He wished he could see it one more time—the arch of the neck, the graceful lines, the flowing mane. It had been beautiful. Michael sighed.

An assignment was an assignment, though, so he stood in Manufactory Master's office, surveying the scene. It wasn't as bad as the storeroom, but it wasn't creating, and he still anticipated a long time spent away from his tools. Disheartened, he bent down to pick up a pencil when the great bell rang. "Saved by the bell," he muttered.

CHAPTER

52

I declare an end to the work in this Jubilee posticum." Head Master stood at the edge of the posticum, his ring of pale hair bright in the posticum's light. The apprentices, more somber than celebratory, stood with their classmates in the smaller courtyard.

Head Master took a deep breath. "This posticum, meant to honor Godfrey Wright in our Jubilee Year, has come at a price. Our young friend, Thomas, is healing and will join us again soon. Luc, the former color keeper, will remain in the posticum. After the circumstances of the past few weeks, we feel it would be best to let him stay there. Thus, we will not be seeking other volunteers for the posticum."

Aaron, the former bell ringer, gaped at Head Master.

Phoebe raised her hand. "But why, Head Master? Luc is no

danger to those of us who are not from the Hall of Hue. Why can't we claim this posticum, too?"

Head Master looked as surprised as Ishmael felt. "Are there any who would wish to go?"

Aaron hesitated. Why hadn't he talked to the others instead of just assuming they were going to go, too? He found Ethan standing with the other Manufactory apprentices. Surely he would want to go—he had done the most important work in the posticum. But Ethan shook his head.

How could Aaron go if no one else in the artisan group went with him? The only other artisan he could see was Ishmael. He caught Ishmael's eye. Ishmael shook his head slightly, but it jerked up when he heard Head Master say, "Phoebe?"

"I don't really belong in the Hall of Sound anymore," Phoebe said, glancing at Sound Master. "Nor do I belong with the Hall of Hue. This seems like an opportunity to start over." Though Phoebe's voice was brave, her shoulders were rounded as if she carried a heavy weight, and she twisted the pitch pipe on her wrist around and around and around.

Ishmael couldn't let Phoebe do this—to sacrifice her opportunity to learn as he had once been ready to sacrifice his by returning home. "If anyone should go, it should be me," Ishmael said.

Head Master's eyebrows rose. "Do you wish to go, Ishmael?"

"No," he said with embarrassment. "But it's not because of Luc." He wasn't sure he could explain why he didn't want to go, but it had something to do with Head Master.

Each time Ishmael looked at Head Master, he saw present, past, and future. Within him were movement and sound and color, taste and smell. All things were laid bare: stone and dirt; trees and plants; oceans beyond thought. He saw depths of unimaginable sorrow, loss, and pain. But he also saw unimaginable joy. In them, he saw completeness.

Ishmael wanted to have that same completeness. He wanted to be that whole. As it was, Ishmael only had the past within him, a splintered past with Mam's rough and calloused hands turning the cheese in the brine, a past with Papa digging the well. A past with Jerusha leading Simon back to the cottage, and Luc herding the flocks of sheep into the barn.

That past was mostly without color, without shape, without motion, without sound, scent, or gustation. If he went into the posticum now, his present would become his future. There would be nothing more for him than what he already had. And from the small bits of the elements of Shape and Manufactory and Motion and Sound that had helped him in this posticum, he knew there was more. And Ishmael wanted more. He wanted to understand the work of the other Halls. He wanted to experience it. "I don't think I'm ready yet, Head Master. And also? I feel like there's so much more collaboration to discover. The artisans from the other Halls helped me so much with this posticum that I'm sure there's more to learn—things that would benefit all of the Halls."

Head Master nodded, and then turned to Phoebe. "Phoebe, I confess, I had hoped you would stay here. Your role in the collaboration between the Hall of Sound and the Hall of Hue makes you invaluable to us as we discuss these future collaborations among the Halls." He glanced at Sound Master with a look of disapproval. Sound Master had the grace to look ashamed.

Phoebe's eyes brightened. "Really?"

"Yes, really."

Phoebe seemed to grow taller under Head Master's praise. "I'll stay, then." She stepped back to her place beside Ishmael. He squeezed her hand.

"Is there anyone else who would go?" Head Master looked at the gathered artisans. Before any of the artisans could respond, Lilith lifted a dappled hand high. "I will go."

Ishmael reeled. Lilith?

"But my dear girl," Color Master said, "Remember the danger for Hue apprentices."

She nodded. "I'm aware of the danger."

Ishmael thought back over the past few days—of Lilith's efforts at spreading the color, of her collaboration with Phoebe, of her desire to fight Luc after he attacked Thomas, of her creativity in coloring the animals. Lilith would be a good caretaker.

"If you're determined to go, I will not stop you," Head Master said. He turned back to the gathered apprentices. "Is there anyone else?"

Without waiting to see if there were others who would join her, Lilith turned to Ishmael. "I know this changes our spectrum, but you'll be all right without me."

Ishmael wasn't sure if they would. Phoebe threw her arms

around Lilith. She motioned Matthew, Rebekah, Jacob, and Hannah over. Hannah flew to her side. Rebekah reached for Lilith's hands. Matthew hesitated, then put his arms around Lilith and the group. "I'll miss you," he said to Lilith, in his quiet way.

"You're far better at diplomacy than you think," she said. "You would have been a good diplomat, but you'll be an even better color keeper. Would you give Thomas a message from me?"

"Of course."

"Tell him, *After the game, the queen and the pawn go into the same box.* I'm not the pawn, though."

Matthew smiled. "No. You're not."

"Now you'll be able to right the wrongs around you— something you couldn't do at your home," Jacob said.

Lilith smiled. "Exactly."

Color Master joined them, her hands on Lilith's shoulder and Ishmael's back, and the friends stood that way, holding tightly to each other until the stones began to groan.

Some of the other artisans stood by the archway: Aaron, Thaddeus, Keturah carrying her basket of vials, Gabriel, Dora, and Michael.

"Are you all going?" Lilith asked, surprised at the sight of the other artisans. She hadn't noticed when they each volunteered.

They nodded.

"Michael? You, too?"

Michael smiled. "Yes. This posticum is a part of me now. I don't want to be left behind."

The stones groaned. "Are you ready?" Phoebe asked. "I don't think you have much time."

Lilith reached out and took their hands. Ishmael had the same inexpressible awareness that he had the morning he had released the light to begin the period of creation. This was beauty. This was right. Even though this posticum would be touched with the ugliness of much that was wrong, it was also built on all that was right: the goodness of others, the grace of mercy, the rightness of justice, the generosity of spirit.

The stones in the walls grumbled. When this posticum closed, they knew they would have a long rest before the next one would be needed. They would have time to adjust to the spaces between, to the distance from their neighbors, to the new life within their walls. But for now, the threshold was a thorn, a needle, grit. They wanted it out, and the sooner, the better. The squeeze that had once been simply annoying grew painful, and once they closed this posticum shutting off the cruel-hearted brother, they were finished interfering.

Head Master sensed the impatience of the stones. "It is time."

The apprentices looked at each other. Gabriel only had the basket of seedpods. Likewise, Keturah carried only vials of scent for the fauna. Few had the tools they would need, but the memory of Luc being shut out of his posticum was still fresh.

Murmurs were heard through the crowd, and tools were passed forward. A clamp, a hammer, a pencil, a ruler, a sphere, a knife, a pulley. Each apprentice took the tools of their trade, thanking the givers.

Ishmael handed his new prism to Lilith. She grasped it in both of her hands. "Thank you. Really, Ishmael. Thank you."

"Apprentices, please take your places within the posticum," Head Master said.

Lilith pulled away from them, joining the other apprentices inside, their arms full of tools and gifts. Head Master nodded toward Ethan. The Manufactory artisan shoved a lever under the threshold, wiggling it until it was under the stone. Then two other apprentices joined Ethan as they thrust their weight on the lever, popping the stone from its place, and the posticum closed instantly.

The stones in the walls of the Commons shivered and sighed with relief. Their penance was served.

Outside of these walls, down the hill or in the market, no one heard the grinding of the stones as they shifted. Most likely, no one smelled the fresh scent of the cold air, a scent that might have reminded someone of a newly born babe. No one in the village knew of the beauty of shape and dimension, of lines and circles, nor the grace of motion, the elegance of manufactory. No one would have seen the color of completion.

Few people did.

ACKNOWLEDGMENTS

The Commons in my world has been peopled with extraordinary individuals for whom I am deeply grateful.

Representing the Hall of Shape is Mary Kate Castellani, a dream editor, who put order to my chaos and shape to what was often formless. She knew exactly how much line and how much circle was needed. I am grateful for her editorial skills, her astute questions, and her goodness.

In the Hall of Manufactory is the Bloomsbury group, a crowd of people who know how to take stardust and turn it into a book. They championed this story and brought it into being and for that I'm grateful: Erica Barmash, Anna Bernard, Bethany Buck, Beth Eller, Cristina Gilbert, Melissa Kavonic, Jeanette Levy, Cindy Loh, Donna Mark, Lizzy Mason, Linda Minton, Brittany Mitchell, Oona Patrick, Emily Ritter, Claire Stetzer. Many thanks also to Ian Schoenherr for his illustrations.

Michelle Witte, an agent in the Hall of Motion, understands how publishing moves: she found the perfect home for my manuscript. Plus, she uses Wonder Woman stamps. I'm so thankful that she is my advocate.

Much love and gratitude to my fellow Hall of Hue apprentices and masters, my Vermont College of Fine Arts community, those who bring color to this world of ours. Special thanks goes to Sarah Ellis and Tim Wynne-Jones who aided me with early drafts. Kathi Appelt and Martine Leavitt gave me a foundation and a springboard. Julie Berry, who is a kindred spirit and friend for the eternities, read draft after draft. S3Q2, my Beverly Shores group, and in particular, Varian Johnson, generous friend and willing dance partner, thank you.

The people in my Hall of Sound listened to me as I talked out plot and story problems, character and motivation. Much gratitude to William Johnson, Adi Rule, Erin Moulton, and Cheryl Coupe.

Early readers and workshop members make up my Hall of Scent. Their influence was a balm to me. Sue Gong, Catherine Linka, Mima Tipper, Larissa Theule, Rachel Wilson, Linden McNeilly, Mary Winn Heider, Sue LaNeve, Jennifer Taylor, Amy Rose Capetta, Anna Jordan, and the members of Sharon Darrow and Alan Cumyn's workshop (Erik Talkin, Mari Talkin, Carol Lynch Williams, Galen Longstreth, Maha Adasi, Simon Fill, Pam Watts, Margaret Crocker, Paul Houser). I am grateful for your encouragement.

And finally, in my Hall of Gustation are those who feed my soul: William, Samuel, and Will Johnson, my three most beloveds; Robin Woodruff (because truly I owe it all to her); and Beth Slazak, who always, always makes me laugh.